Black Forest Redemption

Black Forest Redemption
Published by Even Before Publishing
a division of Wombat Books.
P. O. Box 1519, Capalaba Qld 4157
www.evenbeforepublishing.com
www.wombatbooks.com.au

© Amanda Deed 2012

Cover Design by NetManCorp 2012

Layout by Even Before Publishing

National Library of Australia Cataloguing-in-Publication entry
Author: Deed, Amanda
Title: Black forest redemption / Amanda Deed
ISBN: 9781922074256 (pbk.)
Dewey Number: A823.4

Black Forest Redemption

A Jacksons Creek Novel

Amanda Deed

Acknowledgements

First of all I would like to thank my hubby and best mate, Morry, who puts up with my hours at the computer and no-so-perfect housekeeping, while I invest my time in these novels.

To my three amazing children, I love you very much, you keep me on the fine line between sane and loopy, although that could be debated.

To my extended family, all my friends at SECC, and the network of Aussie authors, you're awesome, I am proud to be part of the family and am always overwhelmed by your support and encouragement.

To Jacquie V, my partner in insanity, or is it inanity? You know how much I value your friendship. There isn't enough hot chocolate in the world...

To Rochelle Manners, I honour your passion and commitment to the Aussie Christian Fiction market. May you be richly blessed for all you sow into us authors.

Finally, to Jesus Christ be all the glory and honour, the maker and lover of my soul, my Saviour and my God, without You I am nothing.

Chapter One

Ballaarat, November 1854

Tony blinked at the cloud of dust billowing up from the dry street as the Melbourne-Ballaarat Coach pulled up before him. Two women who stood nearby coughed and waved the dust from their eyes, watching with interest as the coachmen jumped down from the box and opened the doors. Only the wealthy travelled this way and the townsfolk were curious about who would step out.

Sure enough, the first to be assisted from the coach was a pale, frail looking woman who seemed to sway on her feet a little. She wore very fine clothes. She lifted a lace handkerchief to her nostrils and made a sound like a groan. 'Oh, that has to be the worst twenty-five shillings I've ever spent.'

'Nonsense *Mamá*,' came a musical voice from within the coach. 'You are simply not well enough to enjoy it.'

A small, leather-shod foot poked out and found the step, then with a whoosh the rest of her flounced out, ignoring the offered hand of the footman.

'Oh, dear Lord,' one of the spectators said in horror and turned her back. 'I cannot look at her.'

'Why, her dress does not even touch the ground! You can see her ankles.' The second woman gasped and the two hurried away.

Tony, on the other hand, stood as one transfixed. Before him stood a beauty so exotic he did not note the length of her dress, nor her bare arms. He saw a vision of deep, shimmering red, trimmed in black, with the prettiest face smiling above it. She looked around her, seeming unaware of the crowd of shocked onlookers. 'So, *this* is Ballaarat.' She let out what sounded like a satisfied sigh and turned in a circle, clapping her hands.

Her mother, who leaned on another female from the coach, reached out to her with a loud whisper. 'Here, Stella. Put your bonnet on.'

With barely a glance her way, The Vision took the hat and thrust it over luminous dark hair, still making a slow circle.

She has more life in her little finger than I have in my entire being. Tony gazed at her in astonishment. He felt as though he had only ever seen the world in shades of grey, but now saw colour for the first time. She looked at him once, giggled and then continued to twirl.

'Anarosa. Estella.' A man's voice came through the folk gathered on the roadside and soon his body followed, pushing his way between gawking men.

Tony recognised Mr William Mattherson from the Commissioner's Camp.

Mattherson stopped short. 'Good God! Estella. What is that you are wearing? Rosa, could you not give a thought to your daughter's modesty?'

'Oh, there you are my darling.' The languid woman smiled as he took her hand and kissed it. 'You know I ...'

'Papa!' the girl named Estella squealed and threw herself at him.

He embraced her awkwardly and then pulled away from her. 'For goodness sake, Estella, show some decorum.' He nodded to the footman for him to bring their bags, beckoned the maid and herded his family away towards the Commissioner's Camp.

Tony watched The Vision fade from his view like an extinguishing flame and shook himself free of the spell she had wrought on him. *Trouble*, he told himself with resolve. *That's what one so spirited will induce. As if I need more of that.*

'It is more comfortable this way, Papa.' Stella tried to convince her starchy father. 'These English dresses are no good for this hot climate. I make changes and *voila* — much cooler.'

'Maybe so.' He scowled. 'But you open yourself to gossip wherever you go. Put on a proper dress.'

'Papa,' she pleaded, 'We just arrived. Did you not miss us?'

'Of course I missed you,' he said in a gruff voice. 'But I did not expect to see you dressed like a hoyden. Rosa, why did you not put a stop to this?'

Her mother, looking queasy from the long journey, reclined on a chaise lounge while Jemina, the maid, administered some cure-all elixir. 'You know how she is, William. She *will* have her way.'

'It is but a few inches.' Stella rolled her eyes.

'And no sleeves, or gloves — in the *daytime*,' he pointed out.

Stella opened her mouth to argue further, but decided she would have more luck convincing a rock to move.

'William, you seem distressed. Is all well?' Her mother could always read Papa better.

His shoulders rose and fell with a grunt. 'After I sent word for you to come and join me, things became unsettled here in Ballaarat. A man was murdered and then the diggers held a protest which turned into a riot. A hotel was razed to the ground. Last week, the miners held a Monster Meeting on Bakery Hill. They want reform. I wonder at what price.'

'You suspect rebellion?'

'Possibly. But it was too late to tell you to stay. You had already departed from Sydney. If the trouble grows worse, we may need to call in reinforcements.'

'Do you think it is unsafe?' Her mother looked alarmed.

Her father turned to pour himself a glass of whiskey. 'Truly, I cannot say. We must hope for the best.' He tried to smile, but concern dominated his features.

A week had gone by, but no matter how many times he went to the Post Office — a good excuse to be near the government camp — Tony had not encountered The Vision again. *Perhaps she is not even living there.* He had assumed the Matthersons lived at the camp and thought he might see her about town. To feel alive for a moment again, that's all he wanted.

He had seen miners of all kinds of diverse nationalities — English, Irish, Scottish and even American — but nothing of those dark luminous locks. He had seen strange sights aplenty observing the Chinese population, for they seemed to arouse much suspicion among other men. Their ways were far different from everyone else with their pigtails and strange clothes, the way they carried loads at either end of a pole across their shoulders, even their religion. But nothing stood out to him so much as The Vision's shortened sleeves and hemline, and of her, he'd seen not a glance.

For a certainty, she would have none of him. She came from a wealthy family. He was skint more often than not. When he used his logic, the ratio between the sexes would not stand him in good stead either. He estimated one woman to every four men in Ballaarat, and most of them were already married. The remainder often turned to prostitution to survive, leaving very few for men who would want a wife. Those ladies could afford to be choosy.

'G'day.' A voice drew his attention from measuring grain into sacks.

He straightened and turned to the counter. 'Can I help you?'

'Yeah.' Two men stood there, one small and wiry, the other huge. 'We need some grub before we go and make camp. Just arrived in town.'

Tony brushed the hair back from his forehead and gave them a dry greeting. 'Welcome to Ballaarat.' He filled their list of provisions from the storage containers behind him.

'Hey, you know where the best place is to find gold?' the wiry one asked.

'If you can find it.'

The man laughed. 'Course I'll find it.'

Tony shrugged. 'You can try the Eureka Lead. You passed it on your way into town. But, you'd be even better off going back where you came from.' He tallied their purchases.

The man laughed again and paid for his goods. He put out his hand. 'Name's Smith. Bobby Smith.'

'Tony Worthington.' He shook Smith's hand.

Smith's beady eyes gleamed. 'Pleased to meet y'.'

A flash of bold colour through the window caught Tony's eye and with a lurch, he darted around the counter and out the door, coming to an abrupt stop outside. The Vision strolled down the street with a lilting step, shrouded in dark green taffeta, her maid trailing behind her. *Proper to the ground.* Tony grinned.

Smith and his comrade had followed him out and must have noticed his line of sight. Smith gave a long, low whistle. 'That *is* worth a bolt outdoors, now ain't it?'

'Mmm.'

'Have y' introduced yerself yet?'

'Nah.'

'Why not?'

Tony shrugged his shoulders.

The next thing he knew, Smith had jogged over to her and bowed with a flourish. 'Ma'am,' he grinned. 'I got a friend who'd like to meet y'.'

The Vision stopped and turned in his direction. With an arch look, she eyed him up and down and flashed a smile that made Tony feel he would melt into the ground. She turned back to Smith. 'Tell him, if he wants to meet me, he can come and do it himself.' She leaned in and whispered in his ear, although her eyes slid to Tony, then turned and flounced off down the street.

'What did she say?' Tony asked when Smith returned to him.

Smith spat on the ground and furrowed his brow. 'Said she don't like pewsy-somethin' men. Do y' know what that means?'

'Pusillanimous?' Tony let his shoulders droop. 'Yeah, I know what it means. She thinks I'm a lily-livered coward.'

Chapter Two

'Grog for three, thanks Bill!' Tony had to raise his voice to be heard by the barman.

Bill nodded and set about filling three pints.

Tony closed his eyes and let the merry strains of fiddlers wash over him. Flutes too. And the clump-clump of dancing feet upon the floor boards. All accompanied by singing which sounded more like a chorus of howling dingos than a melody, interspersed with whoops and laughter.

'Here y' go, mate.' Bill shoved the tankards over and Tony flicked him a few coins with a nod of thanks.

Tony carried the beers to a table in a quieter corner of the Ballaarat Hotel where his two new acquaintances sat. They had that all too familiar look in their eyes that told him their lust for riches would blind them to the harsh realities of the diggings. He had seen enough tragedy for more than one lifetime, both in his own family and here amongst the squalor known as Ballaarat. He wished they would listen to his advice.

Now, as he sat on an uneven stool, his dull eyes scanned the room full of jovially drunken diggers. Naught seemed amiss this evening. There had been a good strike at one of the mines today and now the particular digger in question celebrated with his mates. He returned his gaze to his companions.

'This does not happen often, I can assure you.' Tony indicated the revellers with a nod of his head. 'More often than not, these men are brawling. They are frustrated. Most of them have wasted all of their savings on an empty dream. You should return to your homes whilst you still have money in your pockets.'

Bobby Smith rolled his tobacco around in his mouth and spat on the ground. 'We can't lose. Our boss has funded the operation.' He said with a smug grin. 'You got family?'

Tony nodded. 'I have a sister who lives over Sunbury way.' The mere mention of Penny brought a twinge of guilt. She had written him a letter two months ago that she was in dire straits. Their childhood home had been inundated by a flood and she had lost horses and other livestock. Penny had sounded so lonely and in need of help. He should be in Sunbury with her, especially now she had no-one but a farmhand to help her, but she had described him as a reliable fellow, so he'd felt justified in staying in Ballaarat. Besides, he couldn't go back there.

'So why don't you follow your own advice?' Smith asked with a wink.

'Long story.' Tony did not wish to talk about that part of his life with anyone, let alone two strangers. He pulled his pipe out of his pocket and ran his finger over the engraved surface. His father had come to Ballaarat two years ago to plead with him to come home. He'd given him the cherrywood pipe as a peace offering — carved with his initials and a sprig of wattle flower on each side of the bowl.

Tony had still been belligerent back then. The visit had not ended well. The last time he'd spoken to his father, they had argued heatedly and Anthony Worthington senior had left. 'I came to see my son, instead I found a stranger.' They were the last words he ever heard his papa speak.

He would not readily admit his biggest mistakes and saddest memories to anyone. He stuffed tobacco in his pipe and studied these newcomers as he did so. The one named Smith was small and weedy and his close-set eyes reminded Tony of a weasel. He talked the most of the two. Morris Burns was quite the opposite — a large and heavy built man, with brown, unkempt hair, a long, bushy beard and hard brown eyes. His nose was crooked, and his oversize hands had numerous scars on them, giving Tony the impression he had been in many a fight.

As Tony finished lighting his pipe, Burns excused himself and went in search of the outhouse.

Smith winked to a waitress traipsing past. 'So, what does one do for entertainment 'round 'ere?' he asked. 'Apart from drinkin' grog, that is.'

Tony shrugged. 'Some blokes like to sit around their camp fires and sing and tell yarns. Sometimes we have horse races or prize fights, and sometimes we have theatre with music and dancing.'

'Burns would like the fightin'.' Smith's green eyes gleamed and he spat again. 'You should see him. I ain't seen him get beat yet.'

'Perhaps he would like to enter the next competition.' Tony brushed his wayward hair back from his eyes.

'Maybe.' Smith leaned in closer and Tony could smell his rotten teeth. 'What about the *other* entertainment?' He grinned in an unsavoury manner.

Tony grimaced as he pulled smoke through the pipe. He hated to see men so shameless in their lust. Still, he answered the man's question in spite of the sick feeling it gave him. 'You'll find the fallen angels on Esmond Street.'

'Fallen angels?'

'Women who came here to make a new life, but found it impossible to survive.' He sighed. He felt sorry for those girls. Many came here with the promise of bountiful work in domestic service to find most of the populace were single men living in tents.

'Maybe I should go a courtin' with that pretty piece of fancy we saw yesterday, eh?' Smith threw him a wink.

Tony refused to be baited. 'Good luck.' He drank from his mug and wiped the froth from his mouth with his sleeve.

'Whereabouts you reckon they found gold today?' Smith indicated the carousing diggers with a jerk of his head. 'Maybe we should try there.'

Tony shrugged. 'Probably somewhere down on the Eureka Lead. Don't know for sure. I gave up the hunt for gold long ago.'

Burns returned and Smith told him of the prize fighting. Burns grunted and gulped down his beer.

'So, why'd you stop digging?'

A flash of white showed as Tony laughed, albeit a scornful laugh. 'You really have no idea, do you?'

Burns frowned and looked at Smith.

'No idea about what?'

'Haven't you kept up with the news?' Tony looked from one to the other, incredulous. 'The diggers are required to pay thirty shillings per month for a licence to mine a claim that measures twelve feet by twelve feet.'

'Yeah. So?' Smith didn't seem to get it.

'It's exorbitant, that's what it is. Most miners have difficulty paying it. In addition, they have to travel long distances to the nearest government office to buy the licence, costing them time they could be working their claims.

'Recently, the governor has ordered for licences to be checked twice a week, which has aggravated the diggers to say the least. Men are often working up to one hundred feet down in a wet and muddy shaft, and if they keep their licence on them it gets wet and the ink runs. Yet, the police make them climb out and produce the licence, or face a five pound fine.

'Many of the Traps are ex-convicts and get half of each fine they collect, so of course they treat the miners without mercy. I've heard of men who have been chained to felled logs and left in the hot sun, or hauled off to prison in their sodden clothes, for the simple crime of not carrying their mining licence.'

'That bad, eh?' Smith looked grave.

'Yes, it's bad.' Tony wanted them to understand. 'The diggers are angry. They recently had a meeting on Bakery Hill — ten thousand of them — to petition the government to change the laws. They want the Licensing Commission abolished and the system re-designed. They want the right to vote and they want the right to buy the land and not just lease it.'

Smith shrugged and spat black tobacco juice on the floor. 'Well, that's a good sign ain't it? They're doing something about it.'

Tony sighed in exasperation. 'It would be a good sign if the Commissioner or anyone actually listened or cared. But they don't, and this is going to end in bloody violence the way I see it. Reinforcements for the Redcoats arrived in from Melbourne today, and they were attacked on the way into town. Tomorrow the diggers have planned a Monster Meeting on Bakery Hill. The miners from all the camps around here will come out in force to protest their grievances. You should leave before it gets ugly.'

Smith looked at Burns who grunted and then turned back to Tony.

'Nah. Come too far to turn around and go back. She'll be right. I reckon you worry too much.'

Tony opened his mouth to say more, but changed his mind. 'Your choice.' He gave a shrug and slumped further over the table, his whole being fatigued, and not merely with physical weariness. *Why do I even bother?*

'You goin' to the meetin' tomorra?' Smith interrupted his thoughts with a question.

'I'm not a digger. Why would I go?'

'Aren't you even curious about it?'

Tony shrugged again and tucked the pipe back in his pocket.

'Well, like you say, they could be out to stir up more trouble. It could affect the whole town, whether you're a miner or no. I wouldn't miss it fer anythin'. How 'bout you Morris?'

The burly man grunted in reply, but clearly he would attend the meeting along with his comrade.

'They will incite a rebellion. Why sound so gleeful?'

'Yeah, well, if they do, I'm gonna go to the meetin' to see for meself.'

'I suppose you have a point.' Tony sighed in resignation. 'It could be useful to know what they are up to.'

''Attaboy!' Smith slapped him on the back with enough force to cause Tony's beer to splash out of the mug. He gave an unconvinced 'humph' in response, pushed his stray brown hair away from his brow and stared out the nearest window.

'Estella, please don't fly into a rage over this,' her father pleaded, and she could see his patience wearing thin. 'I have already booked your passage on *The Admiral*. The ship leaves early next month and you will be on it.'

Her dark eyes flashed at him in defiance. 'I have no wish to be presented at court! Papa! You cannot send me to England! We just arrived and you would send me away again so soon?'

He came to her and took her hands in his, his eyes filled with entreaty. 'You know I just want the best for you, my dear. Your Great Aunt Tabitha offered to sponsor your coming out. I should have sent you last year, but then your *abuela* passed on …'

Stella sighed. It had been a sad loss. *Abuela* Ofelia, her grandmother on her mother's side, had been the one person she felt understood her and she had grieved for her a long while. Indeed, the whole family had mourned so deeply that other matters were not always attended to. Thus, so far, she had escaped her visit to England.

'… and this past year your *mamá* has been so ill, I needed you in Sydney by her side while I came here. But she is getting better now. Besides, it becomes far too dangerous for a young lady here in Ballaarat. Your mother and I discussed it at length last night. It is time you learnt how to be a lady. Perhaps you will find yourself a respectable husband.'

Stella stiffened. 'Must I? Papa! You know I have no interest in balls or tea parties or any such nonsense. Give me a steed and a mountain trail and I'll be happy.'

'How can you be so sure of something you've never done? I see you have been concocting fantasies in your head again.'

'It is *not* a fantasy Papa!'

His face grew red and he looked like he would burst. 'I'll not have my daughter careening around the bush astride a horse,' he exclaimed. 'You have been raised to better things. And for someone who has no interest in needlework, you certainly seem to have the knack.' He indicated the short sleeves of her dress which she had modified to her tastes.

'That does not mean I enjoy it.'

'Estella! You will do as *I* think is best for you.'

Stella tossed her exotic dark waves and stamped her foot on the floorboards. 'I wish I were a boy. Then I should do as I pleased.'

'Enough of your impudence, Estella!' her father growled. 'You are not a boy, and there is no point wishing it so. You will obey me and leave for England next month. The Baroness is expecting you.' He straightened his jacket and attempted to placate her. 'You shall return to Melbourne in a few days with an acquaintance I have formed here. Then you shall travel under the chaperonage of my good friends, the Stantons. They are trustworthy and they will look after you. In a year or so, if and when you return, then perhaps I will buy you a pony. You know your mother and I planned this for you long ago. Please don't make such a fuss.'

Stella glowered at her father. 'If you make me board that ship, I shall never forgive you!'

He returned her glare. 'So be it,' was all he said and he turned away from her.

Back in her room, Stella paced back and forth. Her fury had not as yet subsided and she spat a string of abuse towards her father. *I hate him! He can go to the devil!* How could he be so inconsiderate of her feelings? How would he know what was best for her? Why should he be so determined to turn her into a proper *señora* and marry her off to a rich man? Just because he had relatives in the peerage! In her mind he had become a tyrant from whom she yearned to break free. She needed adventure, not dull conversation with stuffy aristocrats. She needed to be outdoors, not cooped up in some stuffy parlour sipping tea. How could he be her *padre* and not know her at all? Even if she managed to return without a husband, she knew he would try to marry her off to some old gentleman with grey hair and a sour face at the first chance he got.

England! Even that one word made her stomach turn. Why not Spain, the land of her mother's ancestors? She could learn of their ways. No, Papa believed they were too wild. *Abuela* had told them all, many times, of her youth and the adventures she had experienced. Her father did not approve of their traditional dance with all their swishing skirts, or the way Spaniards courted death with angry bulls. In his eyes one should not *behave in such a manner.* A wicked grin spread on Stella's face. Lucky for him *Mamá* was a quiet, manageable sort of lady. The feistiness had skipped a generation and Stella had inherited a full share.

Stella sank onto her bed and dropped her head in her hands. *Abuela* would have confronted Papa. She knew the way Stella's heart yearned to fly. *Abuela* had said she felt the same at seventeen. She would have known what was best for her, but she had passed on, and her *mamá* had been too sick these past months to argue. Now no-one but herself would plead her cause. And her pleas fell on deaf ears. She could not face boarding that ship. To embark on that journey meant the end of all her dreams. She would never see her beloved Australia again, let alone ride the open country on a horse or have any kind of adventure in her life.

A gentle tap came upon the door.

'*Sí*' Stella hoped it was not her father.

A young girl poked her head in.

'Jemina.' Stella let out her breath in relief at the sight of her maid. 'Come and brush my hair out.' She moved to her small dresser and sat in front of the mirror.

The girl stepped in and closed the door behind her. 'Mr Mattherson told me you would need me.' Jemina brushed the long thick waves. 'Why so sad this morning, Miss?'

Stella's eyes grew dark and her eyebrows knit together. 'Did he tell you he wants to be rid of me?'

'No *senorita.*' Jemina shook her head. 'He loves you.'

Stella folded her arms and grunted. 'What would you know? You are just a child.'

Indeed, Jemina only preceded her by two years, but Stella was in no mood to be appeased.

The maid shrugged and continued to brush.

Stella watched her reflection in the mirror in morose silence. The gentle brush strokes soothed her angry emotions. She loved the feel of it massaging her head and even more she loved to watch the sheen that appeared with each stroke, reflected in the morning light. She admired her olive skin, another of her Spanish attributes, smooth and flawless. Her lips too, were an asset to be prized. She could form them into a brilliant pout when she wanted to. She studied her squarish jaw-line and sighed. She deemed it her one imperfection. *Why, if it wasn't for my hair, I should look ...*

Her eyes lit up with wonderment. The melancholy disappeared from her face and instead she appeared deep in thought for a long time. Jemina soon put the brush down and plaited the thick tresses into one long braid, which she then wound into a tight bun. Minutes passed before Stella jerked in her chair. 'Jemina! I have an idea!'

'Mmm.' The maid only half listened. 'I'm sure it's very clever.'

'Yes it is, Jemina, *very* clever.' She was glad the young girl did not look at her reflection, for she would have seen a wicked gleam in her dark eyes. 'In fact, it's *perfecto.*'

Chapter Three

'Papa, I am going shopping.' Stella poked her head into her father's study and kept her voice cheerful.

Her father looked up from his desk with raised eyebrows. He seemed a little surprised his daughter no longer sulked. 'Are you?'

'Yes. I need to purchase some things for my trip to England.'

Papa sat back in his chair, gazing at her intently. 'You have decided to accede to my wishes, then?'

'Well,' she rolled her eyes, 'arguing with you serves me no purpose.' She moved to her father's side and planted an affectionate kiss on his cheek.

He smiled up at her and patted her hand. Then his forehead creased into a puzzled frown. 'What could you possibly need that you could find in Ballaarat? Why not wait until you reach Melbourne?'

Stella went to the window and drew the lace curtain aside, pretending embarrassment. 'Papa. There are things that shouldn't be discussed with a gentleman, even if he *is* your father.'

'I see.' He coughed awkwardly. 'You will take Jemina along, won't you? I do not wish to see you strolling the streets unaccompanied.'

'*Sí*, Papa.' Stella tried not to roll her eyes.

'Well, enjoy your morning then.'

'I intend to.' She touched his shoulder as she passed. '*Adiós Padre.*'

'Mmm,' was all he replied, his head already bent over his papers.

Stella paused one last time at the door and flashed a roguish smile at the figure of her father. *He is too easy to fool.*

When they arrived at the store, she sent Jemina on a trivial errand to keep her out of the way. Stella waited across the street and watched those who passed by, ignoring the bold stares of young men, having already discovered there to be a shortage of females in this budding town. The gentlemen seemed to soak in the vision of her as though they were thirsty.

Stella noticed a shy-looking boy headed for the store and intercepted him. Handing him money, she asked him to go in and purchase a few items for her. She held out a list. 'It's all here.'

The lad glanced at the items. 'Are y' sure?'

'Yes.' She nodded and privileged him with her most brilliant smile. 'Then you may keep the change for yourself.'

He tipped his hat to her. 'Yes, ma'am.'

'Remember to have them wrapped in paper for me,' she added as he turned into the store.

He flashed a shy grin and nodded before he door closed behind him.

Tony caught a glimpse of The Vision as she paced outside the store and felt curious as to what she was about. Her maid was nowhere to be seen. He remembered her rebuff from a few days earlier and chose not to go out and see her. She already saw him as a coward; he did not need her to add sticky-beak to that belief. Still, it satisfied him to watch her for a few minutes. He absent-mindedly served some more customers, while often shifting his gaze to the beauty outside the window. At least something lovely still remained in this world. The trouble in Ballaarat increased every day, adding to his worries.

The police had gone into the Gravel Pits on a licence hunt and had been met with an angry mob. Rocks had been thrown and a few guns fired. The Riot Act had been read and a few men arrested. Following that, the angry mob had converged on Bakery Hill and burned their licences. They had erected a flag with the symbol of the Southern Cross constellation embroidered onto it, and stood around it swearing an oath.

'We swear by the Southern Cross to stand truly by each other to defend our rights and liberties,' the mob had called in chorus, followed by a hearty 'Amen.' A shiver ran up Tony's spine at the memory. It was as though they had formed a regiment. He could only wonder where it would all end.

He watched as the young lad he had just served exited the store and handed The Vision the parcel of goods he had just purchased. A frown creased his brow. *What is she up to?* He could not help but speculate. He stepped around the counter and headed for the door. He would ask her — even if it meant being labelled a nosey-boots.

Before he could pass through the door, a bunch of diggers burst in. The looks on their faces made him stand still as another cold shiver crept up his spine.

'We are here to requisition supplies for the Reform League.' Their loud voices resounded through the store.

The store owner, Parkin, came out from the back. He frowned. 'What is it you want?'

'Food, weapons, anything to help us fight.' One surly man grated.

'And if I refuse?'

'See for yerself how much business y' keep once people find out you're a traitor.'

Parkin stood and stared at them for a long moment. Then his shoulders sagged. 'Fine. Take what you need.'

Tony edged back to the counter while his heart hammered in his chest. *Is this the beginning of a war of sorts?* If they had formed a regiment and were collecting arms, it would make sense. It did not bode well for the township.

He soon learned a lot more. The miners talked as they stuffed bags with provisions, proud of their actions. They had built a stockade up at the Eureka Camp and were soon to commence militia-type drills, preparing for a fight with the military and government officials.

Tony gave an involuntary shudder. Could a war break out? Hadn't they heard about the American Revolution? Thousands had died in that fight for independence. Of course, this was not so widespread, but ...

Tony's gut tightened with familiar fear. *Where will it all end?* He knew he lived on the brink of dire events, imagining the worst a bloody battle could do to the town. As he measured grain into sacks, he tried to swallow his burgeoning fears.

When the reformers left, Tony managed to relax, if only a little. Before long, he excused himself to take a stroll and shake out his taut nerves. 'I need fresh air,' he told his employer.

Parkin grinned at him. 'I'll say you do. You're as white as a dove in the snow.'

'I am?'

Parkin flashed him a sympathetic smile. 'Listen, the military will have the diggers in order before long, don't you worry too much. Go and have your dinner break.'

'I don't think I can eat right now.' Tony tried to lighten his words with a chuckle, nodded to Parkin, and stepped out into the street.

An aimless walk around the busy streets only served to increase his concern. Down by the government camp, officers boarded up buildings with firewood and corn and hay bags. Clearly they expected some kind of attack. Tony felt sick with dread.

He ducked into the Post Office, where they also made preparations to protect the building and collected a letter. At first, he had expected another letter from his sister, but when he turned it over he didn't recognise the hand writing. *Mr Harrison Blake, Blake and Blake Solicitors. I wonder what this is about.*

He shoved it into the pocket of his moleskins and headed back to the store. Comforting words from his sister would have been welcome. In her most recent letters she had begun to mention a newfound faith. She had even suggested that he should attend church and find out for himself what Christ was truly about.

God.

What difference could God make to his life? Ballaarat resembled more a hell-hole of rebellion every day, he'd failed to find gold and he had failed to show his father that he could make something of himself. Tony knew another moment of regret. If only he'd been able to make Papa proud. But, it was too late for that. Papa was dead and buried.

Guilt nagged at his thoughts. He had failed his father and now he had failed Penny. And by the look of Ballaarat, he might not live to make anything right. Perhaps his sister was right. *Maybe I should go to confession or something.* Perhaps that would put his mind at rest. He opened the door of the mercantile. *Tomorrow I shall find a rector of some sort.*

'Any better?' Parkin asked, but then stopped and stared at him.

'You look worse!'

Tony leaned on the counter. 'They're boarding everything up. The town could be under attack at any moment.'

Parkin sucked in a deep breath. 'Good Lord.' He began to pace, turning this way and that, seeming unsure of his actions. 'I must go to my wife.'

'Of course you must.'

'But the store ...'

'I shall take care of it.' The words were out before Tony could stop them. He would much prefer to run and hide. *Although, this place is as good as any to take shelter in.* It was well built.

'Find some boards and cover the windows, will you?'

'Yes, sir.'

'Right.' Agitation made Parkin animated. 'I'll be off then.'

Tony sank to the floor behind the counter and tried to rein in his rising panic. He banged his head back against the wooden cupboards and bit hard on his lower lip. *Get a hold of yourself, Tony. You have to protect the store now.*

Stella felt the pressure of her father's hand against her lower back as he guided her down the street at a quick pace. Her mother clung to his other arm and Jemina trotted close behind them.

'Papa, why do we have to go to the store?' she complained.

He looked grim and in no mood to suffer her arguments. 'I've already explained it, Estella.'

'Will they really attack the government camp?'

'So they say.'

Her mother stifled a fearful cry. 'Oh William.'

Her father's hand left her back momentarily as he patted his wife's hand. 'There, there, Rosa. You will be safe in the store.'

'And who shall protect us when you go back to the camp?' Stella halted her steps.

Her father reached back and clasped her by the elbow, pulling her along with them. 'The store is a sturdy building — the strongest in town. It will protect you and the other women and children in there while the menfolk defend other areas.'

They had arrived, and her father let her go to assist her mother onto the low verandah surrounding the store. Stella stood in the middle of the street and examined her 'protector'. The store did look well built. A shadow passed over her and she gazed up into the sky. Dark clouds filled the heavens and she felt the wind gust about her. She shivered.

'Come on, Estella.' Her father frowned at her.

She stepped onto the verandah and her eyes fell on that gentleman who worked within the trading post. He had nailed a board across one of the windows, and now straightened to face her, his expression pale and distressed. 'Are you our defender, sir?' She gave him a wry smile, sure he would be of little use in a crisis.

The man shrugged. 'Guess I am.' He went back to his preparations.

Inside, fearful women, brawling children and squalling babies crowded the mercantile. She rolled her eyes. *Is this what I have to put up with?* Papa gave them both a fond farewell, brushing a kiss on her forehead before he went back to the Commissioner's Camp.

Stella sighed and surveyed the room. She found a corner as far from the noisy children as possible, although her mother and Jemina motioned for her to join them. Her plans had been ruined. Well, not ruined exactly, but postponed. *Why must I hide like a little mouse, when I could just as well take up a musket and fight alongside the soldiers? I shall have to carry out my plan tomorrow, that is all.*

She noticed the storeman had entered and wove his way through all the women to the counter. She thought him quite handsome but for the slump of his shoulders and the dull look on his face. He seemed uncomfortable amidst so many of the feminine sex. Or, did he worry over the diggers' threat? *Pusillanimous.* She remembered their almost-meeting of a few days earlier and smiled to herself.

It surprised her when he came over to her. 'Tea?' He looked down at her with question in his eyes.

'Pardon?' She had not expected he would even approach her.

'Would you like a cup of tea?' He raised his voice a little.

Many voices around them rose with a resounding 'Yes, please.' The storeman seemed startled and Stella giggled at him. *A short stay in this building may not be so tiresome, after all.* A little attention from a well-looking man might be just the thing to divert her.

She cupped her hand about her mouth and whispered, 'You cannot very well offer me a cup and leave them to go thirsty.'

He turned around to take in all the expectant women gazing at him and then looked back to her. 'I suppose you are right,' he said with a grim smile. 'Would you care to help?'

Stella had the urge to tease him a little. 'Why don't you ask Jemina, over there? She's a maid.' She sat up tall and craned her neck to see the young girl. 'Jemina! Help this gentleman make some tea.'

'Jemina is busy attending me,' she heard her mother's cross reply.

Stella looked up at the man and gave a resigned shrug. 'Very well, I suppose I have nothing better to do.'

'So grateful for your assistance,' came the dry reply as he offered a stiff bow and then helped her to stand.

'We have not been formally introduced, sir,' she reminded him. 'I am Estella Mattherson.'

A strange look came over his face and she noticed the colour deepen in his neck. He bowed over her extended hand. 'Pleased to finally meet you, Miss Mattherson.' He straightened and proffered his elbow. 'My name is Anthony Worthington. Shall we?'

A gentleman, too. Stella felt impressed by such cordial manners in the midst of this chaotic situation. She took his arm and he led her into the back of the store where a small stove sat. He ladled water from a bucket into the kettle. Stella glanced around and soon located the tin of tea leaves. She spooned some into the kettle.

'I recollect you were eager to meet me, Mr Worthington,' she said boldly, keeping her eyes diverted.

He cleared his throat, but waited a moment to answer. 'Whatever gave you that idea?'

Did he wish to bait her with sarcasm, or did he simply forget? 'Your friend. The other day.' Maybe that would jog his memory.

Mr Worthington lifted the kettle and placed it on the stove. 'My friend made an assumption and acted of his own accord.'

Stella knew a moment of awkwardness. 'So, you didn't want to meet me?' She busied herself collecting tea cups and saucers from a small cabinet.

'No — that is — yes — I mean — not more than anyone else.' He shrugged. 'I shall get more from the store.' He made a hasty departure into the front.

Not more than anyone else? Did he mean to insult her? Stella found a few tin cups to add to the collection she had set up on the small table and banged them down without ceremony. She had thought she might enjoy teasing this man, but instead he irritated her.

When he came back, fists grasping almost a dozen tin mugs, she aimed a very different arrow at him. 'I heard the diggers are planning an attack on the Commissioner's Camp this very afternoon. There are *thousands* of them, armed with guns and pikes and anything else they can find.'

He stopped and she saw the colour drain from his face. She grinned wickedly at him. 'You aren't afraid are you? I heard this store is bullet-proof.'

'I am not afraid.' His voice sounded hoarse. 'Neither do I look forward to the event.'

Stella sat down on a nearby chair and pretended to examine her fingernails. 'I wish I were out there fighting them. I would show them what happens to rebels.'

'You have a lot of gumption, Miss Mattherson. Have you ever seen the damage done by the tip of a bayonet? I daresay you might change your mind if ...'

A loud crack filled the air, accompanied by a bright flash and the unanimous scream of all the ladies and children in the next room. Mr Worthington jumped full into the air with a gasp. Even Stella felt her blood go cold.

Chapter Four

It took a few seconds for Tony to realise that the instant flash and thunder of a close lightning strike, not gunfire, had startled them. His heart beat in a rampant fashion in spite of that knowledge. Overhead, the skies opened up and heavy rain began to pelt on the roof. More lightning and thunder followed. He put a grateful hand over his heart.

'A storm.' He breathed out.

Miss Mattherson's eyes gleamed in mischief, although her face had gone a little pale for a moment. 'Did you think the insurgents were upon us?'

Tony shook his head and went into the store front. It took a few moments to reassure the women they were not under attack. A few of them dissolved into tears, the tension too much for them. Friends held each other and spoke soothing words. He ducked back into the back room. A cup of tea would give them some comfort.

He gazed at Miss Mattherson's profile. Indeed she was far more beautiful up close and her eyes sparked like flint on stone. When still and quiet, she remained The Vision he had mused over the past few days. In conversation, she became something entirely different. He doubted there was any real malice in her bones, but she was full of mischief, none the less. The women in the other room trembled and fretted, while this young girl seemed to relish the threat of invasion. *Or is she that naive?*

The kettle boiled and she set about pouring the tea into the cups. She seemed content enough to do it on her own, so he backed out and went to sit behind the counter. He pulled the letter he had received from his pocket and broke the seal.

Dear Mr Worthington,

First of all I must introduce myself. I am Harrison Blake, nephew of the late Thomas Blake, solicitor. It has been my responsibility to sort through my uncle's affairs, and in doing so I came across an account he had with Mr Anthony Worthington, your father.

Through communication with your sister, Penelope, I have learned of your father's passing, so it now behoves me to inform you of matters pertaining to your father's estate. It may surprise you to learn that Mr Worthington left in his will an entire property, independent of Ellenvale Station, in bequest to you.

The letter dropped from Tony's hand as he gasped. How could this be? *Papa said he would cut me off when I left home.* Indeed, Penny had never mentioned the will, so he assumed embarrassment had kept her from informing him he had been left with nothing. *A whole property other than Ellenvale?* This news shocked Tony to his core. He had been certain his father still hated him when he'd fallen to his death. Could he have had a change of heart? With questions firing through his mind, he picked up the missive from Blake again.

It would serve best if you can make a journey to see me in Melbourne, so I can impart the finer details to you in person. I trust this news will be received with gladness in spite of your loss and I look forward to hearing from you in the near future.

Yours sincerely,

Harrison Blake

Tony sat deep in thought for a long time while Miss Mattherson handed out cups of tea around him, and he tried to convince himself he was now a land-owner. It seemed more than unreal. Why had Penny never mentioned this property in her letters? Where was this land? What kind of property was it? There were so many questions and no answers. He would have to make a trip to Melbourne to find out.

It was a good time to leave Ballaarat with all the trouble around. *I'll finish up tomorrow and head off on Sunday.* He didn't like to leave Parkin without help, but it seemed his life would finally turn around.

'Here's your tea.' Miss Mattherson's voice broke into his thoughts.

'Thank you, ma'am.' As he took the cup, his fingers brushed against hers, sending a thrill through him. He sipped at the hot liquid, trying to ignore the effect she had on him.

The young woman sat down beside him in a rustle of deep pink taffeta, her tea balanced carefully in her hand. 'You seem happy of a sudden, Mr Worthington.'

'Good news, I think.' He folded the letter and tucked it back into his pocket.

She let out a dramatic kind of sigh. 'Good for you. At least one of us can rejoice. Did you know I am to be shipped off to England?'

He turned his head to look at her. She was leaving? He had not even begun to know her. She wore a lovely pout which made his stomach do a somersault. 'You don't want to go?'

She let out a scornful laugh. 'Is it not obvious? My parents want me to be presented in polite society in London. I am being forced against my will.'

Tony sighed. How could his chance to know this exquisite woman be stolen from him so easily? 'It is unfair.'

Miss Mattherson sat up straight and turned to face him square on. Her eyes were alight with fire. 'You agree with me?'

Realising how his words had been taken, he stammered. 'Well ... I ...'

'Mr Worthington.' Her eyes were wide. 'You are my only hope. Help me convince my father I should stay.'

'I ... I'm not sure ...'

'No, you are right. He wouldn't listen to you.' She sat back, her mind clearly moving through ideas in quick succession.

Her zeal to stay made his pulse rise. He wondered if it were somehow possible for her to remain in Ballaarat, although some experience amongst genteel folk would probably be good for her.

'I know!' She turned to him again, her face flushed with excitement. 'If I were married, he could not send me away, could he?'

Tony was taken aback. It seemed her ideas had no bounds. 'Well ... er ... no ...'

'*You* could marry me.'

The words felt like pins and needles all over him. Could it be that simple? Could he find a property, a wife and a future in the space of a few minutes?

'I am very pretty, am I not? I don't care even if you live in a bark hut. I will be a good wife.'

Tony felt numb. The Vision he had dreamed about had just offered herself to him ... as an alternative to England. The notion sobered him. He didn't want to be an alternative; he wanted to be the first choice. *And she is entirely too bold to propose to me at all!*

'No, Miss Mattherson.' He swallowed, uneasy.

'What do you mean, no?'

'No, I shan't marry you. It is not for you to ask.'

A frown creased her brow. 'Very well, you ask me then.'

'No.' He closed his eyes and turned away from her. 'I suspect an encounter with the peerage might be exactly what you need.' A set-down from a British aristocrat might put her in her place.

She was furious. He could feel the heat emanating from her. He waited for her to unleash her rage upon him, but the rebuke didn't come. Without a sound save a scornful sniff and the swish of her skirts, she got up and moved to the opposite side of the store.

Indignant, Stella sat by her mother and Jemina. When asked about her sour mood, she did not see any point in admitting what had transpired between her and Mr Worthington.

'I dislike being shut up in here with so many women and noisy children. When may we go home?' In truth, the sooner she could be rid of this place and the noncompliant Mr Worthington, no matter how attractive he might be, the better.

'As soon as we are sure the insurgents have been dealt with.' Her mother patted her hand in a lethargic fashion.

Stella leaned her head back against the shelf behind her and closed her eyes. Why could not Mr Worthington see the value in her plan? *Surely he thinks I am pretty. I saw the way he looked at me the first day we arrived.* She had half convinced herself he was smitten. Now, it seemed, she had been wrong. *Never mind, I shall revert to my original plan.* The corners of her mouth turned up as she remembered the package under her bed. If only she could go home.

The storm passed and the light faded. Mr Worthington busied himself lighting lamps and feeding them all. Stella did not intend to go near him again, so felt relieved when Mr Parkin came in and assisted him for a time. They opened numerous tins of meat, heating them on the stove, and boiled potatoes, which they then mashed with butter. It could not be called a feast as such, but it proved to satisfy their hunger.

Stella averted her eyes when Mr Worthington came for her empty plate.

'Did Mr Parkin bring any word?' She heard her mother ask.

'Nothing yet, ma'am. Looks as though you'll have to spend the night here.'

He moved on to collect more dishes and Stella sighed. *All night!* If she could go out to the Eureka Camp, she would give those diggers a piece of her outraged mind. *Why don't the military do something?* She wondered why the rioters had not yet been put down.

The night afforded little sleep, often disturbed by howling infants and the discomfort of a hard floor to rest on, not to mention the stop-start of the rainstorm outside. Stella wondered if Mr Worthington had fared any better, but refused to go and ask him. There would be little use befriending the man, even if she did find him rather handsome. There seemed to be a hidden strength in him, too, but he was of little value to her plans now. He refused to aid her in any way.

Soon after a breakfast of salt pork and hard biscuits, she took the example of a few other women present and took a turn about the store to stretch her legs a little. She had not taken much notice of the other ladies until now, but now noted many of them were not much older than herself. They all had at least one child wriggling in their lap. Looking at them, she decided she much preferred her unmarried status to theirs. *Thank goodness Mr Worthington refused me.* She giggled to herself. *Soon I would be just like them.*

The longer Tony remained cooped up in the store with a bunch of nervous women, the more his unease over the rebellious miners grew. He kept himself busy, providing them with food and drink, but his stomach was tied in knots and he could not eat at all. He had not slept a wink. He had given up the single cot in the back room to an elderly woman. Between his worries and the needs of the ladies, he was kept up all night.

With naught to keep his fears at bay for any length of time, he set about re-arranging the shelves. He tried to think what customers looked for most when they entered, and put those items in the most prominent positions. He often had to excuse himself, stepping over a child here, or a woman's legs there. But, although he felt a little guilty for disrupting them, he knew he had to keep moving or cower behind the counter — and *that* could never be an option.

He let out a sigh of relief when, mid-morning, a knock came at the door and Smith and Burns entered. Smith slapped him on the back with a deep laugh.

'Shoulda known you'd be in the best place in town — surrounded by women-folk.' His eyes browsed the room as if in search for a female of his liking.

Tony flicked the hair from his brow. 'Not exactly my choice, but ...'

'Someone has to do it, eh?'

Another slap made Tony's shoulder heave. Smith flashed him a perverse grin.

'Have you heard about the rebellion?' Tony changed the subject.

Smith shrugged. 'The diggers have built a stockade — tipped over wagons and everything — and they are running drills like an army. Not sure what the Redcoats are doing. Maybe waiting for the diggers to attack. I dunno.'

Tony blanched. 'I hope not.'

Once again, Tony felt the thud as Smith cuffed his shoulder. 'C'mon. Nothing wrong with a bit of excitement. Makes life interesting. Eh, Burns?'

The big man nodded.

'Yeah, well, I would rather do without this kind of excitement. It would be nice if I could go home.'

Smith leaned back and laughed. 'And leave these pretty sheilas? Would y' like me to take over?' He rubbed his hands together.

'I'll be fine.' Tony shrugged.

The two stayed for a while and helped where they could, although Tony noticed they only served drinks to the prettiest of girls, including Miss Mattherson. At least he did not have to continue on his own.

He hoped Parkin would return sometime, so he could give him

notice. Tomorrow he wanted to be on the road to Melbourne and away from this place. Thoughts of his own property increased the worried knots in his stomach. Where was this property? How big was it? Did he really own it at all? Or could it be a big hoax?

The day stretched out into the late afternoon and still they had no word. Miss Mattherson finally came to speak to him again, which, in spite of his doubts, made him glad. By her smile, he could tell she no longer remained angry with him.

'I apologise for my forward behaviour last evening,' she told him, although she did not appear to be embarrassed by it. 'I see now I should not have asked you.'

Tony gave her a wry smile. 'Will you propose to someone else now? My friend, Mr Smith, perhaps?'

Her spine stiffened and she let out an offended humph. 'I shall not propose to anyone. I have no wish to be married.'

'A big change from last night.' He was glad he had refused her. If she knew how tempted he felt by her offer ...

She screwed up her face at him. 'Marriage would be too cumbersome, I think. I would soon be laden with children and household duties.' She shook her dark head. 'I wish to be free.'

Tony felt his heart twist. She was too beautiful. Life was unjust. He let his eyes drop to the floor boards. 'Don't we all?'

She grinned at him in the way he had already come to know as a tease. 'Well, where you are sure to do nothing about it, I on the other hand, am sure *nothing* shall stop me from obtaining it.'

He stared into her fiery eyes and gave a mock shudder. 'I am most grateful I am not your father.'

She tilted her chin up and laughed for a moment, then stopped and looked back at him, as if to read his thoughts. She frowned a little. 'Why, what a ridiculous thing to say.'

She stood up and began to flounce away, but halted when the door opened and her father stepped in.

'Good afternoon ladies,' he announced. 'I bring word about the uprising. Most of the rebels have retired to their huts. As tomorrow is the Sabbath, we do not expect them to continue any further action and you are safe to go to your own homes.'

Chapter Five

Tony watched The Vision depart and sighed. The time he'd spent with her had been too brief, even if in strained circumstances. She'd made it clear she no longer intended to marry, but it did not change the way his heart thumped when he looked at her.

He pushed these thoughts aside and tidied the store, then locked the door and went in search of Parkin. The sooner he could get to Melbourne and find out the truth about this property, the better. He would be away from the miners' unrest, away from dangerous men and away from the hopelessness that surrounded him.

On his way to Parkin's house, he met the Reverend Taylor returning to his own home. Tony had heard of this man of the cloth from his employer. Despite his intention to visit him, he'd been caught up looking after the store. The reverend looked up when he saw Tony and smiled.

'Good evening, sir. How are you this fine day?'

Fine day? Is he living in the same Ballaarat I am? Tony paused and dipped his hat. 'Reverend Taylor, is it? I cannot say this unrest increases my peace of mind. Do you not fear the insurgents?'

'Ah, yes,' the clergy said with a nod. 'The rebellion. I had the privilege today, of an interview with the Resident Commissioner. I have just come from there now, in fact. We talked at length on the state of affairs and he assured me the uprising will be brought to an end shortly. I feel confident there is naught to be concerned about tonight.'

Hearing assurances that came from Commissioner Rede himself gave Tony a little relief. 'I am glad I happened upon you, Reverend. I have wished to speak with you.'

'What's on your mind, lad?' He motioned for Tony to walk with him.

Tony launched into his story, stuttering a little at first, but growing confident as he progressed. It felt good to talk about his worries. He told the reverend about his concern and guilt over Penny, his anxiety about the situation in Ballaarat and his confusion about what he should do. He mentioned one of the letters he received from Penny. 'She thought I should find out more about God, I suppose. So, here I am.'

The reverend rubbed his chin for a time. 'Why do you not want to go home?'

Tony shrugged. 'There's nothing for me there.'

'And here?'

'There's not much for me here, either.'

'Can you think of anywhere you'd rather be, or anything you'd rather do?'

Tony let his shoulders sag. 'Not really.'

Reverend Taylor sighed. 'Seems to me, you are in need of a little purpose.'

Tony felt like squirming. 'What purpose? Everything I try to do fails anyway. What's the use in that?'

'So you give up?'

'Look, at least I have employment and a few friends.' Tony shrugged again, although he felt uncomfortable under this man's scrutiny.

'And yet you feel lost.'

This time Tony squared his shoulders. 'No. I am confused. I am worried about the dangers here.'

'Everyone is worried about these riots. That is natural. Although, the Scriptures say God did not give us a spirit of fear, but of a sound mind. We can cast our cares upon Him and find rest for our souls. Running away serves no purpose. You will find the same problems somewhere else.'

'I'm not running away.' Tony's irritation rose. Just like everyone else, this reverend thought him a coward. 'Listen, I think you misunderstand me. I need to know if I should go and aid my sister. What is the right thing to do?'

'Do you wish to appease your guilt, escape your fears, or do you genuinely wish to help her?'

Crikey this man is direct. He opened his mouth and closed it again. 'I don't know.' He mumbled.

'What I suggest is you go and pray. Ask your Father in Heaven what He wants you to do.'

'But, I don't know how.'

Reverend Taylor's mouth curved into a benign smile. 'Talk to Him like you are talking to me.'

Tony looked at him. 'That simple?'

'That simple.'

The minister made him feel things he didn't want to feel, and he had more questions than when he first encountered him on the street. *How could he know me so well, and not know me at all?* He remembered the letter folded in his pocket and the reason he was on the way to Parkin's house.

'I still believe I shall leave town. I have received what could prove to be a great boon.'

The reverend looked at him for a time as if to measure his sincerity, then dipped his head. 'Very well, Mr Worthington. I pray it is so. And I also pray you find what you are looking for.'

Tony's brows creased together in a bemused frown. *What am I looking for?* 'Thank you, sir. I wish you well.'

That reverend is rather odd. Tony half-jogged towards Parkin's house. *He says the strangest things. As if I am on a search. Whatever for?* He shrugged his shoulders as he approached Parkin's front door and knocked.

He found the store-owner's home in an uproar. Parkin paced back and forth before his fire place like a mad-man, while agonised groans drifted from the bedroom. A young maid rushed out of the room and out the back, soon returning with a bucket of water. Tony could hear another voice in the bedroom making soothing noises.

'Sorry to disturb you, sir. It appears you are about to become a father.'

'I hope so, lad. I hope so.' Parkin pulled a handkerchief from his pocket and wiped his brow.

'I cleaned up after the ladies all left and locked the store.'

Parkin managed to murmur his thanks despite his understandable distraction.

'I know this is not a good time,' Tony ventured, 'but I have had news about my late father's will. I need to leave town for some time.' He watched his employer for any signs of comprehension, but Parkin made no reaction.

'It means I must give you my notice. I want to leave tomorrow.'

Parkin stopped pacing as the news sank in. 'Oh, lad. Tomorrow? Can you not wait a few days?'

'I thought it would be appropriate with the trouble about.' Tony brushed the limp hair from his brow, uncomfortable.

'But my wife is about to give birth. I count on you to run the store until she is well again.' Parkin sounded frustrated.

'But, I ...'

'How will I find someone else at such short notice? And someone of your calibre, too? I don't mind telling you, you have a knack for business, young man. It would be a shame to lose you.'

Tony had no answer. He racked his brain for someone who might fill the post, but came up blank. His shoulders slumped forward as he heaved a deep sigh. 'Very well, I shall wait a few days.'

Parkin came over to him and slapped him on the back, his eyes bright. 'You're a good man, Worthington. I am grateful. Perhaps I shall ...'

At that moment the sound of an infant's cry filled the air. The maid appeared in the doorway, flushed and excited. She curtsied. 'It is a boy, sir.'

'A boy. Ha!' Parkin thumped Tony on the shoulder again. 'Did you hear that, Worthington? I have a boy!' He turned back to the maid. 'May I go in?'

'In a few minutes.' She nodded. 'She is well and the baby is healthy.'

Tony was forgotten amongst the commotion and he let himself out. He strolled to the Ballaarat Hotel for a mug of beer in honour of the birth before he made his way back to his hut. Amidst all the current strife, a healthy boy had been born. At least there could be joy in spite all the dissention. *Perhaps it's not so bad after all.* Reports were that most of the diggers had left the stockade and only one hundred and fifty men remained there. They had all gone back to their tents and huts to spend the evening carousing around their fires. With any luck that would be the end of it. He hoped so. He had promised to stay until Mrs Parkin recovered enough to be left at home while Mr Parkin worked at the store.

Stella paced up and down in her room, nervous anxiety coursing through her body. It was now or never. *My other option is to go to England and prance around ballrooms.* She balked at the idea. *No, I must do this.* She stared at her bed. Then, as if she had made up her mind at last, she reached underneath her mattress and pulled out the package wrapped in brown paper and tied with string. She opened the parcel and laid the contents on her bed, staring at them with a secretive smile. The time had come to put her plans into action. She went to her door, opened it and called for Jemina.

Back inside her room she rewrapped the package, placing it beneath the mattress again, and paced the floor once more. She ran through her plan in her mind, to be sure she had not forgotten anything important.

'Where is that *criada*?' Five minutes had passed and Jemina hadn't appeared. She was about to call the maid again, when a gentle knock came on the door.

Stella flung it open.

'You called me, Miss Estella?' The maid bobbed a curtsey.

'Where have you been, Jemina? I have waited here an age.'

The young girl begged her pardon.

'I need your assistance,' Stella told her. 'But you must promise to say nothing to anyone … *especially* my father.'

'*Sí*, miss.' Jemina nodded.

'If you do tell, I shall have you horse-whipped and sent away!' Stella threatened.

Jemina paled at these words and assured her mistress she would not breathe a word to a soul.

Stella threw her a baleful look and then flounced over to her dresser and sat down. 'I want you to cut my hair.'

'Wh... what?' the maid stammered, paling even further if that were possible. 'Y... your hair?'

'*Sí*, Jemina.' Stella nodded. She swept her hand across the back of her neck. 'My hair. Off!'

The maid had no choice but to obey, but Stella could see her resistance. Jemina grimaced in horror as the luxurious dark waves fell to the floor one by one. She noticed the maid's pleading looks several times as she prepared to clip another lengthy curl, but Stella never flinched.

Stella's image in the mirror did hold a hint of regret as she saw her crown of beauty drop to the ground, but the defiance in her eyes overpowered it and she tenaciously held to her decision.

Just you wait, Papa. You shall be sorry you sent me away.

With the deed done, Stella gathered a scarf and tied it over her short locks to hide them and donned her night dress.

'Pull yourself together Jemina, or Papa will guess.' She frowned at the maid, who still trembled. 'And if he guesses, I shall still have you horse-whipped.'

Jemina collected a dust pan and cleaned up the severed tresses, placing them in a paper bag Estella had produced for her. 'Why do you do this, Miss Estella?'

Stella let out a cheerful laugh, although her eyes glittered darkly. 'I am sure I will be a lot cooler now. Thick hair upon one's neck is stifling, don't you agree?' She handed the maid the full bag of hair. 'Make sure you dispose of this where no-one will find it — tip it in the out-house.'

Jemina curtsied with a sniff and went off to do as bidden, glancing both ways out the doorway before stepping through.

Stella went to the window and looked out. She guessed the hour grew late. *Papa will be in soon.* She went to her bed and pulled back the covers, settling herself with a book while she waited.

Sure enough, not too many minutes later she heard a familiar tap on her door. 'Come in, Papa.'

'I apologise for my lateness, my dear,' he said as he stepped in the room. 'Jemina was — why are you wearing a scarf?'

Stella touched the material on her head as though she had

forgotten all about it. 'I wanted to try something. I always find my hair is excessively knotted in the mornings. I thought if I slept with a scarf, it might be a little better.'

He chuckled. 'I see. Yes, you are a turbulent sleeper. Always were. I would find you the wrong way up on your bed when you were an infant.'

Stella laughed, pretending to enjoy his anecdotes. 'What were you saying about Jemina just now?'

'Oh, yes. She came in from the out-house looking ashen. When I asked her what ailed her, she told me she thought she'd almost stepped on a snake out there.'

'A snake? How awful!'

'Indeed.' Her father nodded. 'Of course, I had to take my lantern and make sure it was safe. I can't have any of my dear family in danger.' He brushed her cheek with his finger.

She took hold of his hand and gave him a pleading look. *One last try.* 'Papa, will you not reconsider sending me to England?'

He heaved a tired sigh and looked at her with sad eyes. 'No. You will go and make your curtsey to the queen. And I would appreciate it if you ceased complaining.'

Stella let her eyes fall to her lap. 'Very well, Papa. As you wish.'

'Good girl.' He leaned down and planted a kiss on the top of her bent head. 'Sleep well, my dear.'

'*Adiós* Papa.'

He left her then, and she let herself fall back on her pillow. It was obvious he did not understand her at all. *If only Abuela were still alive. Now I have to look out for myself.*

She turned down her lamp and waited until the house had quietened, often moving about her room so as not to fall asleep. When she believed everyone must be sound asleep for the night, she waited a little longer — the last thing she wanted was to be caught.

Stella drew back the drapes on her window and saw the moon rode high in the night sky. Soft light filled the room and made it unnecessary for a lamp. As soundlessly as possible she pulled the package out from under her mattress. She took off her night dress, bound her chest to flatten her breasts, and put on the clothes from within the package. Removing the scarf from her head, she brushed her shortened locks, then pulled a hat down over her head. She dug through the clothes in her trunk, right to the bottom, and hauled out a pair of sturdy boots she had hidden there, then wriggled each foot in and pulled the laces tight. Stella peered at her reflection in the dim light and nodded with satisfaction. *Just as I'd hoped.*

She reached beneath the mattress for a letter she'd written earlier and placed it on her dresser, then shook her head. *Too obvious.* She shifted it so only a corner protruded from beneath her jewellery box. *There, they won't find that in a hurry.*

In a satchel, she placed spare underclothes, her grandmother's Bible — a treasured keepsake — her hair brush, hard biscuits, a flask of water and all the money she had saved, which numbered a few pounds. *It should be enough to keep me going until I find work.*

Taking one last look around her moonlit room, Stella tried to think of anything she might have missed. With a little shrug, she slung the satchel over her shoulder and hoisted the window open. She swung one mole-skin covered leg over the sill and then the other, pulling the window down again behind her.

Stella edged around the house towards the street. Standing in the shadows, she noticed a lot of activity down the street around the Ballaarat Hotel. *They're open late.* Or early, as she supposed it to be by now. She turned around to head the other way past her house, when a familiar figure moved into the dim light shining from the hotel windows.

Papa?

Stella shrank back into the shadows. Why would he be there at this hour? Curiosity nagged at her thoughts. *What if he sees me?* If she were caught now, her freedom would be lost. She looked down at her masculine clothes and booted feet. Even if he saw her, he would not recognise her. She pulled the hat down further over her brow and inched closer to the hotel. *I will see what he is up to, then I shall leave.*

Rather than approach the front, which would make discovery inevitable, she flitted across the road in the shadows, skirted around the back of the neighbouring property and edged up the side alley. She kept low, below the windows and hugged her body against the wall, creeping inch by inch towards the lighted windows. She glanced up and saw one opened to allow fresh air to enter. *Good. I shall hear what they are up to.*

Beside the open window, she straightened, keeping her back pressed against the wall. She tried to slow her excited breathing in order to hear words as they drifted through the small gap. From a few phrases, she gathered they were planning a strategy of some sort.

Holding her breath, she dared to move her head to see inside. Men were gathered around a table with what appeared to be a map on it. She noticed Commissioner Rede there as well as the police and military leaders, along with her father. They pointed to the map as they discussed their plans. The phrases 'Eureka Camp' and 'Stockade' drifted to her ears.

Why are they discussing the rebellion in the middle of the night?

And then she heard it — the important information ... 'attack at dawn.' Stella gasped and jumped back from the window, hoping she hadn't been heard. She retraced her steps, her heart pounding in her chest, and hid behind another building. There she crouched motionless, sure she would soon hear footsteps behind her.

Chapter Six

Minutes dragged by, but no sound pursued her. Finally she could breathe out in relief. *They mustn't have heard me.*

Common sense told her she should run — leave Ballaarat like she had planned all along. But a longing for adventure screamed out for her to stay and see the battle take place. *How I wish I were a soldier.* At that she remembered her father kept a pistol in the house. Stella felt her heart flutter. *Should I even dare?* She bit hard on a fingernail as she contemplated the possibility of holding a gun.

She sat in the dark shadows for some time, vacillating in her decision, but in the end the temptation became too strong. Keeping watch for any movement, she managed to sneak back to her home, slid her bedroom window up and climbed in. She pulled off the boots so her footsteps would not be heard and then tiptoed to her father's study.

Stella knew he kept the pistol locked in a drawer, but she also knew where he kept the key. She pulled back the curtains, allowing the moonlight to slide across the furniture. It shone enough light for Stella to accomplish her task. She picked up a silver smoking case and pried it open, finding the key inside. She then used the key to unlock the desk drawer.

There lay the pistol, its dark metal gleaming in the silver light. Without hesitation to think or question her actions, Stella picked it up and thrust it into her satchel, along with a box of lead balls which she also found in the drawer. A smug smile crossed her face. *Now I shall know what it is like to be a soldier.*

Minutes later she had returned to the road, hurrying towards the

Eureka Camp, although she still kept to the shadows. As she approached the stockade, she noticed all was quiet. Stella had not come so close to the camp before, and saw for the first time the fortress the miners had built.

In the flickering light of a dozen campfires, she noticed wagons tipped on their side for part of the wall. The diggers had built part of the stockade from cut logs, tree branches, materials from the mine shafts and even sand bags. Inside their protective fence, the men appeared to be asleep by their fires, many holding weapons. Stella shook her head as she took in the scene before her. *Not much of a rebellion.* She guessed there were about 150 men gathered there. *Why would the Commissioner order an attack on such a small gathering?*

She remembered her father telling them in the store that most of the rebels had gone home and they did not expect an attack. *So why are they talking strategies in the middle of the night? Did Papa know back in the store what the authorities considered?* She wondered if she should warn these unwary men about the imminent ambush, but then remembered they were the ones who had caused all the trouble in town.

Stella furrowed her brows. *They shall receive their punishment soon enough.* With quiet steps, she backed away from the stockade and found a secure hiding place between a few large boulders. There, she could view the men inside the camp and also watch the military approach when the time came.

Making herself as comfortable as possible on the hard ground, Stella began the wait for dawn. She peered into the night sky. Surely, it could be no more than an hour or two away. She withdrew the pistol from her satchel and examined it in the moonlight. *I wonder how it works.* She had seen men operate a gun from a distance before, but had never done it herself. It looked simple enough.

She studied the lever at the top. *I think I have to pull that back.* It clicked into place. *Then aim and fire.* She pulled the trigger, aiming at the ground in front of her and felt the release. *Simple.* Now she had but to load it. Stella collected one of the small lead bullets from the box and dropped it into the muzzle. She screwed up her face as a recollection struck her. *I think I need to poke it down with something.* She felt around on the ground in the dim shadows for a thin twig. *This shall do.* She poked it in the hole, making sure her bullet went right down the end. *There, now I must wait.* Stella sucked in a satisfied breath and sat back to wait, the gun resting on the rock beside her.

Stella jerked awake at the sound of a shout, then gunfire burst out around her into the still night air. She sucked in a few deep breaths and tried to make out her surroundings. Dawn approached, as she could tell by the grey line on the horizon, and along with it came the regiments of the Redcoats and the Police. She watched as they swarmed into the Eureka Stockade, guns blazing and bayonets stretched out before them.

She grasped for her pistol with trembling hands. Nervous excitement thrilled through her body. This was it! She cocked the barrel and aimed the pistol towards — what should she aim at? It was hard to tell who were miners and who were soldiers in this semi-darkness.

She could hear the screams of men as they were shot or stabbed to death. A tent went up in flames to her left and the scene lit up in an orange glow before her. There! A digger tried to run away. She aimed the pistol at him and pulled the trigger.

Nothing.

The ball rolled out of the muzzle and dropped to the ground. Stella's brow creased. What was wrong with this gun? She picked up the ball and pushed it into the mouth again, following it with her handy twig. Again she cocked, aimed and fired.

Again nothing.

Perhaps it's the bullet. Stella grabbed her satchel and rummaged for another ball. As she turned back to load it into the gun, she looked up. Running almost directly towards her, she saw one of the rebel miners. His face held a look of sheer panic and then, when she realised he would see her at any second, his body jerked upwards and pain shot through his face. Then he slumped forward to the ground, not even five yards to her left. A dark stain spread on his back.

Stella heard the footfall of a horse approaching and pressed herself up against the boulder. Peering around, she saw one of the Redcoats reach down from his horse with his bayonet and plunge it into the fallen digger's torso, not once, but several times.

Stella held her breath. It was savage and brutal. She felt bile rise in her throat and pressed her hands tight across her mouth. She could not be sick. She must not scream. What if the soldier heard her? Would he do the same to her? *Oh God! Oh God! What am I doing here?*

As soon as the mounted soldier moved away, Stella grabbed her satchel and fled towards the Melbourne road. She choked back sobs of terror as she ran with all her might, the sounds of war still ringing out behind her, the smell of gunpowder fresh in her nostrils. She did not look back, although she expected any moment to receive a ball in her back like the man she had witnessed. She paused, only once, to retch on the side of the road. She knew it would matter little if she insisted she was William Mattherson's daughter. They would kill her anyway. Those men were bent on murder — she had seen it written on the soldier's face.

Stella ran and ran. Even when her breath came with difficulty, she barely slowed. She wanted to put the horrid scene as far behind her as she could. '*Adiós* Ballaarat.' She felt a surety she would never, *ever* return.

Tony slept restlessly. He tossed and turned on his canvas cot. Dreams floated through his mind like so many ghosts sent to torment him. He saw Penny caught, waist-deep in swirling water and though she tried to wade forward the current pulled her back. She held out her hands toward him, crying out for him to save her. Tony couldn't move. He felt frozen to the ground, as though his legs were encased in stone. Sweat broke out on his brow and neck. He wanted to yell, but no sound came out.

Then he saw another man, a stranger, wade through the torrent as though it were a trickle, lift her and carry her to safety, setting her on her feet right before him.

'Why didn't you help me?' The sodden woman showed the hurt in her eyes. 'You left me to drown!'

Still unable to move or speak, Tony could only listen to her accusations in grief. He could feel his heart pounding hard in his chest.

Strangely, Penny's form moulded, like a chameleon, into Estella Mattherson before him. 'Why won't you help me, Tony?' The apparition continued to burden him with guilt. 'They will take me away. Help me!'

Two faceless thugs came up on either side of her, grabbing her by the arms. Miss Mattherson screamed. 'No! Tony, do something! Tony!'

The sweat streamed from his body now, and his heart beat so fast it felt like a humming bird lived in his chest. He wanted to help. He wanted to demand the men let her go, but he was incapable of either. He felt like a statue, a heart of flesh encased in immoveable rock.

The two men dragged Miss Mattherson away. He heard one of them utter a malicious threat and then he laughed. It was a strange laugh — it came like — like — what did that sound resemble? The laugh sounded like ... a gun shot.

Tony bolted upright in his bed, the dream still clinging to him as did his sweat-soaked shirt. But something else forced its way through his sleepiness. More gunshots. They weren't part of the dream. And they continued to fire in quick succession in the distance.

Tony crept out of his hut and listened. The noise came from the Eureka Camp. He could hear voices shouting, groaning, screaming. *What is happening?* He noticed the horizon began to lighten as dawn approached. *Surely not an attack ... at this hour ... and on the Sabbath?*

He ducked back inside his hut. *That's it. I am not staying another minute.* His heart still drummed as it had in the dream. He gathered his few small belongings into his swag, plunged his canteen into a bucket of water to fill it, and headed out.

'Where are you off to?' A voice spoke to him out of the semi-darkness. He had not yet walked five minutes. He kept to the Melbourne road and walked with his head down, trying to ignore the sound of bloodshed to his left. He had supposed he, in turn, would be ignored. He looked up, startled, then let out a relieved breath. 'Smith.'

'We were just coming to look for y'. Make sure yer all right, y' know.'

'I'm fine. I'm leaving town. What's happening over there?' He nodded in the direction of the Eureka camp. The gunshots began to dissipate now, but Tony could see wagons and huts alight with fire at the stockade.

Smith's eyes were bright, as though he revelled in the riot. 'Word is the Redcoats ambushed the diggers in the stockade — caught them unawares.'

'What?' The news shocked Tony. He continued to walk, although a little slower. Cries still rang out in the dim early morning.

'I managed to sneak away. It's not pretty. Saw one bloke get the bayonet in the gut over an' over. Saw another fella shot even after putting his hands up to surrender.'

Tony swallowed. He felt sick in the stomach. 'That's why I'm leaving. I've had enough.'

'Yeah, we figured we'd go too. Not that we don't enjoy it 'ere. A bit too dangerous if y' know what I mean.'

Tony could only agree.

'Hey, we've got a cart a bit further along. Y' wanna join us?'

Tony pressed his mouth into a grim smile. 'Can't say I wouldn't like company.'

'This way, then,' Smith said, veering a little towards the Eureka Stockade.

Though he didn't like the direction, Tony followed him. The smell of smoke stung his nostrils and the mournful cries of women met his ears. It struck him as odd that the magpies continued their cheerful warble in the midst of such horror. Soon, a line of men were marched by, escorted by the bayonets of the military. Many of the men bled from open wounds, some limped.

A soldier carried the Southern Cross flag — the captured flag. 'We have waked up Joe!' He called with sick glee. Other Redcoats called out in cheerful response, 'And sent Joe to sleep again!'

Tony could hear a dog howling. He peered in the dull dawn to where the sound came from and saw a terrier sitting atop a dead man's chest. Someone picked the pup up and took it away, but within minutes the animal had returned to its master, howling again. Tony felt his heart sink. *Senseless.*

He saw a woman in deep distress with an ashen child clinging to her skirts who stood beside a tent. She made unintelligible noises as she pointed at the tent, which had gaping holes in the canvas. Tony shook his head as he realised the holes were from swords and her husband probably lay within, dead.

'How much farther is your cart? I've seen enough of this,' he told Smith, nausea building in his gut.

'Just over yonder.' Smith pointed.

Tony could see the cart now. Smith jogged ahead and stopped there with a strange grin.

The next thing Tony knew large hands gripped him from behind, one big arm wrapped around his chest while the other pressed something over his mouth. He tried to cry out but it to no avail. Burns — he assumed it was he — easily overpowered him. A strange smell assaulted his nostrils, but before he had time to analyse what it could be, he felt reality leaving him and a black cloud filled his vision. The last thing he recognised was Smith spitting on the ground as the sound of death and loss still rang in his ears.

Chapter Seven

Angus McDoughan stretched himself full-length as he woke, his toes poking through the wrought iron rails at the foot of the bed. *Another day with me lovely wife-to-be.* He could not keep the delight from his face if he tried. The past few weeks had turned everything around for them.

Two months ago, Ellenvale Homestead had been inundated with floodwaters rising from the nearby Jacksons Creek. Angus rolled onto his side. He could still see the watermark on the sandstone walls. *Thank Ye Lord for the good Ye've brought out of it.*

Not only had the flood uncovered gold on Ellenvale Station, but the events which surrounded the find — although painful in part — had led to his betrothal to Penny Worthington. A contented sigh escaped him as he sat up.

When he strolled into the kitchen, he went straight to Penny, slid an arm around her slender waist and whisked her around in a circle. 'Good mornin', sweetheart.'

Soft pink diffused her cheeks as her smile spread and he chuckled his delight.

'Good morning, Gus.' Penny giggled as he kissed one of her rosy cheeks.

'You two make me feel quite ill with yer carry on.' Gertie, the maid, slapped his arm as she passed with a fresh pot of tea.

Angus watched her walk to the table, a glint in his eyes. 'Do I detect a note of jealousy?'

'Angus!' Penny shot him a warning look. Not too many weeks ago, Gertie had been infatuated with him. For a moment he regretted his teasing words.

'Ha!' Gertie laughed, and Gus breathed a sigh of relief.

He turned his attention back to Penny. 'I've been thinkin' ...' He reached around her to pick up a boiled egg from a bowl on the table.

'Careful, they are still ...'

'Ow!' Gus juggled the egg and tossed it back into the bowl.

'... hot.' Penny covered her mouth to try and hide her smile, but Gus could see it in her eyes.

'Don't ye be laughin' at me, lass.' He wagged a finger at her.

She shook her head, unable to hide her mirth. 'Don't ye be callin' me lass, then.'

Gertie erupted in laughter at Penny's attempt to mimic Angus's Scottish accent.

Angus feigned a frown and sat down at the table.

'So, what were you thinking about, my love?' Penny asked when she joined them, setting bread on the table.

Angus sobered and looked at her. 'We need to get a mining licence and stake a claim. I'm a wee bit concerned Foxworth might try to claim it before we do — after all the land does no' belong to ye, it's only leasehold. Aye? And what if word gets out ...?'

She nodded. 'You are right, of course. We must do it at once. You should take Gordon out and peg out some claims — perhaps one for each of us to cover more ground. Then, I suppose a trip into the city is in order.'

Angus threw her a wink. 'Aye, and we could find ourselves a good reverend to perform a leg-shackling for us while we're at it.'

Penny rolled her eyes at Gertie. 'As though I were some kind of prisoner.'

Gertie giggled again.

'Aren't ye? Held captive by the iron strength of me love?'

Penny gave him a soft smile and her eyes lit with a warm glow. 'Well, when you put it like that ...'

On an impulse, Gus lifted her hand and kissed it.

'Good Lord! Are you two gonna be like this all the time now?' Gertie interrupted their moment of tenderness.

Angus laughed. 'Aye.'

Lips still quivering with mirth, Penny looked at him. 'Seriously Gus, you don't think we should wait?'

Gus searched her gaze. Could she be having second thoughts? After all, just over a month ago she believed him a traitor. He swallowed his fear, but his voice came out weaker than intended. 'Why would ye want to wait?'

Penny put a hand over his and squeezed, offering him a smile of reassurance. 'Only that I have written my brother about our betrothal. I would like him at the ceremony — to give me away.'

Angus knew a moment of relief, but at the same time he wondered about Tony Worthington. He had not been back to Ellenvale since he'd walked away from the family ten years ago. 'Do ye think he'll come? I'd no' want to see ye disappointed or hurt.'

She sighed, a wistful sound. 'I hope so. I presume he has heard from Mr Blake about the cattle station by now. That should give him extra incentive to leave Ballaarat — not to mention the tensions there.'

'All ri' then. How long would ye like to wait?' Angus knew it was important to her. He would have to be patient.

'A few more days, perhaps, up to a week. Tony is usually prompt with his replies.'

Stella's legs ached. The sun rode low in the sky and she knew it was yet early in the day. She had walked for hours on end and felt exhausted. Her feet hurt in the unfamiliar boots. This road did not compare to an easy stroll in the garden. She had climbed up several hills and then descended into deep valleys. She had rested briefly on two occasions, but wanted to put distance between her and the horrors of Ballaarat. She did not wish to be caught up any time soon. Besides, if she stopped for too long she would become drowsy. She had not slept all night.

Each time she heard horses approach, she hid herself behind bushes or boulders, whichever served the purpose better, and hoped those Redcoats had not chased her down. Even an encounter with other people would not be welcome. It would inevitably lead to questions;

questions she did not wish to answer, for she had no answers ready.

I must create a story for myself. What is my name? Stefan? Sounds too close to my own name. Billy — after Father? Yes, that is simple enough. Billy Watson. Pleased with her creativity, she went on to fabricate Billy Watson's history and reasons for travelling, although she found it hard to focus. The image of the brutal murder she had witnessed kept playing in her mind. She would never forget the look of terror on the man's face, nor his agonised cry as he died.

She shook her head to clear her thoughts. *Where will I go anyway?* She realised she had not considered her destination in her haste to depart. She shrugged. Melbourne was as good a place as any to start.

Hiking made her thirsty. She paused to drink from her canteen. She had almost emptied it already. She looked around her. *I must keep a lookout for a stream.* She shifted her satchel from one shoulder to the other, rubbed the sore muscles in her legs and pushed on.

By the time she figured it was mid-morning, her walk had reduced to a stagger along the road. Exhaustion, trauma and lack of sleep dragged at her consciousness. The heat reflecting off the road made her feel more sluggish. *Perhaps a little rest would be all right.* She eyed a shady hollow near a stream with longing. It seemed a peaceful spot to stop. Gum trees drooped over the trickling water, while the occasional kookaburra called in the distance.

Stella stumbled from the road and sat down, making sure she would not be seen from the track. She pulled the dry biscuits from her pack and noticed as she did, the box of ammunition. She felt sick at the memory. *Why did I think it would be an adventure to shoot a gun? Thank heavens I couldn't get it to work!* Where was the pistol anyway? She made a quick search of the bag and then thought back, with a little reluctance, to the gruesome ambush. *I must have left it there.* She took the box of lead balls and tipped them into the stream. *I never want to touch a gun again.*

She lay back and chewed on one of the dry biscuits a little before weariness took over. Within minutes she drifted to sleep.

When Tony came to he found himself in a cart, lying beneath a canvas tarpaulin. He tried to sit up but then discovered his hands were tied behind his back and his legs were bound together at the ankle. He also became aware of a gag tied tightly on his mouth. At the same time he became aware of the pain those ropes caused, as well as a dull ache in his head. He groaned as a wave of pain assailed him.

His mind remained in a fog of unconsciousness and a few moments passed before he could remember what had happened to him. Then, as the recollection of Smith's wicked grin and Burns' arms holding him surfaced, he jerked in anger and tried to fight against the cords which held him. The struggle made the pain worse and he soon fell back, exhausted from his efforts.

Why had his friends tied him up? *Why would Bobby Smith drug me?* His groggy mind found it difficult to focus on any details. What did they want with him? The effort it took to focus on these thoughts drained his strength. The moment he formed a thought, it disappeared as though it were a wisp of vapour.

Fear crept in and beads of sweat formed on his brow as his panic increased. *I must escape.* He writhed and twisted in an attempt to loosen the binds, but his weakened state made his efforts ineffective. He gave up and lay still, panting through his nose. He peered around in the dim light under the tarp and looked for anything he could use to cut himself free. He saw what appeared to be a couple of satchels filled with food, his own bag which he had packed so haphazardly that morning in the far corner, and a pile of camping equipment and a few blankets folded beside him, but nothing with a sharp edge to it.

The wagon swayed as it moved along and Tony wondered where they were taking him. He had no idea in which direction they had travelled or what time of day it was. If, by chance, he did escape, how would he find his way back? How far had they come?

He lay there, his mind raising one question after another while he tugged at the cords around his wrists on occasion until, at last, the cart lurched to a stop. He heard the two men jump down from the driver's seat and the next thing he knew one of them pulled back the cover. The sun blinded his eyes momentarily as Burns jerked him up to a sitting position. The gag was torn from his mouth and a flask pressed against his lips.

'Drink this,' came Burns' gruff voice as he tipped the water down Tony's throat.

Tony coughed and sputtered, much of the water lost down his chin and onto his shirt, but managed to swallow a few mouthfuls. As soon as the ruffian took the flask away, Tony fired questions at his captors, although his jaw felt stiff from the gag. 'Why are you doing this?'

'That's none of your concern,' Smith answered, and spat on the ground.

'What makes you think you will get away with it?'

'No-one saw us.' Smith shrugged. 'Thanks to the miners' rebellion, no-one paid us heed.'

'Someone will be looking for me!'

'Will they now?'

This silenced Tony and he knew a moment of despair. In truth, no-one in Ballaarat would take much note of his disappearance. Perhaps Parkin would, when he opened the store on Monday morning, but where would he be by then? His sister, the one person who might care about him, lived miles away at Ellenvale Station and she would have no idea anything had happened to him.

These men had chosen their prey well. Tony Worthington could vanish from the face of the earth and it would be months before anyone cared to look.

Before he could speak again, the gag was once again tied around his mouth and Burns shoved him back down in the cart. The tarpaulin was tied down and they began to travel again, while Tony could do naught but lay there and attempt to fathom what Smith and Burns had abducted him for.

His mind a little clearer now, he thought of a possible explanation. Did these men have something to do with his previous employer, James Bentley? That man had been accused of murder and while he had first been acquitted, he had been re-tried and found guilty of manslaughter. Many questions were raised over the case, especially when the mob of diggers rioted over it and razed the Eureka Hotel, Bentley's pub, to the ground. In truth, it was those events that fuelled the fire for the current tensions and rebellion.

Had Smith and Burns worked for Bentley ... or his enemies? Some thought the murder to be a set up by those involved with the sly grog industry. Bentley's legitimate tavern was too successful for their liking.

But, had not Robert Smith and Morris Burns arrived in Ballaarat at least a month later? An easy ruse to accomplish. *Perhaps they were already residents of Ballaarat.* Perhaps Smith and Burns weren't even their real names.

Did they perceive Tony as a threat to the success of the sly grog industry? Did they fear he would testify on behalf of Bentley, or that he would support the petition for his release? In that case, what did they intend to do with him? *Do they plan to murder me?* Tony felt his heart lurch. But then another idea struck him. *Wouldn't they have done it already?* It would have been an easy thing under the cover of the gunfire during the Eureka riot.

Tony groaned. It was too much to piece together. *I've got to get away from them.* He needed to focus on that one thing. A way to escape. But, while his head ached, his wrists burned and the cart swayed, he found it hard to concentrate for long. The air beneath the tarpaulin felt thick and hot and Tony found it difficult to breath, especially with a large knot stuffed in his mouth.

The ruffians stopped again for a short while, once more forcing water down his throat. Tony felt the need to gulp in fresh air while he had the chance and almost choked on his drink. Smith then gave him some bread and told him to be quick about it. Nausea from the rocking cart, added to Tony's anxiety, made the food come straight back up again. Smith looked at him with disgust, poured his canteen over him — Tony assumed to wash the bile off — and shoved him back down in the cart. Within minutes, he felt the cart lurch forward and the journey continued.

Stella woke to the click-clack of hooves on the dirt road and the rumble of cart wheels along with it. *How long have I been asleep?* She peered into the sky, shading her eyes against the glare. The sun still rode high in the sky. Perhaps she had dozed for an hour or so.

Dragging her satchel through the dust, she scurried to the nearest large tree and pressed herself up against the trunk. Her legs felt stiff all over and throbbed with pain and the soles of her feet burned. Even her shoulders were sore from bearing the satchel. She shook her head and tried to clear the cloud of sleepiness from her mind. *What I would give for a ride in a cart.*

Her eyes widened and a smile turned up the corners of her mouth as an idea streamed into her mind. She waited until the cart had rolled by and then darted from tree to tree until she stood at the road side. Crouching low, she dashed to the middle of the track, behind the cart. She kept her head down out of sight and maintained pace with the cart. She fiddled with the corner of the tarpaulin which covered it until she worked it loose. Then, with a graceful pull, she heaved herself into the cart beneath the canvas and lay there holding her breath, hoping not to be discovered. She did not move a muscle, afraid one of the two drivers would sense her movement.

At least they weren't soldiers with bayonets. Stella shuddered.

The air was heavy and moist under the cover and as she relaxed, the lack of sleep threatened to take over once more. Her eyelids dipped with the sway of the cart until the realm of dreams reclaimed her.

Chapter Eight

Stella jerked awake to the sensation of falling. She tumbled towards the side of the cart as the wheel dipped into a sudden pothole. She braced herself in fright, but could not stop herself from crashing into the wall where she bumped her nose on the boards. At the same moment, something heavy crashed against her back, sending a shock of pain through her and slammed her shoulder further against the side of the cart. She barely held back a sharp cry as tears welled in her eyes. She pressed her hands to her face, making every effort to remain silent.

When the wave of pain eased, she tried to push whatever had fallen against her away. A pile of blankets blocked her view, along with the dim light, but it seemed the 'something' was warm. She even thought she heard it groan. She froze in alarm and wandered what occupied the cart with her.

Stella refused to make sudden movements and attract the attention of the drivers, so she resisted the urge to get on her hands and knees to investigate. Curiosity plagued her, but she would not move or speak and give her presence away. She tried to edge away from the body, but had little room to move.

Left without an explanation, Stella's mind wandered. She imagined a poor, sick dog in the cart beside her. Perhaps he had been bitten by a snake and now suffered terribly from the poison in his system. The body seemed to shiver behind her, adding credence to her theory. Indeed she was sure she could smell stale vomit as well. The poor mutt needed to be nursed back to health. *I'll take care of you.* She hoped these men would let her join their expedition and they would all become fast friends.

Tony drifted in and out of wakefulness. One thing he did know. He no longer rode alone in the back of the cart. He had felt the warmth of another body block his fall when the dray lurched in a rut. How the person had gotten there, he had no idea, but they would be sorry when they found out who they had hitched a ride with. *Unless, of course, they abducted someone else while I slept.* He quickly dismissed this idea. Surely he would have woken. *If I could just turn over to see who it is. If only I could warn them.* The gag remained firm around his head and his wrists and legs were bound tight as ever.

Tony had lost track of time. Hours had passed, possibly even a full day when he felt the motion stop. He heard one of the men leap down from the wagon and then the canvas cover was dragged back. Tony felt, rather than saw, the other person sit up behind him. The unexpected movement in the back of the dray caused Smith to recoil and let forth a string of expletives.

Tony squinted against the sudden light and craned his neck around to see who the stranger could be, but the lad faced towards Smith whose expression had transformed from one of shock to irritation. He spat on the ground and his eyes narrowed to a menacing stare. 'It seems we've got a stowaway, Morris.' He said in a tight voice. 'How did he get in ... and when?'

Affronted, his comrade growled. 'I never saw nothin'.'

'Yet, here 'e is!' Smith waved a hand towards the intruder.

At this the boy spoke up. 'Please do not blame Mr Morris here. I climbed in while you were in motion.'

The two men looked at him as though surprised he could speak.

'I apologise for my sudden appearance.' The lad cheerfully jumped from the back of the cart. 'I became weary of walking. I should like to join you on your trip to Melbourne, or wherever you are headed. Are you off to the goldfields?'

'Goldfields?' Smith repeated with a dumbfounded look.

'In Bendigo, perhaps? Or Goulburn?' the boy replied. 'Ballaarat is not so well at present, is it?' He looked from one to the other. 'I, too, want to find gold.'

Smith and Burns looked at each other and then back at him.

'I can be very useful,' he told them when they didn't speak. 'I can look after your horses. I can cook. I will even nurse this poor dog of yours.'

With that, the lad turned to look back towards the wagon and gasped when he saw Tony tied up and gagged there. He saw two wide eyes stare at him before the boy spun back to face the two drivers again. The men ogled him intently, studying his response. The youth glanced back over his shoulder at Tony, who tried again to free himself from his trusses. The boy's eyes darted back to Smith and Tony noticed his shoulders relax.

'Why, aren't I stupid?' the boy laughed. 'My mind had run away with me so that I thought I lay next to a sick animal. It is quite clear now. An ungrateful cur, no doubt. You must have caught him in the act of thievery or some such. You are quite right to keep him bound until you reach the police. You never know what treachery he might perform.'

Smith spat on the ground and shrugged. 'Yeah. Capable of anythin', eh Morris?'

Burns grunted.

The young man's head bobbed up and down. 'Well, gentlemen.' He rubbed his hands together. 'I hope you don't mind if I join you.'

Smith looked at him with a scowl. 'Trouble is, we do mind.'

The big man folded arms like tree branches across his chest. 'Ya want me to get rid of 'im?'

Smith spat again while he stared contemplatively at their stowaway.

Tony yanked at his bonds, writhing around on the bed of the dray. He tried to yell against the gag in his mouth.

The lad seemed to grow uneasy for a moment, but then his courage rose again. He held the dangerous men with a defiant stare. 'My father is very powerful and he will have men out looking for me even now. It would be better for you to release me immediately than be caught doing me harm!'

Smith continued to stare at him with menace, not at all perturbed by this information. Instead, an evil smile lit his face. 'Tie 'im up, mate, I need to think about things.'

The adolescent gasped and tried to make a run for it, but Burns caught hold of him in a lightning grasp, and bound his slender arms and ankles. 'You wanted to join us didn't ya?' Burns let out a course laugh as he placed their new prisoner beside a tree and lashed him to the smooth trunk.

Tony found himself deposited at the base of a tree close to the writhing urchin, and then Burns lashed him to the trunk there. Burns removed his gag and Tony opened and closed his mouth in an effort to stretch his aching jaw. His mouth and lips felt dry and he wished for more water. Their captors prepared camp some distance away — but not so far they couldn't keep an eye on them. Burns had left them with a dire threat to keep their mouths from hollering for help.

Stella sat still, her bottom lip clamped between her teeth and her face averted from the other prisoner. As soon as his gag had been removed and she could see his face, she recognised Mr Worthington from the Ballaarat general store. *Of all the people, of all the places, of all the carts I could have climbed into ...* What would become of her now? Those two ruffians had to be the most hostile folk she could have hitched a ride with. The man, Smith, clearly had it in for her, and Burns appeared to barely contain a desire for violence. She shuddered. *How could I have chosen so badly?*

Fear churned in the pit of her stomach. The first day of her adventure had ended and she'd witnessed a horrible murder, trudged for miles up and down hills and now found herself lashed to a tree while two thugs contemplated her future. She had not planned it this way. On top of that, she could be discovered at any moment by Mr Worthington beside her. She wriggled against the binds which held her fast. Somehow during the night, she would have to get away. If she could escape, perhaps she had a chance to survive and continue on her way. One thing she knew; she would have to be careful of every word and every move.

She knew Mr Worthington would soon realise it was she, in spite of the lowered voice she used, the masculine clothes and the hat pulled down over her brow. As long as he didn't see her face, she might avoid detection. *But, if he recognises me, he is sure to tell. I must not look at him.*

Thankfully, the man beside her did not attempt to be friendly. She heard him grunt a few times, and saw from the corner of her eye that he rested his head on his knees. *He is probably bruised from the rough ride all trussed up like that.* She felt a little sorry for him. She opened her mouth to ask him how he fared, but he lifted his head and spoke before she got a word out.

'Fool!' He gritted, his eyes fixed on their captors. 'You've gotten yourself in a right mess now! What kind of addlebrained whelp would stowaway in a stranger's wagon?'

This offensive criticism did naught but make Estella angry, her compassion forgotten, and her dark eyes flashed with defiance. 'How was I to know they were kidnappers? Much though you can talk. You obviously weren't clever enough to escape them!'

A scornful sound emitted from Mr Worthington's throat. 'You know nothing about me!' he reminded her. '*You* should not have hitched a ride in the first place. Why such a secretive getaway? Did your father beat you?' He said this without compassion but with sarcastic derision, as though there could be no reason great enough to hide away in an unfamiliar wagon.

Stella glared at him and narrowed her eyes. '*You* know nothing of *me!* And I'd thank you to keep your theories to yourself!'

'As you wish,' Mr Worthington hissed, his head slanting her way for a moment. Stella was quick to show him the back of her head and an angry silence fell between them.

Soon enough Burns brought them a plate filled with chunks of cheese, salt pork and fruit, which he administered to them one by one, freeing their hands for a few minutes to feed themselves. Stella found it hard to force the food into her mouth while her stomach churned so much. Smith wandered over, carrying a tin mug filled with steaming tea. He seemed to note the animosity between them and flashed a twisted smile. 'Friends, I see.'

Both prisoners glared at him but kept their silence.

While Burns retied her wrists together in her lap and then lashed her to the tree once more, Smith nudged Stella with his boot to gain her reluctant attention. 'What's yer name?'

Remembering to keep her voice lower, she replied with a scowl. 'Billy Watson.'

'What are y' runnin' away for?'

'I'm not running away!'

'Ri'. And yet, y' been hidin' in me dray.'

'I wanted a break from walking.'

'So, if yer not runnin' away, why would yer father be out lookin' for y'?' Smith watched for her response, like a hawk scours the ground for the smallest movement before he swoops.

Stella had trapped herself with her words. She opened and closed her mouth, wishing an idea would come.

'You still haven't told me what you want with *me*?' Mr Worthington's resentful voice rang out, drawing Smith's attention away from her. 'I never told anyone I believed Bentley was innocent, or that I thought you sly grog people wanted him out of the way, so why abduct me?'

Smith shook his head. 'This has no ...' he stopped short. Then he lifted a greasy finger and wagged it in Mr Worthington's face. 'You been causin' trouble in Ballaarat.'

Stella believed it sounded more like a question than a statement, but Mr Worthington reacted like an accused man. 'I swear I said nothing! What do I care if sly grog is sold aplenty? Bentley is well and truly stitched up. He'll be in gaol a long time, no matter if I tried to do anything about it. For heaven's sake, I didn't even sign the petition, so what do you want with me?' Mr Worthington's voice rose in desperation. 'You came and pretended to be mates while *spying* on me all the while. I am a fool to have thought you sincere. So, now what? Do you intend to kill me? Tell me!'

Smith stood back and eyed him with a secretive grin, then pulled Burns aside towards the campfire. 'Well, well, well. I'll be darned. It seems our friend ...'

His voice trailed off as the distance increased. Stella watched Mr Worthington from the corner of her eye as he let his head fall back against the tree trunk, his eyes closed tight. She saw his Adam's apple bob up and down as he swallowed hard.

The light faded fast and Stella could feel the chill on the air already. She had never spent a night in the open before, although before things turned sour, she had looked forward to it. She had imagined it would be part of her adventure, sleeping beneath the stars. She could hear the musical sound of cicadas ring out in the stillness, and the intermittent croak of frogs from the nearby stream.

It would be difficult to enjoy the evening sounds with the knowledge that those horrible men slept not fifteen yards away. She wondered with a little trepidation how she would fare. *Will I even survive the night?* She felt the knot in her stomach again and continued to tug at the ropes around her.

'Do you really think they will kill you?' she ventured to ask.

Mr Worthington's shoulders drooped forward and his head hung. 'Probably. I can't think of any other reason they would drag me out here. I'm Tony, by the way.'

'Mm-hmm.' Stella would not admit she already knew that.

'Is Billy your real name?'

Stella sniffed in contempt. 'Why wouldn't it be?'

She heard Tony suck in a deep breath and let it out again. 'Look, I'm sorry I ripped up at you like a bear before,' he apologised in a strained fashion. 'I had a devilish sore head from the drug they used on me, not to mention being trussed like a pig all day and being bumped and pitched around in that infernal cart. And Ballaarat was a bloody mess this morning. My temper is sore as an ox.'

Stella stared off into the trees and offered only a shrug. 'I suppose it was ... unpleasant.'

'To say the least.' Tony sighed. 'Anyway, pleased to meet you, Billy Watson.'

Stella kept her face averted but frowned. 'I'm not pleased at all. You must think I have feathers for brains if I am to be pleased at this situation.'

Tony sounded frustrated. 'That is not what I meant ...'

'What do they mean to do with *me*, do you think?' She cut him off, too worried about her own skin to listen to his explanations.

'I can't imagine they'll let you go. You made yourself a witness when you stowed away.'

Stella's temper flared again. 'You think it's *my* fault they chose to hold me hostage!'

'Why the devil did you get into that cart?' Tony's voice rose again.

'What right do *you* have to rake me over the coals for it?'

'As if I didn't have enough to worry about already,' Tony growled. 'Now I have a spoilt child into the bargain!'

Stella's eyes widened in fury. 'You need not concern yourself with me,' she hissed with jerk of her shoulders. 'I am not your responsibility!' She turned a scornful gaze over her fellow prisoner and added, 'Much as you are capable of in your state. Weak as a fish.'

She knew she had offended him now as he retreated into silence with a curt, 'I beg pardon, sir.'

At least he would not ask her any more questions, or accuse her. She felt a little guilty for her outburst. She did like Mr Worthington and she knew he did not deserve to be in this situation either, but she did not like to be treated as a child. In spite of her courageous words, deep down she feared the worst. *Is this the end?*

Regret began to find its way into her conscience. Perhaps she shouldn't have run away. Perhaps a happy adventure could only ever be the substance of one's imagination, whereas in reality it led to naught but terror and pain. If she died, she would leave without a chance to say sorry to her parents. She shivered, partly from the cold night air, and partly from the fears which plagued her senses. The ropes had not loosened at all, despite all her writhing.

Burns soon came to see them again, checked their bonds and draped each with a blanket. He departed again to sleep by the warm campfire.

'At least we get to live another night,' Tony grumbled. He closed his eyes and leaned his head against the tree trunk.

Stella wriggled herself into the most comfortable position she could find, though she wondered if she would sleep at all while tied up to a tree, uncomfortable, and fearing what the morrow would bring.

Chapter Nine

The two captives had been shaken awake in the early dawn light. They were gagged again with their arms tied behind them and forced back into the wagon. They were placed facing each other so they could not try to untie one another, and once again the tarp covered them. Thus began another day of constant rocking back and forth as the horses pulled the dray along.

Tony had spent the night with little sleep; one moment shivering in the chilly air, another overwhelmed with fear for his life. In his wakeful moments he turned the events over in his mind yet again, searching for answers. Though he racked his brain, he could not suppose what they intended. If they had wanted to torture and murder him, surely they would have done so by now. But, they seemed to want to keep him alive. For what purpose, he had no notion. In the wee small hours, he had eventually fallen into an exhausted slumber, only to be awoken at dawn to begin another day of travel.

He peered at the lad, Billy, in the dim shade beneath the canvas. The boy had met his gaze once last night, but in that moment, he had noticed something familiar. *Have I met him before?* He remembered back to his time in Ballaarat, but, try as he might, he could not place the chap. *I wonder who you are?*

Billy's eyes were closed at present, long, black eye-lashes splayed across his high cheek-bones. He seemed a mite pale this morning. *Probably terrified, the poor fool.* Yet, at the same time, the boy did not seem desperate for help. He lay still most of the time, but occasionally strained against his binds. *I wonder what is going on in that bacon-*

brained head of his. Had he indeed run away? And from what, or who? Did he find himself in worse straits than before he absconded?

Tony sighed heavily, the air hissing from his nose. What hope did the lad have for a future now? If these thugs were bent on murder, Billy had no chance of being freed. This relentless jolting and swaying while trussed up like roast fowl only served to weaken them. They would be bruised from elbow to knee before this day ended — if they kept up the travel for that long.

He lay there, dazed by the constant pain and fatigue, almost insensible to the passing of time. The journey was only broken by those moments when the two men stopped. Then, the prisoners were dragged into an upright position and forced to swallow water and some stale bread.

During one of these times of refreshment, passionate fury took hold of him and he tried to lash out at the two men. Billy joined in, thrusting his boot into Smith's leg. However, they succeeded only to earn themselves a sound backhand to the jaw and a shove back to the floor of the cart, putting an end to their meal. As the hours ticked by, the more hopeless he felt. How could he possibly escape?

Finally, the two hostages were lifted from the cart by Burns and tied to a tree again. Tony guessed the afternoon grew late by the long shadows on the ground. He glanced around but could not see the road at all. They had driven well away from the main track. Would this be their camp for the night? Or was it their destination?

Burns went off to scrounge around for dry wood for a fire, while Smith appeared to prepare a billy with water and tea. Tony groaned and tried to stretch his weary muscles as best he could, restrained though he was. His stomach growled with hunger and his throat felt parched. He worked his aching jaw where the gag had been tied around his mouth all day. He noticed Billy did much the same as he, but remained withdrawn. It suited Tony well. He did not wish to be burnt by his insolent tongue again. So, it surprised him when the young upstart spoke to him in hushed and confiding tones.

'I say, Tony,' he began. 'I think I know how we could escape.'

Tony looked sideways at the scheming boy, but uttered no more than a scornful sound.

'I am serious,' Billy insisted. 'Listen. The next time they give us privacy to relieve ourselves, all you have to do is distract Burns for a few minutes while I make a run for it. I will hide until you are gone and then I will walk to the nearest town to get help for you.'

Tony shook his head in disbelief. 'If you think I will be a part of this scheme of yours, you are insane.'

The lad scowled at him. 'I can do it, I know I can. I would let *you* run, but you don't have the strength. I am yet in good health.'

'And how do you propose to send anyone to my aid?' Tony rolled his eyes. 'You neither know where we are, or where they plan to take us?'

Billy remained silent for a moment, thoughtful, but then said, 'I am sure I could lead the police back here. I am very good with directions, you know. Then they could follow your trail.'

Tony sighed with frustration. 'Even if that were possible, you heard Smith. If we try to run, we are threatened with a beating.'

The young man looked at him in disgust. 'You would give up? For fear of a few more bruises? You are a coward!'

Outraged by this attack on his character, Tony's face flared red. 'Do you think I will allow a scrap of a lad, barely out of leading-strings, tell me what to do?' He hissed at the boy. 'You are too green to realise how much danger you are in, and far too brazen. Do not speak to me of cowardice!'

Billy's face became livid. 'I am not a child!' he growled through clenched teeth. 'I am almost eighteen. Don't you *dare* treat me like an infant!'

'Almost eighteen!' Tony laughed harshly. 'With not yet a trace of whiskers on your chin, nor yet of strength in your arm? Do not think me such a gudgeon.'

The sudden look of alarm in Billy's face gave him pause, and he looked at him with careful scrutiny for the first time. In a few seconds he noted the thick eyelashes which framed almond shaped, dark-brown eyes. He took in the high cheek bones, the curvaceous lips and the olive complexion that looked all too soft to be a youth of eighteen years. He observed his square jaw line and saw that the chin dimpled in a mischievous fashion. He again perceived the lack of brawn in the willowy arms, and also noticed his hands had long, slender fingers which appeared to be well manicured. The lad's chest showed nothing remarkable, although the loose-fitting shirt could be deceptive. But then he noticed Billy had a waist and hip that were far too shapely to be ...

'Good God!' he exclaimed in shock, and then, his eyes darting towards their captors, lowered his voice again to a harsh whisper. 'You are a woman!'

Billy's — or whoever she was — eyes widened and she shook her head vehemently, her eyes shifting back and forth between him and the kidnappers.

Tony followed her frightened gaze and saw one of them headed in their direction. Smith must have been alerted by his cry. He looked back at the girl, whose eyes now pleaded with him. He knew she wanted him to keep her secret. As though he would put her in any more danger than she already suffered.

Smith stood over them, chewing his black tobacco, and spat in the dirt beside them.

'What's yer father's name?' he demanded, beady eyes watching for her response.

'Go to the Devil! Why should I tell you?' She spat her reply with indignation, and for the first time Tony realised she used a lowered voice.

Smith's snake-like eyes hardened. 'If you ever want to see 'im again, you'll tell me now.' He growled with menace.

The frown on the girl's face disappeared and she became pale. She opened her mouth and closed it a few times, before she mumbled. 'William Mattherson.'

What? How many shocks could a man take? Estella! *How did I not know?*

Smith's lips curled into a wicked smile. 'So, yer not Watson. Yer the brother of that pretty morsel we seen flouncin' down the street. A right Miss Minx that one, eh Worthington?' He turned a conniving grin to Tony and then returned his gaze to Miss Mattherson. 'So, where will I find *William Mattherson*?'

Miss Mattherson let her head fall forward as she realised the worst of trouble had come to her. She informed him her father worked with Commissioner Rede in Ballaarat, upon which her captor's eyes glinted with unholy glee.

'Billy Mattherson.' Smith looked down at her with a malicious grin and spat tobacco juice on the ground. 'You're gonna make me a happy man.' Burns wandered over to join them.

'Why? What will you do?' Her voice became a little weaker.

Smith made a scornful sound in the back of his throat. 'Wouldn't you like to know?'

Tony chose to put aside his astonishment for the moment. He could deal with Miss Mattherson later. For now he needed to get this man to own up to his plans. 'What do you hope to gain by this?'

Smith snickered at him and spat on the ground yet again. 'You two are gonna make us rich!' He gloated over them as though he were a cat with a fat mouse.

Tony's brows knit together. 'How do you figure that, when I don't have a groat to my name? And Miss ... *Master* Mattherson here probably has none either.'

'Ah, but ya have a sister, don't ya?' Smith's snake eyes gleamed.

Tony became alert as never before. 'Penny? What has she to do with this? If you harm her ...' Mid-sentence he realised what their insinuation meant. 'Oh, so it is a ransom you're after, is it?'

Smith nudged his companion with his elbow. 'He's a bright one, ain't 'e mate?'

Burns grunted.

'I'm afraid you have the wrong man,' Tony told them, his face whiter than usual. 'My sister is likely close to penury.' His shoulders slumped forward and his matted hair fell over his eyes.

'Y' haven't heard, then?'

'Heard what?'

'She's just come into a fortune.' Smith watched him intently.

'A fortune? What?' Tony felt sweat break out on his brow.

'She's rich as sin, an' we are gonna relieve 'er of 'er money.'

Tony could hardly breathe. What money had Penny come into ... and *how*? Papa's estate couldn't have been that large, could it? It would be too cruel to lose it again on his account. He wished he had the strength to run away. But where to? He didn't even know where he was.

'What about me?' Miss Mattherson's voice reminded him he had more to worry about than himself.

Smith wagged a finger at the disguised girl. 'Now, don't try an' fool me, y' young jackanapes. As soon as y' mentioned yer daddy's name I knew y' were from a wealthy family. I'd lay odds he'll be willin' to pay a whole lotta money to get his precious son back.'

Miss Mattherson paled again but kept quiet, instead allowing her gaze to drop to her bound ankles.

Smith watched them for a time and then spat black tobacco juice onto the ground. 'I'm goin' off to post the ransom letters and get provisions. You two'd better not try anything, or else Burns here will give yer a tidy beatin'. Ain't that ri' Burns?'

For answer, Burns thrust one clenched fist into his open palm with a grunt.

Tony looked away, refusing to let them see his disgust and fear. Minutes later they saw Smith drive away with the cart.

'I wish I had not left that gun behind.' Miss Mattherson's eyes followed the dray, while her words came out between clenched teeth.

Tony turned to look at her. 'What gun? And what possessed you to dress as a boy and run away?'

'Shhh.' Her eyes darted to Burns who busied himself at the campfire some distance away. 'Please do not make this worse than it already is.'

Tony gritted his teeth. 'Fine. I shall keep up the pretence and call you *Billy*. Satisfied?' He had no wish to see her disguise uncovered. It would indeed make things worse, especially knowing Smith's penchant for pretty girls. Yet, he felt annoyed at her.

'Thank you.'

Tony waited for an explanation but none came. 'Well, are you going to tell me why you are here?'

She turned to him, dark eyes scornful. 'I have been kidnapped, or had you not noticed?'

'Did you need to state the obvious?'

'Did *you*?'

Tony took a deep breath and pushed down an impulse to give her a savage reply. 'Look Miss ... *Billy*, you and I are in this together now. If we are to succeed ...'

'Succeed at what?'

'... if we are to *survive*, we need to come to a truce. Do you think for a moment you can forget you despise me?'

Miss Mattherson's eyes narrowed. 'I don't despise you, but if you had married me when I asked, we should not be in this mess.'

Tony felt his heart leap with yearning at the mention of marriage, but anger soon took its place and he felt the heat rise in his neck. 'I — we — you blame *me* for this? Doing it much too brown now, I think.' He choked on his words. 'If I remember correctly, you changed your mind about marriage. *Too cumbersome*, is how you framed it. And besides, how do you expect it would have changed matters, anyhow?'

Miss Mattherson held her nose in the air and sniffed. 'If you had married me, though I am sure it would have been *quite* cumbersome, I should not have run away and therefore not have been kidnapped. You see, it makes perfect sense.'

'Oh, yes, perfect.' Tony rolled his eyes and his voice came out like gravel. 'However, I was always the intended victim here. If we had married, I would still have been abducted and quite possibly you would be a widow at the ripe old age of eighteen.'

The young impostor seemed to contemplate this for a moment then flashed him a mirthless grin. 'All the better. I would no longer be *encumbered* by matrimony, and more than that, I should be an independent woman, free of my father's control.'

Tony felt the heat in his face deepen. *Hoyden!* The girl was impossible. How would they ever devise a plan together if she insisted on jabbing him with barbs? Tight with indignation, he glared at her. 'I am sure he would be glad to be rid of you.'

Chapter Ten

Estella Mattherson sits beside me, trussed like a suckling pig. It took Tony some time to absorb the reality of this. Worse, was even if he wanted to — and he *did* want to — he couldn't help her for the ropes which bit into his own wrists and ankles — let alone the obstacle of her accepting any help. *Stubborn chit.*

To complicate things further, she still made him feel more alive than he had in years. In spite of her difficult nature, she awoke something which, until now, he had never known existed within him. The desire to protect, rescue, stand up and fight. But he couldn't.

Tony sighed. She hated him, she'd made that clear. Why should he want to help someone who resented him? *I should think about helping myself.*

At least now he knew these men were not out to murder him, and it had nothing to do with Bentley at all. Smith had returned from his errand at dusk, seeming pleased with himself. That could only mean he got his ransom letters off as intended.

Would Penny give up her newfound wealth? *I wonder how that came about. Why didn't she write me about it? Perhaps Papa left her an extra inheritance too.* If he had managed to hide the cattle run from her, it could be the case. But who would have known about it? Her new farmhand? And how did the word get to men in Ballaarat? *No, Smith and Burns arrived in Ballaarat less than a month ago. Did someone send them? But who?* Tony had no answers and no way to find them.

He shifted his position a little and winced, sucking a painful breath between his teeth. The ropes had rubbed his wrists raw and his jaw ached from being gagged for hours upon end. The corners of his mouth were cracked and dry. He wondered how his fellow prisoner fared.

'You awake?' He heard her whisper. She must have heard his frustrated sigh.

'Yeah.' Tony was wary. Would she bite his head off again?

'Me too.'

'Pain keeping you awake?'

She paused before she answered. 'Yes.'

Tony wondered if he'd heard correctly. Did he detect a quiver in her voice? *Don't do this to me.* He couldn't bear the thought she might be crying.

'Listen, I've given your plan some thought.'

'Plan?' There it was again. That wobbly sound in her voice.

'Your plan to escape.'

Silence.

'Since we know they don't wish to kill us, perhaps we could try.' *Heavens*, w*hat am I saying?* 'In the morning, as you suggested, when they give you a little privacy, you could make a run for it.'

Miss Mattherson still did not speak.

'I'm sure you can run fast. Even if you get away and can't find your way back with help, at least you will be free. Do you think you have enough strength left?'

'I think so,' came her weak response, followed by a sniff. 'Are you sure?'

No, I'm not sure, but what else can be done? 'We will be fine.'

The young run-away became quiet again for a time, and Tony breathed out in relief. She hadn't ripped up at him this time. Perhaps she could no longer keep up her bravado.

He leaned back to look into the night sky. The heavens were so vast — who knew how far that inky blackness stretched? The immensity of it made him feel small and insignificant. Could there be a God up there who cared about him at all? How would the Almighty even know where he was? *If You are there, I could use Your help right now.*

The stars sparkled across the blanket of night, somehow offering some comfort. Except for the Southern Cross. Although it shone as bright as the other stars in the southern skies, it had become the symbol of the massacre he had witnessed the day before. The Reform

League had used the familiar Victorian constellation on their flag. Tony wondered if he would ever be able to see that star grouping without the memory of bloodied wounds and deathly screams again.

'I saw someone die.' Miss Mattherson's watery voice broke the silence again.

How did she know what I was thinking about? 'You were there ... at the Stockade?'

'A soldier shot him in the back then stabbed him over and over. It was horrible.' She choked the words out.

'Why were you there?'

'I thought I might be able to help, but ...'

Tony wondered what kind of help she had planned to give, but she clearly had trouble holding back her emotions. It seemed all the trauma of the past two days had caught up with her and he heard her sobbing quietly. He knew if his arms were free, he would have held her tight. No-one should suffer what she had seen or been through, even if they were head-strong and foolish.

'It was a nasty business,' he mumbled. 'I saw awful things as well. But, we have to try to put them out of our minds. We need to be strong to escape tomorrow.'

Finally, she calmed. 'I know they were rebels, but did they deserve such a ruthless end?'

'It seemed a bit rough they were ambushed on the Sabbath, but, I don't know, hopefully justice will be done.' Tony didn't know what hope he could offer her. He began to think he preferred the feisty Estella Mattherson to this weepy impostor. *Perhaps I should try to rouse her wrath.* 'What I do know is you wouldn't have been much help to them if you become a drivelling mess over one dead body.'

Stella couldn't stop her tears and her inability to hold them back made her angry into the bargain. Ever since Tony had suggested her father would be glad to be rid of her, her emotions went downhill.

It was a horrible thing to say. She couldn't understand why he should be so mean. But, when she contemplated it, she realised she had given her papa a difficult time. With that revelation came the fear he wouldn't pay the ransom. *What if he refuses? Will they kill me?* A shudder had shaken her entire body. Images of the man she had seen shot planted themselves in her memory. *Is that my fate now?*

In an effort to push her fears aside, she reminded herself her father had been involved in the ambush on the diggers. *I don't want a murderer for a father, anyway.* The suspicion that he not only condoned the military's actions, but helped plan it, turned her stomach.

What if Papa does *pay the ransom?* That would mean a certain trip to England and its stuffy tearooms. Her life of adventure had ended before it even began. Her hopes spiralled and the tears came.

The constant jostling in the dray had worn her out. Every part of her body ached, especially her wrists, ankles and mouth, where she had been bound. One could not get comfortable tied to a tree in a sitting position all night.

For a while there she believed Tony might be kind enough after all. He agreed to her escape plan and her hopes lifted a little. She tried to imagine herself running free, but every time she pictured it, she saw the digger from the morning who was shot in the back at the stockade. *That could be my fate if I run on the morrow. But then, what good is a dead ransom swap?*

Then, the words were out before she knew it. She had admitted to Tony what she had seen, and off her tears went again. She hated herself for her weakness. Oh, but then he insulted her again. *Of all the ...* 'I am *not* a drivelling mess!'

'No?' Tony seemed to enjoy rubbing salt in her wounds.

'I almost shot one of those rebels dead myself!'

He remained quiet for a moment. 'I thought you said they didn't deserve that end.'

A curse on my weepy words. 'But *they* caused the riot. *Something* had to be done to protect the township. I don't suppose *you* would have been involved. You probably hid in your hut like a little mouse.'

'At least I don't act like a cork-brained fool!'

'Stow it, you two!' Smith's voice echoed through the darkness. 'Go to sleep or I'll send Burns over there to knock y' out.'

Although Stella seethed, she refrained from making another nasty retort. But, she heard Tony utter a curt whisper: 'I wish he would.'

When the sun began to send misty rays through the trees, they were roused from their inadequate sleep by their captors. Stella felt as though the fog which hugged the ground had seeped inside her head, clouding all of her thoughts. She shook her head and tried to stretch her cramped body, biting her lip to avoid crying out.

Memories of the previous night flooded back into her mind and she winced. *I must have looked such a weakling*, she scolded herself at the memory of her tears. Oh, but this morning, she would try to escape. She sucked in a breath of anticipation and felt her heart-beat rise. Then another sobering concept intruded and she grimaced. *That is ... if Tony will allow me to, after the hateful things I said.* She wondered if he would call attention to the plan out of spite. She frowned. *He provoked me, anyway. Drivelling mess ...* 'Hmph!'

Burns came to untie them from the trees and fasten their arms behind their backs. He attended to Tony first and he soon leaned against the tree, semi-awake. Burns headed her way. She stole a look at Tony while Burns pulled her wrists behind her. His head hung forward and his limp, brown hair shrouded his face. *He's dozed off again.* She waited for Burns to quit fiddling around them and go back to his camp fire.

'Pssst. Tony' She hoped he hadn't fallen into a deep sleep.

She saw his body jerk a little as he roused. 'Wha...?'

'Wake up.'

He sucked in a deep breath, shook his hair from his forehead and leaned back against the tree. His eyes met hers, but for a moment he did not speak.

Keeping one eye on their captors, she whispered as loud as she dared. 'Remember what we planned last night?' *But, please don't remember my tears.* She did not wish to be mocked any further.

Tony opened his mouth as though he had something to say, then closed it and gave a brief nod instead.

'Will you distract Burns for me, while I am ... you know ... later?' She was glad he did not mention her moment of weakness. It would only begin another argument, and then there would be no escape.

Tony tried to stretch himself and winced. He looked more awake though. 'Yeah, I can do that.' He seemed thoughtful. 'Which way will you go?'

I hadn't considered that! Which way was the nearest town? *I could run forever and not find a road or a town or even a house.*

'Did you see which way Smith drove out yesterday?' Thank goodness Tony had an answer. 'Follow his tracks to start with, that should lead you to the road. Then you need to choose right or left.'

Stella nodded. Tony's idea made sense. *Right or left?* She had no time to ponder this, however, for Burns returned to force-feed them breakfast.

Stella tried to be compliant, but her heart already raced in anticipation of her flight. She gobbled down a few mouthfuls of cold oats — leftovers from his own breakfast — and managed to swallow some water.

She glanced over at Tony and saw he did the same. She wondered how he would fare on his own with these two men. *Of course he'll be fine. I shall have to find help as quickly as possible though.* Tony had dark rings beneath his eyes and he often grimaced in pain.

Soon enough, Burns came to untie her. He grabbed her chin in his big fist and forced her to look at him. 'Don't you try nuthin', y' hear?'

Stella tried to nod, but he had a tight grip on her face.

'Go an' do yer business.' He shoved her towards the brush that hedged their campsite.

This is it. She took slow, deep breaths in an effort to keep calm. She walked a little way into the bush and found shelter behind a large tree. She knew she had little time, so rubbed her ankles and wrists so they wouldn't feel so numb, and then completed her ablutions. She pressed herself up against the tree in order to peer around the trunk and ascertain whether she had a clear opportunity.

She could hear Tony in the distance attempting a conversation with Burns. *Good, Tony. Keep him busy.* She heard him ask the big man about his prize-fighting days. She noted that Smith occupied himself with dousing the camp fire.

Now is my chance. With the first step she took she felt a searing pain on her calf. 'Ow!' Then came the sensation of something crawling up her leg, beneath her pants. She swiped at whatever nipped her and felt another bite. She screamed and ran towards Tony and Burns, stopping to jump up and down and swipe at the biting insects on her leg.

'Get off me!'

She broke out of the brush to see all three men stared at her with open mouths. 'Help me! I have ants all over me!' She continued to shake her legs, slapping them intermittently.

Smith spat in the dirt. 'Take yer pants off an' shake 'em out.' He seemed to look at her in disgust.

'They're biting me!' She jiggled some more and darted back into the brush. Out of sight she pulled off her boots and almost ripped her pants off, then flicked every ant from her bare legs and gave the moleskins a thorough shake.

She rubbed her stinging legs. There were a dozen red welts where she had been bitten. Stella chewed on her lip as tears threatened. The pain was intense. She inspected her pants before she put them back on, making sure there were no stragglers in them then checked her boots over too, before shoving her feet back in them. She edged towards the tree she had leaned against and noticed a large ant nest at the base. She had unwittingly stood in the middle of it.

When she emerged again, miserable, Burns tied her wrists behind her back. She glanced at Tony and saw a worried expression on his face. His gaze focused on Smith, so she shifted her eyes to the tobacco-chewing ruffian to see that he, in turn, watched her. His black beady eyes studied her with great suspicion and the corner of his mouth twisted into a malicious smirk.

'Never heard no boy scream like that.' His eyes glittered as they continued to wander over her. 'Now I take a good hard look at y', I see it plain as a tree in the desert.'

Stella's heart sank as she realised she had given her secret away through her reaction to the ants. Now she could see why Tony looked worried. On top of that, she had failed the attempt at escape. *Stupid!* She cursed herself.

Burns forced her to sit down and then tied her ankles together. She whimpered a little as the ropes rubbed up against one of the fresh bites.

'Y' must be that pretty morsel I mentioned earlier. But what am I gonna do now? I sent a ransom letter to yer pop about his son, Billy.'

'I ... I ... am his ... only ... only child. It shouldn't matter. He will know it's me.' Stella hated to admit it, but what else could she do?

Smith eyed her for a moment then turned a mirthful gaze to Tony. 'What a stroke of luck. Maybe y' can go a'courtin' while yer all tied up.'

Smith's laugh made Stella's stomach quake and he looked back at her with a suggestive wink. 'Unless I decide to do some courtin' of me own. What do y' say *Miss* Mattherson?'

'I wouldn't court you in a thousand years!' She spat the words out and hoped he heard the disgust in her voice. He revolted her.

'Leave her alone,' Tony said in a flat tone. 'You've had your fun.'

Burns untied him for his turn to make a visit behind the underbrush.

'Y' gonna defend her, eh?' Smith laughed again. 'Y' reckon you've got it in y'?' He turned his gaze to Stella. 'Pewsy-livered weren't it? That's what y' called 'im.' He spat black tobacco juice in the dirt and strolled back to the campsite with a chuckle, repeating the word 'pewsy-livered'.

Chapter Eleven

Tony still shook his head in disbelief when he returned from his ablutions. Whatever small hope he'd held had fallen away the moment she screamed. Burns bound him again and placed him some distance from Stella while he went to assist Smith packing the blankets back in the cart.

'Nice escape.' The dry sarcasm in Tony's voice could not be mistaken.

'There were *ants*!' Stella sounded frustrated.

'Has no-one ever told you to watch where you put your feet out here? There are also snakes to consider.'

'Snakes?' She sounded alarmed and defensive both at once. 'No. I have never had the freedom to explore the bush before. How was I to know?'

'And you had to scream and dance like that? You could have dealt with it behind the bushes in silence and still made good your escape.'

'They were *biting* me!'

'And now Smith knows you're a girl.'

Stella remained silent.

'He's a dangerous man, Miss Mattherson.'

'There's no need to tell *me* that. I'm not *stupid*!' She turned her face away from him, but he noticed her chew on her lip. 'I could not help myself, I tell you. I have bites all over my legs to show for it.'

Frustration finally gave way to sympathy. 'Do they hurt much?'

'Yes.'

'We used to sell a wonderful ointment for that at the general store.

Too bad we can't get some.'

Miss Mattherson flung angry eyes towards him. 'Do you intend to make me feel worse?'

'No. I do wish I were able to help you.' Tony tried to keep a straight face, but the image of her jumping up and down in panic came to the fore.

'What is so funny?' She glared.

Tony guessed she must have seen his lips twitch. 'Well, if we weren't in such a perilous situation, it would be a little amusing.'

She stared at him for a moment and he hoped she might even smile. Instead she uttered an 'hmph' and turned away again.

Burns returned to gag them before he lifted them both into the cart. They faced each other once again and thus began a third day of being jolted around in a wagon with no way to brace themselves.

It was hard to keep track of time beneath the tarp and he dozed off and on. In his wakeful moments, he spent his time gazing at Miss Mattherson. Positioned as they were, he could not turn away even if he tried. Sometimes she stared back at him and he wondered what messages she might be trying to send. He hoped they were pleasant ones. *She is so headstrong.* He wouldn't be surprised if she had measured him up for a helpless coward. *After all, what have I done to help her?* It didn't matter that he was bound hand and foot, he still felt as though he should protect her somehow.

Especially now that Smith knew her femininity. He felt a lump of fear grow with that knowledge. What dangers lay ahead for Miss Mattherson now? If there were a way to escape — would there even be another chance? He would not argue with her if she wanted to try again. She needed, more than ever, to be safe and away from Smith and Burns.

He drank in her beauty like a thirsty man. How could he not have recognised her on first sight? Of course, he had never imagined her dressed as a male. The one thing he could be thankful for in this wretched situation — that he lay facing her. Her eyes always had a glint of strength and determination in them, in spite of her tight bindings. And those long lashes not only framed them, but softened them. Her olive skin was smooth and clear and he remembered how her hair shone in the sunlight.

He wished he could reach out and stroke her cheek, even though the gag partially covered it. Would she recoil from his touch? Probably. He sighed to himself. He knew for a certainty she held him in low esteem.

Stella rocked back and forth in the dray, feeling bruises grow on her shoulder and hip as they rubbed and bounced against the rough wood. Her legs itched incessantly from the bites, and added to that discomfort, part way through the day it started to rain. Not a light sprinkle or drizzle, but a heavy downpour. At first the canvas cover kept it at bay, but before long it seeped in around the edges until it soaked through her clothes as well.

Smith and Burns pressed on in spite of the deluge. Clearly they did not wish to lose time. She managed to sleep on occasion in spite of all the discomfort, but mostly she felt too angry with herself and her captors to rest.

She wondered how Tony could seem to be so relaxed, or perhaps he had succumbed to sheer exhaustion. When he was not asleep however, he stared at her, which she found a little discomfiting. Did he still laugh about her encounter with the ants? *He must think me a silly girl, indeed.* She had failed what had seemed a simple escape attempt.

Stella squeezed her eyes tight as another fear struck her. Smith and Burns knew of her femininity now. That put her in a new pile of danger. The knowledge of what they could do to her chilled her to the bone. She hoped they were not *those* kind of men.

In her frustration, she wriggled her wrists often, trying to get them free. Though the ropes burned and scratched at her delicate skin, she continued to work at the knots from time to time. She needed to make good her escape, and show she could be useful after all. She wanted Tony to be pleased with her efforts, not amused by them.

Little by little she could feel her slender hands work their way out of the binds. Though a painful task, she knew she made progress. At some point in the day, she figured it to be in the afternoon, she finally wriggled one hand free. Then it took but a moment to free the other as well. Wouldn't Tony be impressed? If she could manage to get him untied too, they could slip off the back of the cart. After all, she'd climbed on without the two thugs knowing.

In the dim light beneath the canvas, she brought her hands around in front of her to show Tony, rubbing the raw welts on her wrists. Her hands felt numb from her efforts.

His eyes were closed, his damp hair plastered across his brow, so she reached out to shake him by the shoulder. He jolted a little, but when her saw her arms were free, his eyebrows shot up. He nodded to her, and she saw his eyes direct her to her feet. She needed to finish untying herself.

Just then, the cart lurched to a stop. Stella sucked in a frightened breath through her nose. Had they heard her move around in the back? She lay back in position, thrust her hands half-way through the loops in the rope behind her and hoped they wouldn't notice.

She locked eyes with Tony and he gave her a slight nod of encouragement. Instinctively she knew he wanted her to make a run for it and she nodded to him in return.

She held her breath when Burns drew back the cover, hoping her free arms would not be discovered. Thankfully, he paid no attention to her, instead reaching for Tony.

With one last glance at Tony, she hoped he could read the promise in her eyes. She would somehow return with the police to save him.

Burns pulled Tony up and then lifted him out of the dray, slinging him over his shoulder like a sack of potatoes. *This must be our camp for the night.* Not for her though, she intended to run. It was now or never. Without sitting up, she tossed the rope at her wrists aside and worked to release her feet. She pulled the gag from her head and almost groaned at the stiffness in her jaw.

She inched her way to the back of the cart, keeping as low as she could, then slipped down to the ground. She crept away from the cart on the far side from where she could hear Tony and Burns. She smiled to herself as she realised he attempted to keep the giant from returning to the wagon.

She had gone a few steps when she remembered her satchel. *Abuela's* bible. She figured the two men had already been through it and taken her money, but her grandmother's bible was a sentimental treasure. Without thought for the possible consequences, she crept back to the cart. *If I can just get the bag, then I shall run.*

With her heart beating in her ears, she peered over the edge to see inside. She glanced in all directions but could see no-one. The satchel sat about half-way down the cart. Stretching onto the tips of her toes, she could almost reach it. *Just a little ... bit ... further ...*

Stella gasped as arms gripped her around the waist and yanked her backwards to the ground. She looked up into the face of Bobby Smith, twisted with a sinister grin.

'Thinkin' to escape are y'?' He grabbed her by the arm and pulled her to her feet.

Stella could not speak as fear froze her whole body.

'I'll teach you what happens to young hoydens who don't do what they're told.' He dragged her over towards where Burns stood beside Tony.

She saw Tony's eyes widen and Burns's face creased into a frown.

'Time to teach this one a lesson.' Venom laced Smith's voice. He forced Stella's arms behind her back and held her tight from behind. 'You'll be sorry,' he hissed into her ear.

Burns took a few menacing steps towards her.

'No!' Tony yelled. 'She's just a girl, leave her alone!'

Stella saw Burns's hand draw back. She squeezed her eyes tight, expecting a vicious slap, shrinking back as she let out an ear-piercing scream.

But nothing came. She blinked her eyes open to see Burns fall backwards to the ground. At the same time, Smith abruptly let her go.

Her chest felt tight with fear and she could barely breathe, but she saw what had happened. Tony had managed to roll himself across the ground and thrust himself into Burns's legs — enough to make him lose his balance.

'Now that was a big mistake.' Smith wore a twisted smile.

Burns scrambled to his feet, his face mottled and almost purple. He glared at Tony on the ground before him then picked him up by the front of his shirt. Once again, his huge fist drew back and once again Stella screamed.

Chapter Twelve

Burns showed no mercy. In a black rage, he landed a number of blows to Tony's face and a few more to his torso. All the while Stella screamed at him to stop. She even tried to grab him from behind and pull him away.

'Stop it! Stop it! You'll kill him!'

Before she could get Burns's attention, she felt Smith's arms around her midriff, dragging her back. 'She's right, Burns. That's enough. We don't want 'im dead.'

Burns grunted but let Tony, whose body slumped senseless in his grip, fall to the ground. Still livid, he stormed off into the underbrush.

Stella wriggled and kicked at Smith. 'Let me go!' She wanted to see if Tony still breathed.

Smith's grip tightened around her waist and leaned close to her ear, making her skin crawl. 'Yer a lotta trouble for a young chit.'

His breath on her neck sent cold shivers down her spine. She opened and closed her mouth, but could think of no safe way to argue. She didn't wish to receive a beating like Tony had. She looked down at him and caught her breath. His face already swelled in several places and blood oozed from his nose. She tugged at Smith's hold on her again and this time he let her go. She dropped to her knees beside Tony's inert form.

'Just think, if not fer him, that would be you lyin' there, girly.' Malicious glee filled his voice and it made her stomach turn. 'Think twice afore y' try anythin' stupid again.' She heard his footsteps retreat. A quick glance over her shoulder told her he had gone to the wagon, where Burns had reappeared.

At least he hadn't tied her up again. Now she might be of assistance to Tony. She had no idea how severe his wounds were. She put her ear close to his mouth and nose and felt relieved to hear shallow breath pass in and out. She would have to get him to wake up. His left cheekbone and eye socket had become swollen, so she tapped him on his right cheek. 'Tony. Can you hear me? I need you to tell me where it hurts most. Tony?'

He uttered a deep groan and tried to move, only to cry out in pain and pull his knees up towards his chest. His eyelids fluttered, but only one would open. And that single, pain-filled eye looked straight into hers.

'Stella ...' His one word ended in a cry of pain and he seemed to clench his teeth. She heard what sounded like a few sobs escape from him.

Stella felt tears well in her eyes, making it hard to see and to help. 'What can I do, Tony?' She sniffed and wiped at her eyes with her sleeve.

He drew in a few shallow breaths, but even that seemed painful. When he spoke, his voice came laced with agony through clenched teeth. 'Think ... broken ... rib. Can't move ... mouth.'

Stella wiped her eyes again and examined his jaw line. She felt along the bone to see if she could determine any fractures. *Will I even be able to tell?* She was not a surgeon — that's what he needed. He hissed in pain but she noted his teeth still lined up. 'I cannot feel anything broken.'

'Uh,' he groaned. 'But ... hurts ... bad. Hurts ... breathe.'

'I don't know what to look for. You need a doctor.'

In reply he let out a few more sobs. He knew they could not get a doctor and she could see frustration building in him. *I need to think.* She got up and wandered over to the two captors where they drank their billy-tea as though nothing had happened.

'He gonna live, then?' Smith shot her a malicious grin.

'Yes, but he is in no condition to travel. He needs a surgeon.'

'Too bad. Should ha' thought of that afore y' tried runnin' away.'

Stella could barely hold back a nasty retort. But she knew it would not help the situation. 'May I have some water?'

'Go get some from the stream.' Smith tossed her a billy from the dray.

'Aren't yer gonna tie 'er up?' Burns grunted, eyeing her with distrust.

'She's not goin' anywhere.' Smith didn't even look at her, but poked at the fire with a stick.

'Neither is Tony,' Stella hissed. 'Can I untie him at least?'

Smith glanced up at her, weighing the odds it seemed. 'I s'pose.' He spat into the dirt at his feet. 'Keep in mind what happens if y' think about runnin' again.'

Stella wasn't sure how far she could push her luck. 'M...my satchel. There is a spare shirt I could use ...'

Smith frowned at her, looking irritated. 'Who do y' think I am? Saint Nicholas?'

Stella gasped. 'But ...'

'Get yer blasted satchel an' make it snappy.'

She did not reply but dashed around the cart to collect her bag, noting Tony's swag there as well and grabbed it too. She then scurried to the small creek to fill the billy-can. She hoped she could make Tony a little more comfortable before they put him in the cart. *Please God, help me.*

Back at Tony's side she saw he had drifted again. She untied his arms from behind his back and then followed with his feet. Reaching into her satchel, she pulled out a spare undershirt and proceeded to tear it into strips. The first of these she dipped into the cool water and dabbed at his bloodied nose and lip. His nose had swollen across the bridge to twice its normal size.

The touch of the cold water roused him and he flinched.

'It's all right, Tony, it's only me. I think Burns broke your nose as well. This should soothe it a little.'

'Mmph.' He moved his free hands towards his rib cage.

'Where does it hurt the worst?'

Tony pointed to a section low on his chest.

While she cleaned his face with the cool cloth, often dipping it into the billy, she tried to think ahead. 'I think they plan to put us back in the cart shortly. I don't have much time to help you. Do you think you can sit up ... if I assist?'

'Try.' He gritted out between his clenched teeth.

She took him by the elbow and pulled, while he pushed himself up with his other arm. He groaned but did not pass out again.

Stella went to work and began to undo his shirt buttons. She heard Tony's intake of breath and paused for a moment. 'Sorry, I should have told you. I intend to bind your chest. Perhaps that will give your ribs a little relief.'

He nodded his understanding and let her continue. By the time she had wound several strips of cotton around his torso, Smith approached them. She refastened Tony's buttons.

'I hope you do not mean to travel further today. Tony needs to remain still.'

Smith glared at her. 'Y' know, girly, you've got altogether too much pluck to know what's good for y'.'

'You said yourself you need him alive for the ransom swap.'

Smith drew his hand back as if to slap her and she recoiled in fright. When she flinched, he dropped his hand and spat in the dirt. 'There, y' *do* know yer place after all.' He chuckled. 'As it turns out, this is where we are stayin'.'

'No more travelling in that horrid cart?'

Smith flashed her a malicious grin. 'Y' should be grateful y' didn't have to walk.'

Stella watched him pick up the discarded ropes beside Tony. 'Do you intend to tie us to trees again? Because Tony is in no condition ...'

'Listen girly, yer gettin' a trifle too bossy for my likin'. I can see I'm gonna have to teach yer a lesson if y' don't watch yer tongue.'

Stella dropped her head. She knew she trod on dangerous ground, but Tony's injuries gave her even more gumption than usual. She chewed on her lip to keep a nasty retort back.

'We've got a special place for y', but it's not quite ready. I've gotta tie yer up so we can make camp.'

He moved towards Tony who lay motionless on the ground.

'Do you think that's fair? He can't fight or run. For heaven's sake, he's hardly even conscious.'

'Stow it, girly!' His shout made her jump and she bit her lip again.

Smith turned his gaze back to Tony and spat on the ground. 'Ri' then. I'll leave y' be. But, if y' so much as move an inch, I'll slit yer girly here's throat. I only need one ransom an' yer more important. She was a bonus. Understood?'

Stella felt her blood run cold and Tony's one good eye opened wide in fear. He nodded his compliance.

Smith turned his attention back to her. 'Now, get up against that tree.'

Stella did as bidden, though she knew Tony needed more attention. Smith bound her to the tree then crouched down in front of her. He looked her over with one of those twisted grins that made her heart freeze. 'Such a pretty thing for one so feisty. I kinda like it.' He put a greasy finger out and stroked her cheek. His voice felt like pond slime on her ears. 'I can tell we are gonna have fun.'

'Go to the devil!'

He stood up and spat tobacco juice on the ground. 'Play hard to get all y' like. Makes me want y' all the more.' He sniggered as he walked away.

Stella tried to put his threats out of her mind. They terrified her more than anything else. She had to keep her focus on Tony, else she might lose her nerve all together. She winced as she took in his swollen face again. *That must feel awful.*

He lay almost in front of her and a little on his side, keeping his injured rib off the ground. He shivered with cold and shock, and she could see his breath came in shallow gasps. Stella wished she could help, but for now had to wait till Smith and Burns deigned to untie her again.

Besides pity for Tony, she felt anger and remorse. *If I hadn't tried to get that useless bag, I might have gotten away.* And then Tony wouldn't have been beaten. Or maybe he would have anyway. If he hadn't tried diverting Burns's attack to himself, he would not have suffered as he did. *It's my fault he's so battered.*

She could not stop the tears that sprang to her eyes. She wept against the tree for a good while before her spirits lifted again. But, when they did, they came with thoughts of revenge. The attack on Tony had not served to turn her from plans of escape. She now wanted to be away from these evil men more than ever. To avoid stabs of fear and pain, she tried to develop a new strategy to be free. She needed to get Tony away so he could be treated for his injuries. If only she knew how.

Morris Burns lifted Tony to carry him and placed him by a fire. Tony gritted his teeth in pain all the while. He felt damp and cold, but that paled in comparison to the way his whole body throbbed in agony from the beating he'd received. In spite of his pain, the flames of the fire went to work on his shivering body and warmth began to spread through him.

He tried to piece together what had happened in the past hour or so. He remembered the attack, but then his memory went fuzzy. He had been unable to keep a grip on reality since and could not string two conscious thoughts together. Exhaustion and pain besieged him, often dragging him back into blackness. The only thing he knew to be real was the intense pain in his side and all over his face.

Later, he became aware of gentle sobbing around him. At first he had the notion he heard his own tears, but realised the sound emanated from the tree nearby. *Stella*. Dear Stella. A young girl should not have such a burden to carry. On top of the murderous scene at the Eureka Stockade and being kidnapped accidentally, she now had to witness him get the beating of his life and then try to patch him up as best she could.

How could he help her now? He had been all but rendered useless by his injuries. And he had received them to prevent her from being flogged. *They would have killed her had I not distracted Burns.* He didn't regret his actions, even though excruciating pain followed them. *Better me than her. My life is a waste anyway. Hers has just begun. More than anything I hope she gets out of this safely.*

Were they to travel any further? He remembered that Smith had mentioned their plans. *Where are we?* How could he plan an escape? Would it even be worth the risk? Their first attempt resembled more of a travesty than an escape, and the second attempt had resulted in a nightmare. He supposed the best option was wait to see what opportunities arose.

'Stella.' He whispered through his aching jaw.

He saw her dark, moist eyes flutter open and she tried to blink the tears away. She shook her head a little, indicating with her eyes towards the place where Smith and Burns removed equipment from the dray.

He remembered the warning Smith had given, but he believed simple conversation would not result in murder. 'Thank you.' He whispered, wanting her to feel better. *I think I love you.* That might work. But it also might be slightly insane. *The pain is making me delirious.*

She shook her head again and closed her eyes tight, sending the message she didn't want him to talk to her. She had clearly been shaken, awakened to the dire nature of their situation.

Chapter Thirteen

'Do you plan to untie me at all?' He heard Stella ask in a demanding tone, drawing Tony from his semi-slumber. He guessed she remained lashed to a tree behind him.

'Nope.'

'What 'e means is not yet.' Smith added as he approached. Tony tried to look around, but pain shot through his head and torso. He could hear the tink of iron on iron and the flap of canvas. Stella followed their activity better, for after a moment he heard her voice again.

'Is that a tent?'

'Like y' said, we can't have 'im gettin' sick on us. We gotta keep 'im alive till we get that money. It will be a bit snug in there if yer joining 'im.' Smith laughed a perverse laugh.

'How long are we to stay here?' Stella again.

'As long as it takes.' Smith sniggered. 'No-one's gonna come lookin' for y' here.'

Smith moved around to the other side of the fire where Tony could now see him. He untied a bundle which had been dumped there and proceeded to erect another tent, all the while chewing his tobacco and spitting.

He soon heard Burns heavy tread crunching twigs underfoot as he walked to the cart and back again. There was a slight jingle in his walk with his return.

'What's that?' Stella, ever inquisitive, yet had a tremor in her voice.

'You'll see.' Burns dropped a pile of chain not far from Tony's head. Tony bent his head back to see what occupied the man.

Burns picked up a long U-shaped iron bar with spiked ends. He threaded two chains onto the bar and then inverted it to be sure they didn't slide off again. He planted it in the ground nearby the fire pit, then picked up a large sledge hammer and pounded it in deep, stapling the chains to the earth. With the other end of the chain, he approached Tony. He knelt down at his feet and fastened a manacle attached to the chain, to one ankle.

He must have done the same for Stella as she soon crouched by his side, while Burns moved to assist Smith with the other tent.

'Free but not free, eh?' he gritted as she sat beside him.

'We have enough chain to get from the fire to the tent. How are you feeling?'

'Not good.'

'Try not to move your mouth too much. You still don't know if it's broken or not.'

Even if he wanted to jabber on like a parrot, he couldn't for the pounding in his head. 'Thanks.'

'Are you comfortable?'

Tony clenched his teeth again. *What a cork-brained question.* 'Of course I'm not comfortable.'

Stella's dark eyebrows drew together in a frown. At least she had gotten past her weepiness. He was thankful for that. Her tears made him feel that much worse.

'Don't get surly with me, Tony Worthington, I'm trying to help. Do you want to move into a different position to perhaps ease your pain?'

He had rolled onto his back but that had only increased his pain and difficulty in breathing and he doubted much could be done for his head.

'No. Something to lean on ... help me breathe'

Stella took the two satchels, stacking them atop each other, the softer one on top. She helped him sit up a little and pushed the bags behind his back. 'Better?'

Tony gave a slight nod.

'Is there anything else I can do?'

Leave me alone with my aching head. When he concentrated past the pain however, he realised his throat was parched. 'Water.'

Stella raised her voice to call across the campsite. 'Can Tony have water, please?'

'When we are done 'ere.'

The light began to fade. Tony wondered how long they would be kept prisoner here. Had Penny received the ransom letter yet? *He only posted it yesterday.* It could be a few days yet before she fetched her mail. But, where had Smith suggested the swap take place? Would it involve more travelling? He guessed not. When he contemplated it, it made sense the kidnappers would bring them within an easy distance of Penny. Perhaps there would be another chance at escape. If the pain subsided a bit he would figure out a plan.

'Make sure ya feed 'im good tonight, too.' Smith's voice drew him from his thoughts. He had come over to them with a canteen and bread.

Stella scowled. 'I don't know that bread will do much to revive him. I doubt he can even chew.'

'Mmm,' Smith agreed as he slaked his thirst on the canteen. 'From now on, you can make the food, girly. I reckon y' might know how to cook us tasty grub. Since y' seem to like playin' nurse an' housemaid, that'll be yer job.' He gave her a lurid wink then wiped his mouth on his sleeve, tossing the flask to her. He reached into a pocket for his tin of tobacco, rolled a new wad between his fingers, then shoved it into his mouth.

'I'm *not* your housemaid!' Stella's frown deepened.

Tony closed his one good eye. She would receive a wallop if she kept firing up. 'Just do as he says.' He groaned through his teeth.

Thankfully Stella made no retort.

'Get 'im up,' Smith commanded. 'Give 'im a drink.'

Stella helped Tony to sit up, although it sent waves of pain through his torso. She cradled his head to save him energy, but the effort to open his mouth hurt too much. She tried to dribble water through his slightly parted lips, which he gratefully swallowed.

She tore off a piece of bread and held it up to his mouth. He saw her eyes were filled with doubt. She knew he couldn't bite or chew. Tony took the bread and motioned for her to pour the canteen on it. 'Water.'

Stella nodded with a brief smile and did as he suggested.

'What are y' doin'?' Smith chastised them.

'He needs the bread to be soft so he can swallow it without chewing.'

Indeed, even the soggy bread was difficult to swallow without terrible pain. His stomach felt tight with hunger, but it would not be satisfied tonight. He managed to take in a few mouthfuls before it became too much and then he lay back against the bags.

Smith strode off to his tent, leaving them alone.

'You need more food than that.' Stella insisted.

'Can't.'

'You'll starve.'

'Try tomorrow.' Every word hurt.

Stella nodded and proceeded to eat for herself. 'Perhaps I can make you a stew or broth tomorrow,' she said between mouthfuls. 'I hope they have decent provisions over there.'

Smith returned again with a small flagon. He thrust it toward Tony and commanded him to drink. Tony did as bidden with Stella's assistance, and felt the burn of strong whiskey slip down his throat. The liquor stripped his already raw throat and he coughed violently. At the same time he cried out from the explosion of pain in his chest.

'That'll help y' feel better.' Smith gave a harsh laugh, and motioned for him to drink more.

In spite of his first reaction to the drink, the warmth of alcohol did much to revive him, and he was thankful for this small mercy.

The light had faded and although they stayed by the fire for a time, not much could be done in darkness. Smith and Burns retired to their tent and left them to take care of themselves.

'You take the tent.' Tony offered. 'Get some sleep.'

'You need it more than I.' Stella rose and he heard her chain jingle as she moved around. 'There's enough room in here for the both of us. And they've left us a couple of blankets.'

'Regular hotel, eh?'

She came back to his side with a light giggle. 'With all the modern conveniences.'

'Bring blanket. Fine here. Can't move anyway.'

'No. You should sleep in the tent. I can stay here.'

'Not leaving you out here.' *Why does she have to argue all the time?*

'Fine. I'll sleep in there with you.'

'Not proper.'

'I don't care about propriety.' She gave a little frown and shrugged, her dark eyes glittering in the firelight.

Tony made a noise which sounded like a half-groan, half-laugh. 'Forgot about that. Short dress, short sleeves, boys' clothes, gun ... proposals. Anything you wouldn't do?'

She stared at him for a moment, but he could see her anger rise yet again. 'Fine.' With a curt nod she rose to her feet. 'Sleep out here then. I'll see you in the morning.' A few seconds later he felt something drop at his side. 'There's your blanket.'

Tony groaned. Now he'd offended her again. But how could he tell her he admired her assertiveness. She had more mettle than he'd ever had. Pluck to the backbone. Where any other girl would cringe in fear, Stella came out fighting. Sure, she had her moments of weakness, but that intrepid spirit soon rose up again. *She must be covered in bruises and grazes herself, yet she is busy looking after me.* He couldn't think of anyone he would rather have been abducted with.

He raised his hand to explore his swollen face and winced. Burns had done a good job on him all right. He wondered how long it would take to subside — till he could open his left eye again. *I must be a sorry sight.* Penny wouldn't even recognise him if she came to make the swap. What if she refused to believe it was him? After all, she hadn't seen him since his sixteenth birthday. *Ten years.* It had been too long. A new wave of guilt besieged him. He should have gone home long ago.

Stella curled herself into a ball, pulled the blanket tight around her and listened to the night noises. In the distance she could hear the hiss of the breeze high up in the trees. Closer, she recognised the occasional owl call, the rustle of leaves when a creature moved through the underbrush, the high-pitched hum of a mosquito around her ear as it searched for a place to feast, and the crackle and spit of the nearby camp fire.

Why did Tony have to be so belligerent? *It is not as though I suggested some shameful impropriety. He needs to be warm. We both need to be warm.* She hoped the fire and blanket would do the trick.

She stewed over how Tony had summed up her behaviour. It stung her that he thought so little of her. *Why does no-one understand I don't want to sit around sipping tea? Is it so wrong to want more from my life?* Why did people make so many rules about how one should behave? Surely society had exaggerated the definitions of proper decorum.

She remembered her grandmother again. She had often quoted rules from the Bible. What were they? *Do not lie ... do not steal ... do not murder ...* She couldn't remember any more than that. If they were the basic rules of good behaviour, then what did a few inches off the hem of her skirt matter?

She wished Tony could look past all that. *Why can he not just see me as a pretty girl?* It would be nice if he looked at her the way other boys had — with admiration. Instead, he said spiteful things to her and made her angry. But then, he *had* thrown himself at Burns to prevent him from hitting her. She sighed. Who else would have taken a thrashing in her place?

She would have to make sure he healed quickly. And they would have to figure out a plan to escape. This time, they would have to plan it well. They could not afford another mistake. And if they did fail, it could cost her life. Stella drew in a deep breath and let it out slowly. She was prepared to take the risk, but only if she felt certain they could pull it off.

Stella groaned on the inside. She shouldn't even be in this situation. She should be safe at home in her bed. Everything had gone wrong from the moment she chose to leave. *Dear God, what have I done? I never should have run away.*

God. She remembered her *Abuela's* Bible again. Her satchel remained outside, propping Tony up. She would have to wait until morning to fetch it.

Abuela had always talked about God in affectionate and familiar terms. So many stories — some almost unbelievable, some thrilling — but they all showed God's miraculous power. God had rescued His people in so many ways, from different kinds of trouble. She said the stories were all in the Bible and they were all true. She had also said God loved her. *Well, God, if You love me, I could use Your help right now.*

At least she would sleep better now she had shelter and no ropes tying her arms and legs together. And she could lie down. The shackle on her right leg restrained her movement a little, but not enough to disrupt her. It was a relief to be able to scratch those bites when they itched. After two nights of little sleep and days of bumping around in the cart, exhaustion dragged at her. But, although weariness begged to take over, it still took time for her to drift away with troubles circling around her mind.

Stella eventually did sleep, and soundly. When she opened her eyes again, the sun had already crept a good way past the horizon. She wondered that her captors hadn't awoken her and demanded breakfast. *Perhaps they have died in their sleep.* She knew it to be a vain hope and a spiteful one at that. It seemed they also needed to recover from the long journey.

I must check on Tony. She pushed the blanket aside, stretched her somewhat cramped body and stepped out into the summer sunlight. She took a moment to examine her clothes and realised they had become rather grimy. And she smelled like she needed a bath. *I wonder if they will allow us to bathe at all.* The bindings she had wrapped around her chest to flatten her breasts had worked themselves down to her waist and would fall off if she unfastened her shirt. *I shall broach it with Smith when I see him.*

Putting the desire of a wash aside, she moved to the inert form of Tony, her chain chinking as she walked the few steps it took to cross the distance. She knelt on the ground and gently shook his blanket shrouded body. He had pulled it right up over his head, she assumed to keep warm. No response came.

Stella caught her breath as a sudden fear surprised her. Could *Tony* have died during the night? She pulled the blanket back from his face. The black bruises around his eye and nose stood out in stark contrast against the pallor of the uninjured parts of his face. He lay very still.

'Oh!' Stella could not suppress her shock. He looked almost lifeless. She laid one hand on his chest and leaned down to put her ear close to his mouth. She felt the rise under her hand and the hot breath from his mouth on her ear. He yet breathed.

'Tony.' She patted his cheek and felt it warm beneath her hand ... too warm.

He groaned then and his one good eye fluttered open. 'Stella.'

She frowned at him. His stubborn propriety had made things worse. 'I told you you should have slept in the tent with me. Now you have a fever.'

Chapter Fourteen

Ellenvale Station, Sunbury

8ᵗʰ December, 1854

Angus guided the horse down the steep driveway toward the homestead. He had taken the seven mile ride to Aitkens Gap to see if a letter had arrived from Tony yet. Alas, nothing amongst Penny's mail came from Ballaarat, and the news he did hear in The Gap would not give her any hope. He frowned, wondering how she would receive what he had to say.

When he came in from the stable, she already waited on the verandah with an expectant smile, but when she saw his grim face, her expression fell.

'Nothing, yet?'

He shook his head. 'I'm sorry, sweetheart. Your brother has no' written. But, I might know the reason why.'

Penny's chin came up and she searched his eyes. 'What is it?'

Angus pressed his lips together. 'Let's go inside an' fetch a cup of tea.'

'Now you make me feel uneasy.' Her eyes were wide, but after another gaze into his eyes, she entered the kitchen and put the kettle on the stove.

Once seated by the fire in the small parlour, Angus handed Penny her mail — a few letters and a small package — and a newspaper. 'There were a lot of talk about Ballaarat, love. Unpleasant stuff.'

'What? Tell me?'

'The miners revolted and set up a stockade. Last Sunday mornin'' the military an' police attacked. Many diggers were arrested, some wounded an' some were ... killed.'

Penny's hand flew to her mouth, her eyes wide pools of fear. 'Tony?'

Angus put a comforting hand on her shoulder. 'We can no' know for sure.'

She stood up, pushing the mail aside, and paced before the fire. 'He couldn't be. He would never go near such a skirmish. You know as well as I do he did not work amongst the diggers. He has a post in the store.'

'I'm sure yer ri'. But, Ballaarat is all locked up. The businesses are closed, no-one is workin'. The town is under Marshall Law — at least that's what they're sayin'. I managed to get a copy of The Argus for ye — Monday's edition.' He pointed to the paper she had left on her chair. 'Page five.'

Penny sat down again and hastened to open the paper, reading the article Angus mentioned. She gasped. '*Fifteen are lying dead in the Eureka Camp. Sixteen are dangerously wounded. A German has received five different wounds. The Eureka Camp, as well as the stores and tents in the neighborhood, have been burnt to the ground, and considerable loss of property has ensued thereby.*' She glanced up at him. 'This is terrible Gus.'

'Aye.'

She bent her head back to the paper, reading further. She shook her head. 'No, no, no,' she groaned. 'Dear God, I hope Tony is all right. Listen. *The most harrowing and heartrending scenes amongst the women and children I have witnessed through this dreadful morning. Many innocent persons have suffered, and many are prisoners who were there at the time of the skirmish, but took no active part.*' She looked up at him, alarm creasing her forehead. 'What if they arrested him?'

'Shall we pray for 'im?' Angus knew it was the only thing they could do at that moment.

'Please.'

They both bowed their heads and clasped each other's hands, sending up a plea for Tony's safety and for their own sense of peace. It was a comfort to know they could both turn to the Lord in times of difficulty. Angus thanked God that Penny believed as he did. The

Lord's presence in her life had softened her considerably from the girl he first met six months earlier. Now, to hear her pray and place her troubles in the Lord's hands gave him a great sense of gratitude.

'Amen.' Penny looked up at him with a small smile.

Angus lifted her hand to his lips. 'I love ye.'

Her smile grew. 'And I love you.'

He leaned back in his chair and drank his tea. 'Would ye like me to ride to Ballaarat an' see if I can find Tony?'

Penny had picked up her mail and began to leaf through the envelopes, but her eyes flew to his. 'Would you?'

'Aye. Of course I would. I could bring 'im back fer our weddin'. I want me bride to be happy.' He threw her a wink.

Letters and the small package scattered on the floor as she flew into his arms and landed on his lap with a squeal, almost knocking the cup out of his hands. 'You are a wonderful man, Angus. Thank you.' She pressed her lips to his and for a time they were lost in the wonder of each other.

'Ahem.' They heard a deep throaty sound from the doorway and pulled apart with a giggle.

'Gordon.' Angus grinned. 'We were just ... er ...'

The black smith laughed. 'I know what y' were doin'. But, I must tell y' Penny, he's not a dental surgeon.'

Penny giggled and hid her flushed face by bending to pick up the letters.

'Very funny Gordon.' Gus's shoulders shook with mirth.

'I see Gertie is not doin' a proper job of chaperonin' you two.' Gordon Johns shook his head as if to scold them, but the dance in his eyes belied his words.

'She's down by the creek washin' clothes, if yer lookin' for her.'

'Nah. Just came in fer a cuppa.' Gordon held up the cup of tea in his hands. 'Did y' trip to town go all right?'

'Aye. I've been tellin' Penny about Ballaarat. There was a battle o' sorts there on Sunday mornin', between the diggers an' the military.'

'Was there?'

'Aye. A sorry business by all accounts. I'm goin' to take a trip out there. Penny's brother lives there, ye know. We need to make sure 'e's ...' He stopped when he noticed Penny lift one hand to her mouth, her face drained of colour, while the letter in her other hand trembled. 'Penny, what's the matter?'

She lifted terror-filled eyes to his. 'Tony's been ... kidnapped.'

'What?!' Both men said at once.

'Here. Read.' Penny handed Angus the letter with an unsteady hand.

Angus had recently learned to read and write through Penny's gracious teaching. He took the message and concentrated on it for a moment. The lettering more resembled scrawl than writing — uneven and slanting down the page — but he managed to make sense of it.

Miss Penny Worthington,

I am holding yer brother, Tony, for ransom. If you want to see him alive again, you must bring £10,000 to the place one mile north of The Bush Inn, where there's an outcrop of boulders. Turn left on the narrow track and follow it to the creek. I'll be watchin for you every day from Sunday the 10th till Tuesday the 12th of December.

If you don't come by sundown on the 12th, you'll never see Tony again. If you bring the police or try anything foolish, likewise you'll never see him again.

As a token of proof I have Tony with me, here is an item belonging to him, which you might recognise.

I'll be waiting for you,

X

'Dear Lord. This is no' good.' He looked up at Penny's white face with concern etched into his own. 'What did 'e send?'

Penny held up a pipe made of a dark, red wood. He took it from Penny's hands and examined it. He could smell the stale tobacco in the bowl. A carving of wattle flower graced each side along with the initials AJW. 'Is this his? I thought his name was Tony?'

'Anthony John Worthington. Yes, it is his. I've only seen it once. Before Papa went to visit him in Ballaarat.'

Gordon had come closer to spy the letter over Angus's shoulder and now inspected the pipe as well. He looked as troubled as Angus felt. 'What are y' gonna do?'

'Yes Angus, what will we do?' Penny almost wailed. She got up from her chair and knelt in front of him, gripping his arms.

Angus stroked her face. 'I don't see as ye have much choice.

Tony's life is no' worth takin' a risk over. Ye need to get the money an' make the exchange.'

Penny nodded, biting her lip.

'But, I suggest y' go to the police anyway.' Gordon added with a frown. 'They might 'ave an idea of how to get yer brother back without losin' yer money.'

Angus nodded. ''Tis true, they might.'

'But, who would do such a thing?' Penny's voice rang out.

Angus brows furrowed. 'Aye. There's a good question. It seems strange that barely a month after ye find gold, this happens. And the only people who knew about it are the four of us livin' 'ere, the Foxworths and the bank man in Melbourne.'

All three of them looked at each other as suspicion took hold.

'Rupert Foxworth!' Penny growled. Her conniving neighbour had first found the gold on Ellenvale, but had hidden it from her, proposing marriage in order to get her land *and* the gold. It would be like him to do this out of spite.

'I'd lay odds 'e's behind it.' Angus agreed.

'But how do we prove it? 'E's been busy over at Henry's Run supervisin' the shearers this past two weeks. We all know 'e'd deny it.' Gordon's logic sent them into quiet contemplation for a time, but before long Penny jumped to her feet.

'We cannot afford to sit around and devise a plan to catch Rupert out. My brother is in danger. Who knows what this — she waved the letter in the air — this blackguard has done, or is doing to him. The sooner this is over the better.' She went into action, pacing before the fire. 'Gordon, please go and saddle the horses. Angus, can you go and bring Gertie in from her washing and ask her to pack us some provisions? You and I need to prepare for a journey.'

Gordon turned and went out to the stables, but Angus hesitated. 'Do ye think it wise to go yerself? This may be a dangerous criminal we are dealin' with. Perhaps me an' Gordon should go.'

Penny stopped and eyed him with determination. 'Do you know what Tony looks like?'

Angus let his gaze drop. 'No.'

'Neither does Gordon, so how will you know if it is a genuine swap? I am coming!'

Angus had no argument, even though he had no desire to see her in danger, as would be the case at the changeover. 'Someone needs to stay 'ere an' guard the dig.' It would not change her mind, he knew, but it would make her think things through more. They had found a few more small nuggets in the past week — it could not be left unattended.

'Gordon shall remain here and keep an eye on the claim.' Penny barely paused. It seemed her mind raced ahead.

'And Gertie?'

Penny flashed him an impulsive grin. 'Our chaperone. She shall ride with us.'

Angus shuffled his feet. *Gertie might make things more dangerous at the other end.* He cleared his throat. 'Do no' take me wrong, love, but Gertie is of an impetuous nature. I'm no' sure she would handle the swap.'

Penny nodded and pressed her lips together as she thought. 'Then we shall leave her at The Bush Inn while we do the exchange. Does that sound acceptable?'

Angus shrugged. He could not hope for much more. Truth be told, he didn't like any of it. If it could be left with the authorities to sort out, it would be better. But, a man's life was at stake. The risk must be taken. 'Make sure ye bring yer rifle.'

Within an hour, Penny sat aside on her Thoroughbred, Chocolate, Gertie rode on Zimmer and Angus on their new horse, Thunder, a fiery steed with an impatient nature. Gordon walked amongst them, checking all the straps for the third time. Before he allowed them to go, he led them in a prayer for their safety and for Tony's as well, and for justice to be done for the abductors.

'God speed.' He slapped Thunder's hind quarters, sending him off towards the gate while the two women followed behind. 'Come back safe.'

'Thanks mate!' Angus called out as the distance between them increased. He did not intend to slow Thunder down. The animal loved to run. He would soon have to rein him in a little though, as the girls would never keep up.

He tried not to think about the changeover. Anything could go wrong. But, it would be a few days before they had to face it. For now, he would try to enjoy the journey. *After all, I have me beloved by me side*. Angus grinned at his happy fortune. While in town, he would procure a marriage licence. His heart leapt at the happy notion. *Once we have Tony safe an' sound, we can enjoy our weddin'.*

He wondered where the kidnapper held Tony and hoped the scoundrel treated him well. *I hope we find 'im hale an' whole.* If the villain who did this wanted to meet beyond The Bush Inn, then it seemed possible he hid out in the Black Forest. Those two words often struck fear into the souls of those who passed through that region on their way to Bendigo gold fields — or indeed on their way back. It was the favoured haunt of Bushrangers due to the density of the trees, and many a cashed-up digger had been robbed there. *Aye, the Black Forest is a good a place as any to hide a victim.* Angus pressed his lips in a grim line. He had no doubt that extreme danger lay ahead for them.

Chapter Fifteen

The Black Forest

Two days had passed and Tony's fever finally ebbed away. It had not been severe, but it had made him ache all the more. Stella had been a gem. He had watched the way she conducted herself, unable to say much himself due to his painful jaw, and became more impressed by the day. Although he knew she must be a little frightened, she spoke fearlessly to their captors, demanding this and that, but always stopping before she crossed the boundary of their patience.

On the first day, she had done as they requested and cooked for them all, always food that Tony could manage to swallow. But, she had then told them she needed to bathe and asked Smith to fetch her some water. He had not argued, but sent Burns to do the task. She warmed the water over the fire and then disappeared into their little tent with her bag for a time. When she reappeared, she wore a clean shirt, hanging the other — dripping wet — over a branch. What she had managed with a small pale of water was remarkable. She looked fresh and beautiful.

She held out the tin bucket and asked Burns for more water. She heated it once again and then commenced bathing Tony gently, beginning with his swollen face. Apart from painful contact with his bruises, it felt divine.

'Do you mind if I undo your shirt and freshen you up?'

Does this woman have no shame? 'My arms work, you know.'

She dropped the cloth into the pale and folded her arms with a frown. 'Fine. Do it yourself then.'

He had gritted his teeth. She knew very well he couldn't do it on his own. 'Help me sit up.'

She didn't move.

'Please?'

She relented and pulled him up, although he winced at the pain in his side. He unbuttoned his shirt, but again became stuck when he couldn't remove it without pain rifling through him. He didn't need to ask this time. She moved behind him and slipped the shirt off his shoulders. The touch of her hands on his skin sent a shock all through his body. It was a good thing she couldn't see his face. He might have kissed her.

She removed the bandages from his torso and left him to bathe while she washed his shirt and hung it on the branch. The warm air on his wet skin felt pleasant. It mattered not if he had to sit without a shirt for a few hours. He had leaned back against a tree to rest.

Soon, Stella sat nearby, her back to him, with a book in her lap. He wondered why she faced away from him. *Does she think me that ugly?* He figured she still held a grudge at him for insulting her. He heaved a great sigh. *I'm doomed to love a woman who hates me.*

His contemplation had turned to their circumstances. He needed to get his strength back. The pain had been a little less that day, apart from the fever, and he had assumed it would lessen every day. *At least my legs are in full health — if we have to run. But how do we escape? Smith has the key to these dreaded chains.* He looked at the metal spike which pinned the chains to the ground and wondered if both of them pulled on it together, would they be able to pull it loose? It would have to be attempted under cover of darkness, when Smith and Burns were asleep.

Tony had let his gaze drift around the small campsite, examining every detail of their surroundings. There must be some way to break the chains. They were in a small clearing, with enough room for the two tents and the campfire. Beyond that stood dense forest — towering gum trees pressed close to each other, their straight trunks making everything seem dark. The greenery of ferns and other small bushes gave a contrast and filled any space between the trees.

He noted that although the undergrowth was thick and lush, the trunks of the bigger trees were black and leaves grew directly out of them. *Evidence a bush fire has been here some time in the past few years.* The Black Thursday fires of '51 had been widespread throughout the Victorian colony following a drought. Ellenvale Station and other properties on the plains had escaped because the sheep had eaten the grass so short it could not fuel the fire. *Could we be in one of the fire affected areas?* If so, they were possibly near Middle Gully, or along the Plenty River somewhere — and neither of those places were too far from Ellenvale.

Decaying bark and leaves and moss-covered rocks covered the ground, giving off a rich and moist aroma. It resembled a prison cell, albeit a very beautiful prison cell.

In truth, the Black Thursday fires had burnt almost one quarter of the state. He could not be certain where they were. He could hardly even tell the time of day, so obscured was the sun.

Any small branches that may have lain on the ground had been removed, as well as any manageable rocks. Smith and Burns had cleared the area well, leaving nothing for them to use as a weapon.

Perhaps we should wait for Penny to bring the ransom. After all, they wouldn't have to fight to escape then. Or would they? What if the swap went wrong? What if Penny or Mr Mattherson didn't come? How would he run anyway when every breath caused him pain? Anything could happen. No, he needed to think how they could get away before that. For now though, no matter how he racked his brain, he could think of nothing.

He had gazed over at Stella's back. 'What you reading?'

She half turned her head towards him. 'The Bible. It belonged to my grandmother.'

Tony didn't know what to say. Hadn't *he* had religion on his mind of late? 'Oh.'

He saw her stiffen. 'What does 'oh' mean? Do you not approve?'

'Just surprised.'

'Why? You think I'm a heathen as well as a hoyden?'

Tony groaned. *Here we go again.* 'Where did you get it?'

She paused. He suspected she assumed he would insult her again, not ask a question. 'I brought it in my satchel. As I said, it belonged to my grandmother.'

'You were close?' Tony would have liked her to turn around so they could have a proper conversation, but she remained with her back turned. Besides, he could still only manage small sentences anyway.

'*Sí*. I keep it to remember her. She wrote many things in the pages.'

'You Spanish?'

'*Sí*. That is, my mother is Spanish, and *Abuela*, but my father is English.'

It explained the faint accent he heard in her words.

'What you reading about?'

Stella did not answer right away until he wondered if she would. 'I have been reading the Ten Commandments.'

Tony remembered hearing about this list of rules way back in his childhood, but wondered why she had chosen that topic.

'Did you know God spoke them directly to Moses and even wrote them Himself on the stone tablets?' Stella sounded excited.

'No.'

'God came down and spoke as a friend with Moses. Don't you find that remarkable?'

'Never thought about it.'

Stella paused again. 'Do you think He still speaks to people today?'

Tony did not know how to answer her. 'I'm sure religious people think so.' What had Reverend Taylor said? That he could talk to God like a regular person. *Should I tell Stella?* 'I heard a preacher say so, anyway.'

Once again Stella hesitated before speaking. 'Have you ... have you ever spoken to Him ... I mean ... do you pray?'

'Lately. A little.'

She turned toward him then, her eyes full of interest. 'Me too.' She smiled briefly. 'I mean, with the situation we are in, what else is there to do?'

'Try to escape.'

Her eyes faltered and her gaze dropped. 'Last time was a disaster.'

Could she be losing her spirit? Tony hoped not. Her tenacity had been the thing which helped him persevere. 'Not afraid, are you?'

Stella bristled. 'Of course I'm not afraid. But how would you escape in your condition?'

'I'm fine.' Tony ignored the pasty feeling of his skin and the deep ache in his side and face. If she believed pain would prevent him from trying, she was mistaken. *I am not a coward.*

Stella turned her back once again with a sound suspiciously like a snort, and went back to reading.

Tony felt frustrated. They couldn't even hold a conversation for long without an argument. *If only she would stop seeing me as a chicken-livered failure.* He took a deep breath. Somehow, he had to get her to talk again — *without* pointless conflict.

'Did He ever answer you — God, I mean?'

She did not look up from her pages as she answered. 'Not yet. We are still here aren't we?'

'You really think He would help us?' Even though Tony himself had prayed for help, he had no certainty that God would listen.

At this Stella did turn to look at him again. 'This book,' she lifted it up for emphasis, 'is filled with stories of people who asked God for help, and of the ways He rescued them. My *abuela* used to tell me all the time. Maybe if we pray, He will help us.'

Tony couldn't help it. Unexplainable anger rose up in him. 'Those stories are thousands of years old. If God wanted to help people today, He would have stopped my mama from dying.' The force of his words made the pain in his chest increase, but he continued, wrapping one arm around his ribcage. 'He would have given me a chance to tell Papa how much I ... but he died, too. He would have stopped the massacre in Ballaarat, and He would have kept my sister safe from the flood. God has left us to fend for ourselves.' He lifted a hand to his face. That outburst had hurt.

Stella watched him as he leaned back against the tree again, nursing his head and his rib. Her eyes seemed to be filled with hurt. He had stomped all over her hope. *Well done, Tony. Now you have pushed her further away.* But, he could not pretend he felt differently. God had let him suffer one loss and failure after another, if He had even taken any notice at all. He closed his good eye and swallowed.

'I'm sorry you feel that way.'

'Just ... keep reading ... if you wish.'

And she had. For the past two days, between cooking for them all and any other little tasks, she read. She had even ventured to read a few of the stories to him until, though he didn't think it possible, he found a little hope in them himself. She read about David, who had a king hunting him down to kill him, but time after time, God protected him. The nation of Israel, when confronted by a vast enemy, would call upon the Lord, and He would give them a miraculous victory.

When she read about the apostle Peter however, he began to pay close attention. Peter had been arrested and locked in prison. While his friends prayed during the night, an angel came and escorted him out of the jail, as though the chains, bars and soldiers did not even exist. Could it be possible? Could God actually do that kind of thing? Could He somehow free Stella and himself from these chains?

Tony had his doubts. Why would He help now, when He'd never helped before?

Did you ever ask before?

He wondered where that question came from. It was strange. He'd never considered God in his life at all until the past weeks, if he wanted to be honest. Could he expect God's help if he never asked? One usually didn't receive help from anyone else unless one asked. Why would it be different with God?

Ask and you shall receive.

Tony looked around him, to see if anyone stood or hid nearby. The shadows lengthened in the late afternoon light. Of course there wouldn't be, no-one knew they were there. *Where did that voice come from, then? Did I imagine it?* Another idea made his skin turn to goose-flesh. *Could it have been Him?*

'Stella.'

She glanced up from the book and looked at him with an odd expression. 'What is it, Tony?'

'I think we should pray.'

She watched him as if reading his face. 'All right.'

'Together.' He put out his hand and she reached over and put her hand in his. Tony tried not to focus on how nice it felt to have her soft hand enclosed in his. *How do I pray?* He remembered the words of Reverend Taylor — pray as you would speak to another person. He cleared his throat and closed his eyes.

'God. It's me, Tony. And Stella. We are chained up with two evil men and we need help to get away. We'd be very grateful if You could send an angel or something to get us out of here — like You did for Saint Peter. Thanks.'

'Amen.' Stella pulled her hand away, but a grin lit her eyes with amusement.

'Oh, yeah. Amen.' Tony returned the smile and she dipped her head back to the Bible in her lap. Was he mistaken, or did he see a little colour in her cheeks? Did she feel embarrassed to pray with him? It didn't seem to make sense. She originated this whole praying idea in the first place. Why would she be embarrassed by it?

He shifted his gaze to Smith who now adjusted the ropes of his tent. *God I hope You answer soon. Stella is in more danger by the day.* He had noticed the gleam in the weasel-like man's eyes. Any time Stella was near him, he ran his gaze over every curve of her body and he made lurid comments. Tony knew it was a matter of time before he did something unspeakable. He remembered how Smith had drooled over the tavern-girls in Ballaarat and how he'd asked where to find the houses of ill-repute. It turned Tony's stomach to think of it.

He felt his body tense as Smith tightened the guy ropes then headed to their tent to do the same. As expected, he ogled Stella in that filthy way. Tony yearned to darken his daylights, but while the scoundrel only looked, it would not be worth the risk. Instead he tried to draw his attention away from the pretty girl.

'How long are we to be here? It's been two days already.'

Smith spat in the dirt then looked at him. 'If yer sister pays up quick, y'll be home before y' know it.'

Furious at his captor's smugness, Tony tugged at the chains on his feet, succeeding at naught. 'I hope she refuses to pay you a single dime!' He spat the words at Smith, although the effort sent pain through his tender ribs.

The ruffian laughed, taking callous delight in his weakness. Then Smith turned a grave face to him. 'If she does, y' won't live to see another day.'

Chapter Sixteen

Melbourne

Angus, Penny and Gertie arrived at Mrs Mac's Lodging House late in the afternoon. By the time Angus had taken the horses to a nearby public stable and joined the women, Mrs Mac had organised their rooms and provided steaming cups of tea.

'Mr McDoughan, how lovely to see you.' The round-faced, rosy-cheeked hostess ushered him into the parlour, where the others were already seated on a comfortable-looking sofa. Pouring him a cup of tea, she continued her speech. 'I have been telling Miss Worthington all about the nasty business in Ballaarat. Of course, you already know about it, but it is terrible. We attended a large meeting here in Melbourne three days ago. The Government wanted to raise public support for their actions, but instead an outcry rose against the number of miners killed and they had to close the meeting. Everyone I have spoken to thinks the military went too far.'

Angus smiled at Penny — a smile which exchanged the understanding they were in for a regular ear-bashing. Mrs Mac was known to chatter on without giving a space for one to speak. As she handed Angus his tea, she continued.

'The next day — let's see, that was Wednesday — we heard that thirteen people were charged with treason. Goodness me! Surely it is too severe. Anyway, a huge crowd gathered at St Paul's Cathedral to protest against the Government's actions — *especially* those in charge in Ballaarat. They say there were six thousand people gathered at the church.'

'What do they intend to do now?' Angus noticed Penny wore a slight frown, as if to scold him for encouraging the woman.

'I'm sure a commission will be heard. Do you know how many folk died in the clash?' She glanced at them briefly before she continued. 'I hear it is over thirty, and I can tell you most of those were in the stockade, not the military. Then there are scores who were injured. It's disgraceful, that's what it is. What is this colony coming to?' She clicked her tongue and shook her head, then with a deep sigh she looked at Penny. 'So, what is your news, Miss Penny?'

Angus guessed she wouldn't mention Tony, although she did appear a little drawn. Instead she placed her tea on the side table, stood and moved to his side, hooking her hand through his elbow. 'Mr McDoughan and I are engaged to be married.'

'Oh! Oh! Oh! How wonderful!' She clapped her hands then placed a huge kiss first on Penny's cheek, then on Angus's. He heard Gertie smother a chortle of laughter.

'I'm a very fortunate man, I am.' Gus chuckled.

'Indeed you are. Oh! I shall have to get out the good wine and bake you a fine supper to celebrate.'

'There's no need to go to too much trouble, Mrs Mac,' Penny argued.

'Nonsense.' Mrs Mac waved her off. 'Now, you make yourselves comfortable and I shall get busy in my kitchen. It's the excuse I need to make a special supper.'

She didn't exaggerate either. Soon, the lodging house filled with delicious aromas, and when supper arrived, they were treated to a spread of delightful dishes; roasted beef and cold tongue, white soup, poached eggs, green beans in butter, roasted onions and prune tartlets. Mrs Mac sat with them to dine, although she often disappeared into the kitchen to check on her cooking. Angus gazed at Penny with pride. There had been a time, not long ago, when she would have been offended by Mrs Mac's presumption to join them. Even Gertie would not have been welcome at table ... neither him for that matter. A chuckle escaped him.

'What is so funny, dear?' Penny looked at him.

Gus grinned at her. 'You. Sittin' amongst us underlings an' enjoyin' every minute of it.'

A genuine smile lit her face. 'How much I have missed out on over the years because of my pride.' She let out a wistful sigh.

Angus reached out and squeezed her hand, then lifted it to his lips. ''Ere we go again.' Gertie rolled her eyes in mock disgust.

'Don't scold them, lassie.' Mrs Mac shook her short, dark curls. 'It is wonderful to see a couple so in love they aren't afraid to show it. Oh, it does make me miss my dear Mr Mac, though.' She dabbed at a sudden tear with her napkin.

Angus looked at her with compassion. 'I'm sorry. We didn't mean to upset ye.'

She waved the napkin in the air and shook her head. 'No, no. Never mind. I've always been one to cry without a moment's notice. I'll be right as rain in a moment. So many years have passed. You would think by now I wouldn't be so sentimental.'

Angus noticed Penny's gaze drop. It had been little more than a year since her father passed. He squeezed her hand again. 'Grief is a strange an' unpredictable thing.'

'That it is. That it is.' Mrs Mac nodded and sniffed.

A moment of sombre silence fell around the table. Angus knew each of them dwelt on memories of a loved one. He figured Penny had Tony uppermost in her thoughts, hoping he would not be another addition to her recent losses. He kept hold of her hand to let her know he understood until the moment passed and they began to laugh and talk again.

'Did ye sleep well?' Angus asked Penny at breakfast the next morning, while they had a little privacy. Gertie hadn't risen yet and Mrs Mac busied herself in the kitchen.

'A little.' She shrugged. 'I cannot help but worry about Tony. I want to get it all over with.'

Angus stroked her cheek. He wished he could take the burden for her. He drew in a deep breath, and let it out slowly. 'Ye know we canno' do the swap till tomorrow. I know it's hard, but ye need to try to be patient an' relax for today.'

'I do not know how I shall do that, cooped up here all day. We have naught to do but get the money.'

'An' we are no' doin' that till the end of the day. It's safer that way. We can let them know to get it ready, of course, bein' it's a large sum.'

Penny nodded. 'Yes. I agree. But what of the rest of the day?'

Angus gazed into her eyes and caressed her cheek again. 'I have a few ideas. If ye weren't so busy thinkin' about Tony, ye would know what they are.'

A smile lit her face. 'The marriage licence. Of course. And I must arrange some mining licences for our claim.'

'Aye. There ye go.'

'It will not take all day, you know.'

'Then I'll take ye for a walk. I'll show ye things ye've probably no' seen.'

Penny sighed and he saw gratitude in her eyes. 'Thank you for taking care of me, Gus.'

'For the rest of me life, that's all I wanna do.' He leaned back in his chair and heaved a contented sigh. 'The sooner we can get leg-shackled the better. To have an' to hold ...' He leaned forward and pressed his lips to hers for a lingering kiss.

'It will be soon my love, I promise.' Penny giggled when she pushed him away.

Angus chuckled to himself. He looked forward to a life with this precious woman. He envisioned the task ahead and sobered. *Lord, I hope this ransom goes smoothly. Penny does not need another setback right now. Please keep Yer hand of protection over us an' over Tony through this, an' give us wisdom as we act.*

Chapter Seventeen

The Black Forest

Stella lay still in the tiny tent and listened to Tony's even breathing. He had conceded to sleep in the shelter, although inadequate, on the second night. With a mild fever, he needed it even more, lest he become worse. But, by then, she had wondered about the propriety of it herself, and more so once she lay next to him.

Bathing him that day had altered her in some strange way. His naked torso — even though his physique was not remarkable, especially with those black bruises — made her heart flutter in a peculiar fashion. She had to turn her back. She had been thankful for her *abuela's* Bible to focus on.

But then, lying beside him in the tent, although they lay back to back, felt just as awkward. She wished she could snuggle closer to share his warmth. She even imagined how nice it would be if he put his arms around her and held her.

She had to remind herself he saw her as a spoiled child and nothing more. *How can I convince him I am a grown and mature woman? I can be sensible ... I think.* She knew she had an impulsive nature, and it often got her into trouble. *I must try not to speak ...* especially *when he insults me.*

With that resolve, she had kept her words and reactions to a minimum over the past few days. Reading the Bible helped. She had found hope in the words ... and even peace. She wanted to share the experience with Tony, but had been shocked when he had blamed God for the loss of his parents.

Her heart had turned over at his words. *How he must have suffered.* She wondered what he had left unsaid about his father. Something must have happened before he died. She had wanted to ask him more about it, but thought the better of it and kept her mouth shut. He would think her impertinent if she pried. Thankfully, he had not remained so opposed to her new interest and allowed her to even read to him.

Now, after three nights together in the shelter, she determined she would sleep by the fire next time. She was sure she had hardly slept a wink, always aware of Tony's presence so close. She knew not if he saw her any differently, but she knew beyond doubt her own feelings had grown. She opened her eyes. Sunlight and a light breeze played chase with the eucalypt canopy above and the shadows of leaves danced on the white canvas. Bird calls all around heralded the morning. Another day as prisoners.

Tony had prayed yesterday. It had surprised her. But, she supposed, with little else to do but sit around and wait for his wounds to heal, he probably had spent a lot of time in thought. She wondered if he had considered her at all. *There's no point in wishful thinking*, Stella scolded herself. She was nothing more than a thorn in his side — an added worry when he already had enough to struggle with. *If only he could see how much I wish to help.*

Would their prayer be answered? Yesterday, when Smith had looked at her, she had felt fear in the pit of her stomach. It had been the first time she felt truly and deeply afraid. The first couple of days since he discovered her sex had been uncomfortable — he had made her feel like she needed to put a thick, spacious overcoat on to cover her figure. His words and threats had sickened her, but she had not taken them seriously. But yesterday, something burned in his eyes which made her skin crawl and sick dread had coursed up and down her spine.

When would Papa come? She hoped it would be in time. *If he comes at all.* And if not him, then it must be God, for He must be the only one who knew where they were. Tony did not have the strength to break free and defeat two thugs. If God cared, like her *abuela* said, He would surely rescue them.

'You awake?' Tony's foggy voice broke into her thoughts. She had become used to his short sentences of the past few days. How long would it take for the pain to subside, she wondered.

'Yes.'

Tony rolled onto his back and blinked in the soft morning light. 'I can see out both eyes.'

Stella glanced at him. 'I noticed the swelling had subsided a little yesterday. It was partly open then.'

He reached up and prodded the tender areas of his face, much as he did every morning. 'Not so sore there. The nose is still awful.'

'How about your jaw?'

'Stiff. But better.' He carefully felt the left side of his chest. 'Rib's still tender.'

Her mind still on Smith, Stella mumbled an acknowledgement. 'Tony, can you think of any way at all we can escape?'

Tony looked at her, one green eye surrounded by black shadow and the other surrounded by white. 'Thought you didn't want to risk it?'

Stella opened her mouth then closed it again. She couldn't tell him how terrified she'd become of Smith. 'We can't stay here and wait around. What if my father does not come?'

'He'll come.'

'How can you be so sure?'

'You're his daughter. He'll come.'

'But, what if he does not come in time?'

'For what? They're not intent on murdering us.'

Again she hesitated, wanting to tell him her fears, but unsure how to voice them. 'Smith ... he's ...'

Tony stared at her for a long moment, as though he tried to read her mind. 'We could throw a lighted stick at their tent while they're asleep — burn it down. But then we'd likely kill them and we'd still have no key.'

'Could we dig that huge spike out of the ground?'

'They'd discover us before we got very far. Why not threaten them with the knife when you're cooking?'

'They don't let me touch it. Burns takes care of all the cutting. What would it serve anyway? They would easily overpower ...'

'Plannin' an escape, eh?' Smith's harsh voice came from outside the tent and both of them jumped in fright.

Stella clamped a hand over her mouth to keep a scream from filling the air and she noticed Tony stiffen.

Smith drew aside the canvas tent flap and stared at them with a ferocious glare. 'I've told y' before. Y' try anythin' an' yer'll get a worse beatin' than last time. Maybe I'll even send the girly to an early grave.' He pulled a knife from his belt and caressed the blade.

Stella swallowed hard and backed as far away from him as she could, her whole body trembling.

'We are not going anywhere.' Tony said in a low voice. 'Just passing the time, Smith. As if we could get away if we tried.'

Stella wondered what he meant by that. Had he spoken those ideas merely to humour her? *That's what you do with a contentious brat, isn't it?* Furious, she let out a string of expletives, her fear forgotten. '*He may be a coward, but I would wrap this chain around your throat if I had the chance, you base-born maggot!*'

Smith's face twitched and he jiggled the knife in his hand. His lips drew back in a sneer that revealed his rotten teeth. 'Y' better watch what y' say, girly. I'll make y' sorry y' ever stepped foot out of yer house.' He spat black tobacco juice at her feet.

Stella let out a scream of rage, her anger propelling her forward towards her captor, but a strong hand grasped her arm and held her back. Smith dropped the canvas flap and left.

She turned on Tony, her chest heaving. 'Let go of me! Pathetic ... useless ... are you incapable of action?'

Tony stared at her for a long while, his hold still firm on her arm, although he seemed to wince in pain at the effort. She writhed and bellowed at him in frustration, but his grip felt like a vice. 'You need to calm down, Stella.'

'He will *kill* me, didn't you hear?' She hissed through clenched teeth.

'He has no such intention, Stella. He wants to scare you.' Tony spoke with a quiet voice. 'I know you are afraid.'

'And you did nothing! You laid there and let him threaten me.'

'Roaring at him and threatening him does not make things better, Stella.'

She glared at him, seething. 'You think it's *my* fault he threatened me?'

Tony's face flushed with colour, but his words remained gentle. 'He is a twisted man, Stella. It is like throwing oil on a fire. You are already in enough danger without making it worse.'

'I want to go home!' Stella buried her face in her hands and sobbed and her anger released through her tears.

The hand that had gripped her arm now slackened and he rubbed her shoulder instead. 'It will be all right, Stella. We will get out of here, one way or another.'

Tony rose out of the tent and sat by the small fire which Burns had re-ignited from the remaining embers. Though it was now summer, the mornings remained cool, especially in the dense bushland. Besides that, their captors would want their little cook to make them tea and breakfast soon.

Stella's words had cut deep. Once again she had called him a coward and had made it clear she held him in little esteem. The things she had said ...

Tony picked up a twig and fiddled with it, breaking small pieces off and tossing them into the flames. What did she want from him? He had merely tried to keep Smith calm by pretending he didn't seriously consider escape. Partly, anyway. Truth be told, he also wanted to rouse Stella's ire. She had looked so terrified before. But he hadn't expected the tongue-lashing she gave. *I guess her fear fuelled her venom more than usual.*

And now her tears flowed again. He wished he had the nerve to wrap his arms around her. He could feel his heart pound with compassion. The poor woman was desperate with fear. But he knew she would push him away if he tried to hold her. *I couldn't take that. It's bad enough she thinks I'm useless.*

It all served to make him think harder on a way to escape. *Come on, God. There must be a way. Please help me find it.* He wanted to believe a Great Being out there watched and waited to help, but he knew he was unworthy of His attention.

He had no idea what plans were made for the ransom swap — when it would be, where it would take place, how it would be done — and he had no certainty Penny would have the money. Smith seemed to be sure she did, but her letters had all told a different story. There were so many unknowns, except he knew they must be free of these two men.

The morning passed swiftly as he sat and contemplated escape. Stella eventually calmed and did her 'chores' before she shut him out with her Bible on her lap. After a midday meal of stale bread and an apple which had begun to rot, Smith sent Burns out to get meat. Burns slung a rifle over his shoulder and strode off into the bush to hunt a wallaby.

When Burns' footsteps in the underbrush had faded from their hearing, Smith stood still and stared at the two of them. He held an apple in one hand and his knife in the other, which he tossed up and down. With Burns out of the way for a couple of hours, Tony guessed Smith intended to unleash his evil on them.

Sure enough, he finished his apple and tossed the core amongst the tall trees around the camp. He ducked into his tent and brought out a length of rope then headed straight for them.

'You two are gonna pay for yer little outburst this mornin'.' He looked down at Tony with a sneer and then spat in the dirt.

'While the cat's away, eh?' Tony wondered if talking would delay the inevitable. He looked out of the corner of his eye to see Stella pale at Smith's words.

'Burns would enjoy this too, but I want the pleasure all to meself.' He licked his lips as though he'd just eaten a tasty morsel and his eyes gleamed with sinister glee.

'Wha... what are you g... going to do?' Stella trembled.

Smith stretched the rope tight in his hands while a smirk twisted his mouth. 'First I'm gonna tie this fella up.' He lunged towards him.

'No you don't!' Tony made to fight him, but in a flash Smith held a knife to his throat and he heard Stella give a scream of fright. He sucked in his breath and froze.

'Now, y' can be nice an' compliant, or I can use this on y'. It's up to you.' Smith leaned close enough for Tony to smell his rotten breath.

Tony let his head drop and remained still. How would he help Stella if he was wounded further? Then again, how would he help her if his hands were tied as well as the shackle on his foot? *God, don't let this happen! Please!*

Smith grabbed his arms and pulled them behind his back. Tony gave a sidelong glance to Stella. Though her face was white, her eyes glinted with fury. Before he knew it, she hurled herself at Smith with a scream like a banshee and clawed at him. 'Leave him alone!'

'Get off me, y' little hussy.' Smith thrust his elbow out and connected with her stomach. She fell back with a cry of pain and rolled into a ball, clasping her midriff and gasping for breath.

Tony swallowed hard at the rage which rose in him, while Smith finished tying him off. 'You'll be sorry for this,' he gritted. 'Stella! You have to fight him!'

'Shut yer mouth!' Smith back handed him in the face and knife-like pain shot through his nose and cheekbone anew. Then Smith shoved him to the ground.

Stella groaned as she tried to sit up.

Smith pulled her to her feet. 'Get yerself in that tent,' he hissed, pushing her forward.

Tony knew some relief to see she resisted him. She spun around and though her face was etched with pain, she glared at him. 'I will not!'

Once again Smith lifted the knife, this time to her throat and Tony heard her sharp intake of breath. He fought against the rope around his wrists, ignoring the burn as it chafed his skin.

'Y' will, if I say y' will.' Smith forced her to turn around again, still holding the knife at her neck. The point of the blade gave her no option but to move forward.

'Please don't do this!' Stella's voice crumbled as she staggered towards the tent. 'I won't try to escape again, or even talk about it. I promise.'

Panic rose in Tony's chest and he heaved at the ropes once again. He felt his cracked rib complain, but refused to acknowledge it. He writhed in desperation and cried out against his binds. *God! Where are you? We need you now!*

He could no longer see them, for they were inside the tent, but he heard Stella scream as she resisted, while Smith grunted as he fought to hold her down. Then he heard the sound of fabric being torn.

'Nooooo!' His voice echoed through the tall trees as he strained against the ropes. Suddenly, the rope went slack around his wrists.

Without questioning how, he wriggled free. Then, in one fluid motion, he picked up the cord and dove for the tent. *God give me strength.*

He threw himself at Smith and with the rope held taught between his two hands, he slipped it over the villain's head and pulled with all his might. He yelled with the effort and the pain which coursed through his torso. Stella scrambled out of the way, panting in fright, and gathered her torn shirt together.

For a few moments, Smith fought against him. He clawed at the rope digging into his neck, but Tony somehow found the strength to hold the rope firm until Smith's body went slack. He held on for a few heartbeats longer and then released him and let the unconscious man collapse to the ground.

Chapter Eighteen

'Did you kill him?' Stella could barely find her voice. Her chest heaved from her battle against Smith and she swallowed hard. Tony had spared her from his clutches just in time. What he had been about to do to her was ... She clutched her torn shirt close to her throat though her hands trembled violently.

Tony looked up at her and wrapped his arms around his chest with a groan, gasping for breath. It must have hurt his broken rib, straining so. His eyes seemed troubled as he glanced from her to Smith and back to her. Then he leaned down and listened to the scoundrel's chest. 'No, he's not dead. Are you hurt?'

Stella shook her head. He stared at her for a moment then checked the man's pockets.

The enormity of what had happened overwhelmed her then, and sobs ripped from deep within her, shaking her small frame. Tony paused in his search and watched her with a slight frown. As he continued his search, his words were anything but comforting. 'We don't have much time. He could come around at any moment. And who knows when Burns will come back.' He found what he looked for and held it up — the key. Without pause, he unlocked their chains. 'Now is our chance to run. See if you can find anything useful, and quick. I will check their tent.'

Stella understood he meant for her to pull herself together. She gulped air in an attempt to control the tide of emotion which had taken over her. Tony ducked out of the tent and crossed the campsite to Smith and Burn's tent.

She watched him go in turmoil of mind. Didn't he care? Oh,

how she wished he'd put his arms around her to hold her. Instead, he brushed her off. But, she couldn't think about it now. She needed to do as he said. They had this one chance.

Her legs were a little unsteady from the fright she had suffered. She managed to find her satchel and her grandmother's bible, barely holding the tide at bay. She wiped at her eyes with her sleeve. By then Tony emerged from the other tent with a satisfied smirk and came over to her.

'Here, put these in.' He handed her a gun and ammunition.

Stella took them and put them in the satchel while Tony checked on Smith once more. She clutched at her shirt. The buttons at the top were gone and her shoulder peeped out where it had ripped open.

Tony came back with the knife and rope. The cord in his hand brought a question to her mind, though she found it difficult to speak at all. 'How ... did you ... get ... free?'

He glanced down at the rope in his hands. 'I don't know. It came loose when I tugged on it. It still seems to have the knots in it though.' He took the satchel from her, shoved the rope in it and slung it over his shoulder, keeping the knife in one hand. Then he grabbed her free hand and pulled. 'Let's go.'

'Don't you need anything from your own bag?'

Tony paused and a small frown creased his brow. 'My pipe. I haven't wished for a smoke these last few days, what with my face all smashed up. But it was a gift from my father.' He bent to collect his satchel and rummaged through it, his frown increasing. 'It's gone. The scoundrel has stolen it.' He looked as though he wanted to go and wake Smith and demand it and he wavered on his feet for a moment. With a groan he dropped his bag and turned. Stella could see it took an effort to let it go. 'There's no time.'

They took off at a run, straight into the dense bush. 'But the track! It's back the other way.' Stella tugged on his grip.

'And it's the first place they'll look.' He turned, picked up a large stick and scratched out their footsteps back to the edge of the trees. He kicked decayed bark and leaves over their tracks to be sure. Once again at her side, he took her hand and led her further away, keeping their pace as fast as they could through the thick bushland. Tony paused often to gasp for breath, clutching his chest, then pressed on again.

They had to find their way around rock formations, climb over fallen, burnt out gums and navigate the rises and falls in the landscape. It was a rugged area, and Stella hoped they gained enough distance.

Tony never let go of her hand, except if the landscape was too difficult to manage while holding on. She felt like a child pulled along by an impatient parent. Her lungs burned, her legs felt like fire and raw spots already developed on her feet, though she knew they hadn't gone far. Was Tony as breathless as she? *He must be.* He had a broken rib and broken nose on top of everything else. When she believed she could run no more, they burst into a clearing, and the sight which met her eyes caused relief to sweep over her.

A group of men sat around a campfire, tin cups in their hands. They laughed at some jest, but stopped at the sudden interruption and all heads turned their way.

'Help us ...' Stella panted out, glad to find assistance, but even as the words passed her lips, she felt Tony's grip on her hand tighten.

'Grab them!' One of the men yelled and the three of them leapt up and darted towards them.

'Run!' Tony yanked her towards the thick bushland again.

I can't! Her body screamed at her. As she turned away however, she saw one of the strangers draw a pistol from a holster.

'Get down!' Tony dove over a fallen log and landed with a groan. Stella did the same, a heartbeat behind him, as the sound of gunfire met their ears.

Stella screamed then turned to Tony in panic. 'Who are they? Why would they shoot at us?'

Tony still rolled on the ground, clutching his rib in agony, his teeth clenched against the pain. 'Bushrangers, I think,' he hissed between shallow breaths. 'We saw their faces. Probably wanted men.'

He pulled himself up and scrambled, still crouched, through the undergrowth, beckoning her to follow. He soon straightened, so they could move faster and dodged this way and that through the trees, while branches slapped against their faces and arms. Stella wondered if they had any hope. They were already exhausted and the men who chased them were fresh. She stumbled and her hand slipped out of Tony's grip. Another scream echoed into the forest as she landed heavily, small branches scratching her arms as she fell.

Before she could gather her feet under her again, she felt a hand fasten around her ankle. She screamed over and over as she kicked and tried to free herself. But the man's grip felt like an iron vice. Tony appeared at her feet then and threw a punch into the man's face. The grip slackened on her foot and she shrank backwards, struggling to stand up.

She saw a second bushranger grab Tony's arms from behind as he went to grab the knife he had long since pocketed, and pull them behind his back rendering him unable to fight. He kicked his legs in a blind panic, though they met with little contact. He roared at his captors to let him go.

Dear God! Not again. Please help us. How could they gain their freedom only to be caught again? And these men would kill them if they were indeed wanted men.

The third man lunged at her. She tried to run, but he had her in his grasp before she made a few steps. She screamed and fought him with every ounce of strength she had left. It was no use. She could not get away. The man Tony had punched was back on his feet and came over to assist.

Then, a sudden shadow burst from behind the trees. A huge figure which resembled a tree trunk fell on the third man with his fists flying. The bushranger had barely hit the ground before he turned and attacked the man who held her. Burns! She recognised his face in an instant.

'They're *mine*.' He planted a rock-like fist in the man's face. Stella went down with him as he fell but rolled to safety.

The stunned bushranger staggered to his feet and charged at Burns, who had turned to fight the man who had Tony. The next she knew Tony crouched beside her as the men continued to brawl. 'Run!' Tony whispered in her ear.

As quietly as they could, they ducked behind a giant gum tree and ran.

'Hey! Come back here! You'll never get away! I'll find you!' They'd never heard Burns string so many words together, but they didn't stop. Surely the trees would hide them.

They ran and ran, though both were exhausted. Stella's lungs burned and she could only imagine how much pain Tony would be in. After what seemed an eternity, Tony glanced over his shoulder, took a few more steps, then looked behind him again. He stopped.

'Can you ... see them?' Stella bent over and placed her hands on her thighs, trying to drag air deep into her lungs.

'Come.' Tony reached out for her hand, turned and headed back the way they came.

At first Stella feared capture, but soon realised Tony had found them a hiding place. A large eucalypt stood before them, but unless you stopped and looked, you would not see the trunk only went a dozen feet or so into the air. The rest had disappeared at some time and the inside had been burnt hollow from the recent fire. Low ferns covered a gaping hole at the base. Somehow, Tony must have noticed it.

'In there.' He motioned for her to crouch and enter and he followed behind.

'Catch your breath,' he panted once they were installed in the charred out centre of the tree.

'Do you think we've ... escaped him ... them?' Stella whispered between breaths.

'Listen.'

Neither of them could hear running feet or branches snapping close by. In the distance they could hear the holler of voices.

'I hope ... they don't ... find us.'

'I doubt it ... now.' Tony hugged his chest as he tried to slow his breath, his face screwed up in anguish. 'Rest here ... a while.'

Soon enough, even the sound of voices died away and they sat in silence.

'Thank God.' Stella sighed out the words.

'It was close. We need to keep moving though.' He ducked out of the tree and held out his hand towards her. She placed hers in it without hesitation and followed.

They'd walked for hours. Tony's legs felt like jelly beneath him, but he managed to keep swinging one in front of the other. They would have to stop soon. The light had begun to fade.

Where are we? He had hoped they would come to a road or track by now, but it seemed the forest grew more dense. Another concern played at the back of his mind. They had no food, and more importantly, no water. They had stumbled across one tiny creek soon after they escaped the bushrangers and had slaked their thirst, but they had seen no sign of water since then. *How could I have saved this woman from one peril to face her with another?* Once again the familiar sense of failure swept through him.

She had trusted him to lead her to safety. She had not questioned him, but held onto his hand and followed him deep into the bush. Now it seemed they would spend a night in the open, and who knows what tomorrow? Exhaustion nagged at him and all the activity of the day had intensified the pain in his rib cage. He searched the bush around them, though he could not see very far, and looked for an appropriate shelter — if such a thing even existed.

'Tony. I'm thirsty.'

They were words he didn't want to hear. What solution could he give? 'Me too. But we've got no water.'

'Can't you find us another creek?'

Tony stopped and turned to her. Her eyes held such hope. *When did she switch from her independence to looking to him for solutions?* He listened for the sound of running water, but could only hear the hiss of wind as it blew through the tree tops. *It must be gusty out in the open.* Even on the ground the breeze could be felt a little. It made it impossible to hear water even if it were there. And who knew how long it would take to find some in the dim light. He let his gaze drop to the ground and his hair fell across his forehead. 'I ... I don't know ... where we are.'

She looked around them, peering into the trees. 'It's getting dark.'

'I know.'

'What will we do?'

Tony scuffed the ground with his boot. 'I guess we have to stay here for the night.'

Stella remained silent. She turned and limped over to a fallen tree where she sank to the ground. He watched her for a time. *She looks so tired.* She no longer bothered to hold the torn part of her shirt up and her porcelain shoulder, smeared with dirt though it was, gleamed in the afternoon light. He turned in a full circle, looking in each direction. 'I guess here is as good a place as any.'

He stumbled over to her and dropped down beside her. His whole body ached. He had to figure out what they should do. He had not much considered their direction while in the desperate moments of escape, even after their encounter with the bushrangers. He glanced at the sun which sank towards the horizon to their left. He supposed they had travelled to the north, possibly the east a little. If they were in the Black Forest as he hoped, they should head east on the morrow, and eventually emerge onto the plains. The problem was, he couldn't be sure they were in the Black Forest, so had no idea where they were headed. If he could figure out where Smith and Burns had taken them ...

'Tony!' Stella's sudden grip on his arm, shocked him awake. Darkness shrouded them. He hadn't even realised he'd fallen asleep.

'What's wrong?' His voice sounded groggy.

'What's that noise?'

Still heavy with sleep, Tony tried to focus on the sounds around them. He sat bolt upright when he heard it. A deep growl or roar filled the night air. Stella's grip on his arm intensified. He smiled at her, though she wouldn't be able to see it. 'That's the koalas.'

'Koalas?'

'Uh-huh.'

'Those cute bears that sit in the trees and eat leaves?'

'The very same.'

'They make that awful noise?'

'They do.'

'Oh.'

Tony found it a little strange, too. He'd been shocked the first time he'd heard a koala growl. He felt sorry for Stella. 'I fell asleep. Sorry about that.'

'Never mind. I did too. But the growling woke me.'

'All the running and walking wore me out.'

'That's an understatement if I ever heard one. I don't want to *ever* have a day like that again.'

She blames me for it. And right she is. 'I'm ... I'm sorry ...'

'Sorry?' Her voice had a sharp edge, but he couldn't see the expression on her face. Sorry would never be good enough. Tension rose within him along with a sense of inadequacy. Coupled with exhaustion, he had little energy to rein in his temper.

'All right! I'm *useless*! Is that what you want to hear? You've already told me as much. Plenty of times. I've led us from one scrape to another. And this time I've got us lost. I have no idea where we are, or how to find our way out? We should have stayed in our chains! You see. There! I am a coward, just like you said!'

He must have shocked her into silence, for she didn't say a word. His chest heaved with emotion. *I may as well be dead for the use I am on this earth.* And this beautiful woman was stuck with him, even though he couldn't save her if he tried. His heart ached with helplessness.

'You're not a coward.' The words were very softly spoken, but he heard them clearly.

'What?'

'You are not a coward.'

Tony felt his anger rise. 'I *am* a coward. I've spent my whole life running. I ran from the memory of my mother. I couldn't even return to help my sister when she needed me. I convinced myself to keep out of the Eureka riots — I was on the way out of Ballaarat when Smith and Burns got me. 'Struth, I couldn't even tell my father what I really felt. Instead I told him I hated him and I didn't want to be his son. Even *you* have seen how much of a failure I am. You said it the first time you saw me, remember. Pusillanimous was the word you used. So, don't try and pretend I'm not!'

Once again quietness filled the air, until Tony believed he'd convinced her. Although, part of him hoped she would argue. He felt as though he could drown in self-disgust at his weakness.

'I'm not pretending.' Her voice was very quiet. 'It was you who diverted the attack from Burns to yourself. You threw yourself at him, so I would not be hit. I did not imagine that. It was you who stopped Smith from ... from hurting me. And you didn't run when those bushrangers had me. You stood up and fought them. *You*. Not someone else. You Tony. It does not matter that we might be lost. At least you tried. A coward would not have done as much. I think you have been very brave.'

Tony leaned forward and put his head on his knees. *She really thinks so? I was sure she hated me.* 'I have wondered several times today whether we should have stayed in our chains. Don't you think that a coward's thoughts?'

'It is not cowardly to have doubts. But I can tell you this: I would rather be lost in the bush with growling koalas than kept prisoner by that horrid man.'

'Hmph.' Tony wasn't sure what to say. Her words had unravelled something deep within. For so many years he had been convinced his life had no meaning — that he had no purpose or use on this earth. Could it be possible someone saw him differently?

'Tell me about your father.'

Could he talk about this? *Will she laugh at me?* She would likely rethink her belief in his bravery. But, the weight of it felt so heavy now. It would be nice to have it off his chest. 'I ... I ... don't know where to start.' He was thankful for the darkness which hid his face.

'What happened between you?'

Tony swallowed. 'I ... uh — when Mama died, I didn't know what to do with myself. I missed her so much. She always gave me direction, but then she passed away. I begged her to stay. But she either couldn't or didn't want to fight her sickness.' He shrugged. How could he express the abandonment he had felt?

'Then Papa wanted me to 'hold my chin up' and get busy helping him with the sheep. He told me to 'be a man' and to stop crying over her. He may have been able to put his grief aside with ease, but I couldn't. I never had his kind of mettle. Penny — my sister — was always made of stronger stuff than I. And I think he liked her better for it. She used to follow him around the station, carrying her dolls along with her. She was very sweet.' He allowed a brief smile, but could not tell in the shadows if Stella responded.

'Anyway, Papa wanted to teach me all about the sheep-run, but I already resented him too much. I resisted every attempt he made for two years. As soon as I turned sixteen, I packed my things and left. Of course, Papa ripped up at me something terrible. He swore he would cut me from his will if I took one step out of the gate. I shrugged my shoulders at him, turned my back and walked away.'

'And you think yourself a coward?'

Tony shook his head. How could she doubt it? He felt tears sting his eyes and brushed them away. 'Yes! It was a weak and craven thing to do. I should have stayed and told him how I felt!'

'Why, when he wouldn't listen anyway? That's why I ran away —
my father wouldn't listen.'

'Then you are as much a fool as I.' Tony growled.

'Why?'

'Because what if you don't get another chance to tell him how you
feel? What if you can't ever tell him you love him again? My father
came to me at Ballaarat. He came to mend the rift between us and to
take me home. He gave me a gift — the carved pipe I mentioned this
morning. But I never gave him a chance. I told him I hated him — that
I didn't want to be his son. And do you know what? He did not say
another word. He just picked up his bag and went home.'

'You see. He wasn't going to listen.'

'No Stella!' Tears streamed from his eyes and he had no power
to stop them. '*I* was the one who wouldn't listen. He wanted to tell
me something ... something about his will. But I cut him off with my
resentment. I assumed he wanted to remind me I was no longer part of
his life. I found out a week ago he purchased a whole new property for
me. For me! And I never got the chance to tell him how sorry I was or
how much I cared about him because he died!'

Years of self-loathing and regret poured out of him then. He felt
Stella place a hand on his arm but he shook it off. What would she
want with such a worthless wretch? She left him alone for a time, yet
sat motionless beside him.

When the torrent of anguish had subsided, he dried his face and
leaned back against the fallen log. 'I'm ... I'm sorry. You must be
convinced by now? You see how weak I am?'

Her voice sounded a little wobbly as she replied. 'I think ... I
think you are a man with many regrets. But I still don't think you're a
coward.'

Something about her statement made him want to laugh. *She
knows the worst of me and still thinks I'm brave.* Her words felt like a
balm to his wounds, a silver lining to this dark night.

'What is so funny?' Stella sounded unsure, or perhaps she had
taken offence.

'I don't know.' He felt as though his chuckle could turn back into
tears without warning.

Stella kept silent for a moment. 'The day we met ... when I said you were pusillanimous ... I was being ... coquettish.'

It had obviously taken her a lot of effort to admit it, but Tony could hardly believe his ears. *She flirted with me?* She hadn't intended to offend him, but had tried to get his attention. *Could it be possible?* Hope winged its way through his soul. Stella, the most beautiful vision he'd ever seen, and the most spirited and courageous girl he'd ever known, was interested in him?

With a slow, deep breath, he peered at her in through the shadows. He couldn't read her face in the darkness, but could see she hugged herself against the wind. 'Cold?'

'A little.'

'Well, come over here then. I know it is improper, but I also know propriety is not high on your list of importance. We have no blankets, so we shall have to keep each other warm for the rest of the night.'

She stared at him for a time, although he couldn't see her face clearly. He couldn't be sure if she wanted to rip up at him for calling her improper, or do as he suggested. In time she sidled closer and he pulled her into him so her body was cradled against his chest, though she stiffened somewhat, and they lay with their heads on the moss-covered ground.

'Just watch your elbow near my ribs.' It seemed a clumsy kind of thing to say, but he couldn't very well tell her how much her nearness made his whole body come alive. *You're on dangerous ground, Tony.*

Another deep growl pierced the air. 'Are you sure it's a koala?' Stella's voice trembled.

Tony shrugged in the darkness and tried to sound serious. 'It could be a Bunyip I suppose.'

Stella bolted upright and sucked in a frightened breath. 'A Bunyip?'

'Have you heard of them?'

'Of course I have. They are monsters that live near water. There have been many reported sightings of late. Oh, Tony could it be?'

Tony chuckled. 'Come and lay down, I'm teasing you. Bunyips don't exist. If they ever did, they're extinct now. It is just a koala, like I first told you.'

Stella seemed to hesitate before she curled up beside him again. 'You're certain?'

'Yes, but Brave Tony is here to protect you, all right?' His voice sounded thick with sarcasm, but she giggled in response.

'How do you know so much about the animals?'

'Mama.' Tony swallowed hard. 'I already told you how she was sick. She would spend her days — in the warmer weather anyway — sitting in a chair by the creek. I suppose Papa believed the fresh air would do her good. She did like to watch the animals and examine the plants.

'After one trip to Melbourne, Papa brought home Shaw's *Zoology of New Holland* and *A Specimen of the Botany of New Holland.* For hours on end she would try to match plants and animals to their drawings in the books. She even persuaded Papa to bring home more articles — anything he could find — every time he went to the city.'

Tony felt a tear slip from his eye. *Here I go again.* Memories of his mother were so precious. He had never mentioned her to anyone in Ballaarat. He swallowed again. 'Whenever I could sneak away from my farm chores, I would go and sit by her. She showed me everything she'd learned. That's why I know about the koalas and such.'

Stella remained quiet for a long while, till Tony suspected she might have fallen asleep. But then he heard her whisper. 'You miss her?'

'Very much.' He almost choked on the words.

'My mother is sickly too. For the past year anyway. But, she just lies around and we are at loggerheads all the time.' She sounded a little envious of his time with his mother.

'Perhaps you should sit with her and listen. You might find she has something of interest to tell you.' Tony could imagine Stella impatient and chaffing to run off on some activity or another, rather than recline with her mother and spend precious time with her.

'Mmm, perhaps.'

Stella lapsed into quiet thoughtfulness. At least Tony assumed she had, else she had dozed off again. Memories of his dear Mama reminded him again how precious Stella had become to him. *I have to get her home to safety. I couldn't bear to lose another dear soul.* Almost involuntarily, his hold around her waist tightened. It would be so easy to lean forward and kiss that pearly white curve in her neck.

'Good night Brave Tony.'

He cleared his throat. 'G'night.'

Chapter Nineteen

Melbourne

By dawn on Sunday morning, Angus had Penny and Gertie packed and in the saddle. They had a long ride ahead of them. If they wanted to give the horses time to rest on the journey and still have time to meet the kidnappers in the afternoon, they had to leave at once. His fiancée appeared very serious this morning with faint shadows beneath her eyes. He suspected she had slept little in spite of their long walk yesterday.

'Are ye all ri' my love?' He gave her hand a squeeze as he looked up at her upon Chocolate.

She gave him a brief nod. 'The sooner I see the end of this day, the better.'

Angus pulled himself into the saddle, holding tight to Thunder's restless reins. 'Shall we pray before we head off?'

'Of course.'

They edged their horses closer and reached out to join hands, Gertie on the other side of Penny. After a quick but heartfelt prayer, asking God to be with them on their journey and through their task afterwards, they nudged the horses forward and left Melbourne behind.

Angus uttered prayers beneath his breath for most of the ride. It was a nervous thing to carry £10,000 such a distance. No wonder the gold which came in from the goldfields had an escort of soldiers. One never knew just where thieves waited to ambush a wealthy traveller. He touched the strap across his chest which held the rifle at his back.

An extra security he felt relieved to have, though he hoped not to need the use of it.

By midday they had reached the Aitken's Gap without mishap. Angus's brows furrowed together as he envisioned the next leg of their journey. They approached the Black Forest — the favoured haunt of thieves and robbers. He dismounted, as did the two women, and he took the horses to the inn's ostler for refreshment. On returning to the tavern, he found the girls had just found a seat in the crowded inn, and were ordering food from the inn-keeper.

'Hungry, eh?' He grinned at Penny.

She nodded with a brief smile. 'I hope their food is edible.'

'I've et 'ere before.' Gertie added her opinion. 'It's not too bad.'

Angus let his gaze drift around the room, small though it was, to take in the other visitors. It seemed a platoon of soldiers filled the building with their red uniforms.

'A detachment on the way to Bendigo I suppose.' Penny must have noticed his interest.

'Aye. With the trouble in Ballaarat, they probably have to send reinforcements everywhere.'

Gertie's eyebrows rose in delight. 'Some of them soldiers is mighty 'andsome.'

Angus and Penny looked at her and laughed as she gazed at the men.

Another man in well tailored riding clothes approached their table, removed his hat and offered a short bow. 'I beg pardon. I hope my men are not too noisy for you.'

Indeed the soldiers were at ease and laughed together over their dinner.

'They're no' disturbing us.' Angus stood and put out his hand. 'Angus McDoughan, at yer service.'

The man's concerned frown turned into a smile, albeit a grim one. The opinion struck Angus that the man looked haggard. He shook Angus's hand.

'William Mattherson's the name.'

'This is me fiancée, Penny Worthington, and this is Gertie.' Angus offered Mr Mattherson a seat with them. 'Are ye takin' these men to the goldfields?'

'Pleased to meet you. No, no.' He sat, though he appeared to be unsettled. 'We have a little mission to accomplish. That is all. I had wondered if you came in from Bendigo, in fact.'

'No.' Penny shook her head. 'We are on our way north — a little mission of our own.'

'Right. That's too bad. I had hoped you could tell me about the road north of The Bush Inn.' He slapped his thighs and rose. 'I suppose I should ask the other few guests here.'

'Very sorry. That's where we are headed, but we've never been there before.' Angus also stood and saluted Mr Mattherson. 'All I know is there is supposed to be an outcrop of boulders about a mile into the Black Forest with a track goin' off to the left. Best be on yer guard. They say bushrangers hide out in the Forest.'

Mr Mattherson's face changed into a serious, even angry mask and he glared at Angus. Before Angus knew what had happened, the man had grabbed him by the shirt collar and leaned his face close. 'Are you the cur responsible for taking my daughter?' His voice was fierce and his grip, unyielding. He heard the metallic sound of swords and pistols sliding from their holsters and he knew the soldiers around him were ready to defend. He heard Penny and Gertie gasp with fright. *Lord, help me!*

'Unless yer Miss Worthington's father come back from the dead, I do no' know what yer talkin' about.' He managed to get the words out, even though Mr Mattherson had cut his supply of air somewhat.

The man gave him a little shake and his eyes bulged out of his head. 'Then why would you mention that section of the road?'

Angus had no idea why Mr Mattherson reacted so violently and he feared it would not end well. He could only be honest and hope it worked. ''Cause that's where we are goin' — where we've been told to go.'

The man's grip loosened a bit, although he still did not let go. '*Told* to go?'

Penny reached up and tugged his sleeve then. 'My brother has been kidnapped.' Her voice came out hoarse and her eyes darted about the inn, clearly hoping no-one heard her who could endanger Tony's life. 'Please let Gus go. I need him to help me get my brother back.'

With that Mr Mattherson released him and sank into the chair again, while the soldiers sheathed their swords and went back to their meals. 'Kidnapped, you say?'

'Yes,' Penny whispered.

Angus still wondered what had caused him to react so strongly. It alarmed him to say the least. He sat down again, though hesitant to do so.

'My daughter has been kidnapped.' Mr Mattherson ran a hand over his face.

'Oh.' What seemed like a united realisation struck them all and they fell into silence.

A bar maid arrived with the travellers' food and deposited it on the table before them. Unlike Mrs Mac's fine food, they were served a simple bowl of mutton stew with crusty bread. But, with Mattherson's revelation, Angus's appetite evaporated.

'Sorry to man-handle you, Mr McDoughan,' Mattherson mumbled.

'No, no. Never mind. Tell us more about yer daughter. Do ye think it's the same man, or men who took our Tony?'

Mattherson looked at him with a glum face. 'If you have been told to turn left at the outcrop of boulders and ride to the creek, then yes.'

'Why have you brought soldiers with you? We were told Tony would be murdered if we involved the authorities.' Penny's eyes were wide with grave concern.

'I don't care what that blackguard says. I will not be manipulated or blackmailed by some swamp rat!' Mattherson's fist crashed down on the table, making Penny jump. All eyes in the inn seemed to turn their way. In a lower voice, he added, 'I am determined to make sure they don't get away with this.'

Angus reached out and patted him on the shoulder. 'Ye'll get no argument from me there, sir.'

'But Redcoats? They will see them coming a mile away.' Penny's thoughts clearly centred on Tony's safety.

Mr Mattherson either didn't hear her, or ignored her fears. 'I don't understand it. At first I believed Estella had run away.' He rubbed his face again. 'She left a note to say so. She thinks I am a bad father, you see. I had planned to send her to England and she didn't want to go.'

Angus watched him. What he had earlier suspected as weariness, he now recognised as the burden the man carried. He could see Penny frown and suspected she wanted to mention her doubts about the Redcoats again. He caught her eye and shook his head in a very subtle way. Thankfully she closed her mouth again.

'She took off with her most valued possessions, and even my pistol, though God knows why she needed it. Safety I suppose. I daresay she does not even know how to use it.' Mattherson gave a hollow laugh. 'The strange thing is my pistol was found when they cleaned up the stockade area. For the life of me, I cannot imagine why she would have been there.'

'She was at the Eureka riots?' Penny's eyes were wide.

'It seems so. That's the night she disappeared. Her mother and I were beside ourselves when we realised she had gone. As if I didn't already have enough to worry about with the bloody mess out at Eureka.'

'Have things settled down in Ballaarat?' Angus wanted to know.

Mattherson gave a brief nod. 'The diggers have been very quiet all week. They mourn the loss of a number of their own. Marshall Law has helped. The church men have been busy with funeral services.'

'So how did you find out your daughter had been abducted?' Penny drew him back to the topic at hand.

'When we received the ransom letter. Our maid had been very weepy since Estella vanished until I wondered if there was more to her tears than worry. Anarosa — my wife — questioned her and soon the truth tumbled out. Jemina had cut her hair off and promised not to tell.'

'Why would she do that?' Penny frowned again.

'At first I had no idea. When I received the ransom, it became very clear. The letter mentioned my son, Billy. I do not have a son. I assume she cut her hair and dressed as a boy.'

Penny and Gertie gasped.

'Are ye sure?' Angus couldn't believe a young girl would do such a thing.

Mattherson's lips were pressed into a thin line. 'My daughter has always been ... er ... headstrong. She will do most anything if it serves her purpose. She is not stupid, however. She knows it is not safe to wander as a woman unattended. The scandalous nature of her actions would not have even entered her thoughts.'

'She did all that to avoid a trip to England?' Even Gertie seemed astounded.

'What I cannot put together is how she went from runaway

to ransom captive. How did they know she came from a wealthy background? I assume the villains spied on her for a while and took their chance when they saw her run. Although that would mean they had watched my house in the dead of night.' He rubbed his face once more. 'I just don't know.'

The party fell into silence for a time, thinking on all he had said.

'I have to get her back. She is our only child. Before her there were many miscarriages and ...' Mattherson swallowed. 'Anarosa has been unwell for a long time. This will cause her health to suffer further unless I can bring Estella home. I have to find her.'

Angus saw the wild look in the man's eyes and gave him a comforting pat on the shoulder. 'We'll find her. We'll find them both.'

'I hope they have been well looked after.' Penny added her concerns.

'*I* hope they have not discovered Estella's sex.' Mattherson gritted.

Angus frowned. It would indeed be a grave concern.

'Your Redcoats might put them in danger.' Penny returned to her earlier fear.

Mattherson looked at her with bleary eyes. 'These soldiers are some of the best. They know how to creep up on a man without discovery. We have a plan in place, never you mind.'

Angus knew by the resolute look on Mr Mattherson's face that to argue would be fruitless. Obviously he was a man familiar with leadership. Angus suspected he had a military past as well. He turned to Penny and gave her a gentle nudge. 'Why don't ye tell 'im about Tony?'

'Oh, I ...'

'Of course,' Mattherson interjected. 'I should have asked you earlier. Beg pardon, do go on.'

'We recently came into a lot of money,' she began. She did not tell him about the gold discovery on Ellenvale, but did recount the attitude of the Foxworths and how they suspected Rupert might be behind the whole abduction and ransom.

Mattherson listened, but his frown became even more pronounced. 'But, if this Foxworth fellow organised it all, and he is here in the Sunbury region, how would he know about my Estella?' He looked from one to the other.

Penny's eyebrows went up and she shook her head, turning doubt-filled eyes to Angus.

'Perhaps we've got it all wrong.' He gave a helpless shrug.

Penny's face fell. 'But who would do this to us then?' She turned to Mr Mattherson. 'Foxworth is the *only* one outside our property who knew about the money.'

Mattherson scowled and spread his hands on the table. 'Well, it seems we shall not get the answers we need until we find these low-born thieves and bring them to justice. They are the ones who can tell us what happened. I suggest we get on the road and put an end to this abominable affair.'

'Here, here.' Angus began to rise from the table, but Mattherson put out a staying hand.

'You might want to eat your dinner. We've a long afternoon ahead of us and you'll need to sustain yourself.'

Angus looked at his mutton stew and nodded. 'I s'pose yer ri'.'

He nodded to Penny to do the same and she fell to her meal. Gertie, on the other hand, had already finished, having eaten while they all discussed the situation. She followed Mattherson back to his table in order to meet some of the soldiers and they soon heard her giggle at their jests.

Angus reached out and gave Penny's hand a squeeze of reassurance. 'The Lord is with us, me lovely. Try no' to worry too much.'

She sent him a half-smile which he read as gratefulness for his encouragement. 'I shall try.'

Chapter Twenty

Stella lifted Tony's limp arm from over her waist and wriggled free of him. She sat and watched his sleeping form for a long time. The bruises over his eye and nose were still very black. *All the running yesterday must have taken a lot out of him.* She knew how exhausted she had been, and still was, and he had injuries on top of that.

The urge to reach out and brush his hair away from his face came very strong, but she didn't want to wake him. *Besides, he wouldn't appreciate me touching him.* It had taken her a lot of courage to admit to him she had been playing coy with him. But his voice had been so thick with self-revulsion, she had to make him know the truth — that she did not think him a coward at all. Nothing she had said seemed to help at all until then. He sounded so convinced of his contemptibility, it made her heart sick. No-one should hate themselves so.

Now, she knew she had convinced him she had no morals. He probably thought her unchaste now. After she'd confessed to her flirtatious behaviour, he'd had no qualms about holding her close all night. *He thinks me so wanton I would not object.* But she *had* wanted to object. That kind of close proximity had been uncomfortable. It sent bells ringing all through her and her heart had beat rapidly. She gazed down at him and sighed. *Don't you know how attracted to you I am?* She had agreed only for the needed warmth.

She looked up into the canopy of trees. The sun already rode well up in the sky and the air was warm. It promised to be one of those blistering summer days. They needed to find water in a hurry.

Stella noted the tops of the tress did not blow about as they had last evening, yet she could still hear a similar hiss through the bush. *Could it be a stream?* Peering around her, she noticed a short distance through the trees the ground dipped a little. With a brief glance back at Tony, she scrambled to her feet, although her stiff muscles and blistered feet complained. She slung her satchel over her shoulder and went to investigate the nearby terrain, careful to kick a mark into the ground every few steps. *Losing my way back would make things very much worse.*

She recalled the past twenty-four hours. At times she had been terrified for her life, but Tony had been there in time, every time. *Brave Tony.* She remembered his words from the previous evening and smiled. *If only he believed it.* Somehow she had to make him realise he was not only brave, but her hero, the man she wanted to be with for the rest of her life. *But he wouldn't want a shameless flirt for a wife.* A tear sprang to her eye, unwelcome, and she brushed it away.

As she hoped, the ground dipped further, until the sound of rushing water became unmistakeable. Not only did a creek run through the small gully, but a waterfall cascaded into it perhaps fifty yards away. In no time she scrambled over moss-covered rocks and around trees till she stood at the base of the modest waterfall. She knelt down and cupped mouthful after mouthful into her dry throat. She lifted her gaze to the white, tumbling water again. *While Tony is asleep, now would be a good time to wash.* She removed most of her clothes, stood beneath the icy water and rubbed every trace of grime from her body. *The only thing I am missing is soap.*

The invigorating wash helped lift her flagging spirits. Hiding behind a large rock — in case Tony emerged — she removed her underclothes, wrung them out and put them back on again. She rinsed out her filthy and torn shirt and spread it on a rock to dry. *If Tony hadn't stopped Smith when he did, who knows what might have happened.* She shuddered at the thought and hugged herself.

Stella sat beside her shirt in the sunshine and pulled her satchel close, lifting her Bible out of it. Tears threatened again as she remembered her grandmother. She brushed her hand over the rough leather and remembered all she had read over the past few days. As *Abuela* had said, there were many wonderful stories within the pages, but it had been one of the Ten Commandments which had stayed foremost in her mind.

As expected she had found rules about falsehood, stealing and murder, but the one which had struck her most was 'honour thy father and thy mother'. Those words rolled around in her mind over and over, whether she wanted them to or not. They made her uncomfortable and niggled at her conscience, because she knew she had not honoured her father's wishes. Instead she had run away, gotten herself into dire peril, and caused her *padre* unnecessary grief. *God, have I been so wrong? Please give me the chance to say sorry.*

She opened the cover of the Bible. *Abuela* had written in Spanish on the first page. She ran her eyes over the familiar writing, but for the first time took in the meaning. 'Trust in the Lord with all thine heart; and lean not unto thine own understanding. In all thy ways acknowledge him, and he shall direct thy paths. Proverbs 3:5-6.' Stella wondered why that verse had been so important to her *abuela* she wrote it in the front of her Bible. She smiled to herself. *Abuela had the same feisty nature as me, I wonder if she too struggled against what everyone else wanted for her. If her answer had been to trust in the Lord, then it must have worked. Abuela* had always been happy and peaceful, even though her spirits wanted to fly. Most of the time, especially in recent days, Stella had felt angry and frustrated at her lack of freedom.

She turned some pages of the Bible and continued to read, forgetting all around her.

Tony opened his eyes with a groan. His body ached all over, especially his broken rib. All the activity yesterday must have disturbed it. He sat up with a wince and peered around, but could not see the one thing his eyes wanted to find. Stella. His heart dropped into the pit of his stomach. *She's left me. She probably thinks me even weaker after my outburst last night. She can most likely do better on her own.* Then again, what if something had happened to her? *But, she's taken the bag with her.*

'Stella?' He tried to call her name, but his parched throat made it impossible to create any volume of substance. He rose somewhat stiffly to his feet and squinted into the trees in every direction. He could not see her, but he did see large scuff marks in the ground.

A brief smile found the corners of his mouth. *A trail. She left me a track to follow.* With great relief, he followed her obvious tracks to where the forest descended into a narrow gorge. His ears soon recognised the welcome sound of the waterfall. *Water! Good girl!*

And then he saw her. She sat on a flat rock with her back towards him. The top half of her body was only covered in a thin cotton shift, and that flimsy garment clung in damp folds to every curve. He could see her graceful neck from beneath her short hair-cut, the soft roundness of her shoulders, her shapely waist and ... *Dear God in heaven, save me!* Tony forced himself to turn away as desire swept through him like fire through dry grass. He knew he was in danger of doing or saying something scandalous. 'Ahem.' He forced an alert to his presence behind her.

He heard her sharp intake of breath and figured she jumped in fright as well. She had been engrossed in something on her lap.

'Oh, Tony. Give me a moment. I am almost done here.'

A few heartbeats later, although it seemed like a thousand, he heard the rustle of fabric as she put her shirt on. 'All right. You can turn around now.'

Without a glance at her, he went straight to the water's edge and slaked his thirst then splashed water over his face and hair. He hoped the water would cool his heated emotions.

'I'm glad you found my tracks. How do you feel this morning?'

He sat nearby and dried his face on his shirt sleeves, careful not to touch the bridge of his nose. Finally he dared to look at her, but even then his heart did a somersault. 'Rather sore today. Thank you for finding water. And you?'

'Still tired I suppose, and stiff, and I could eat a large cow right about now.' She grinned. 'But I am all right. Why don't you bathe beneath the falls? It is simply *divine*.'

'I take it you did so.' *That was obvious Tony, now you sound like an imbecile.* Tony felt incapable of intelligent speech.

'Yes. I shall turn my back if you wish to enjoy it.' As she spoke, she manoeuvred herself to face away from the running water.

Tony noticed her shirt no longer gaped open at the shoulder and throat. On closer inspection, he could see she had sewn it up. *How did she do that?* She must have seen the question in his face.

'I had an idea.' Her lips curved in a demure smile. 'I used the knife to make a point on the end of a narrow stick.'

'You did?'

'Yes. It was terribly easy. Thank you for putting it in the satchel by the way, I found it rather handy. I used the sharp stick to poke a few holes in the shirt. Then I unravelled some of the rope to get a thinner strand, laced it through the holes and *voila*, I sewed my shirt. It's a bit rough, but at least it does not hang open anymore.'

'That's impressive for a ...'

Her eyes dropped. 'For a girl who dresses as a boy. I know. But, I've always been handy with a needle.'

Tony had intended to say something more along the lines of her youthfulness, but he let it go. If she only knew how amazed her innovation made him. *She whittled a stick of all things!* He recalled the first time he'd seen her, when her dress and sleeves were shorter than fashion allowed. 'I've noticed your skills in sewing before.'

She did not bring her eyes back up to him, but kept her gaze fixed on the ground. 'Do you intend to go and bathe so we can be on our way?'

Tony nodded and headed over to the tumbling water and took advantage of its invigorating power as Stella suggested. The cold water pummelled his back and his head, washing away the dust of the past few days. He stared at Stella's back from beneath the shower. She was unlike anyone he'd ever met — so fresh and spontaneous. She impressed him and surprised him at every turn. He imagined he could sit at her feet all day and never be bored.

'What shall we do today?' Stella asked him as he hung his shirt over a branch in the sun.

Tony ran his hands through his dripping hair and looked around them at the bushland, not that it gave him any clearer direction. But then he saw something that gave him pause. 'Give me a few moments. I shall be back.' He headed back up and out of the gully, close to the waterfall.

'Where are you going?'

He didn't answer her but kept climbing. If he'd seen what he hoped he did, it might help them find direction. He clambered onto some rocks at the head of the falls and peered toward the top of the trees. Yes. A small mountain rose above them. He scrambled back down to where Stella waited.

He told her of his hunch they were in the Black Forest. 'However, I am uncertain of anything for sure. There is a mountain to the north of us. I believe if we climb it, we shall be able to see exactly where we are. Then we can make a more solid decision on where to go.'

'Up the mountain, then?'

'Up the mountain.'

'All right.' She stood up and began to walk, although she did not look convinced.

It surprised Tony when she didn't argue. 'Come back and sit down. I ...'

'Since when did *you* become my father?' She turned and flung the words at him with a frown.

He looked at her evenly. Her mood had changed, though he could not fathom why. Half an hour earlier she'd been happy and smiling. Had he done something wrong? He couldn't think of anything. Frustration grew in his chest. 'Let's get this straight. I don't *ever* want to be your father.'

As soon as he said it, he knew his words were too rash and he chided himself. He didn't want to be her father, but he *did* want to be the man she called husband. He could not tell her that while they were alone in the forest, however. He was on dangerous ground already. Unfortunately, she seemed on edge this morning and her frown increased. 'Please sit down. I am not yet ready to go. And I should like to know why you agree to go up the mountain against your better judgement.'

'Why is it I must argue with you? You expect a childish tantrum every time I open my mouth?' She sat down heavily on the rock she had just left.

'No. But I can see you don't want to go.' He liked to hear her point of view, even if it might be filled with unconsidered risk. Between them they might hit on a reasonable plan.

She gave a little shrug. 'We have no food and we cannot carry water. If we went west we could be sure to stay alive — we *know* there is a road over there. Unless, of course, we met with any desperate criminals along the way.' She looked him in the eye. 'But, I have decided to trust God, so I will go where ever you lead.'

Tony screwed up his face into a frown. 'Trust God? Where did that come from?'

Her gaze faltered and then she sighed and retrieved her Bible from the satchel. 'I read this earlier.' She opened the front cover and reached out to pass it to him.

Tony glanced at the hand-written verse inside and looked up at her again. 'I can't read Spanish.'

Her eyelids closed as she shook her head. 'I'm sorry. I forgot.' She read the verse to him. 'It made me think, Tony. What if ... what if God answered our prayers?'

'What do you mean?'

'What if God loosened the rope around your wrists?'

How could she know he'd wondered the exact same thing? 'But maybe Smith didn't tie it properly because you distracted him with your attack.'

She considered it for a moment. 'But it came loose at just the right time. Was it a co-incidence or could it be that God helped us?'

Tony didn't want to argue with her, but neither did he feel convinced.

'And what about the fact Burns arrived when he did? What are the odds he happened to be there in the same place at the same time?'

Tony heaved his shoulders. 'Perhaps you have a point.'

She sat up straighter and her eyes brightened. 'Well, I think we should pray again. If God is watching over us, He can lead us out of this forest. This verse says He will direct our path if we trust in Him.'

He remembered the voice he'd heard a few days earlier about asking and receiving. Although it seemed hardly believable, Stella's words made him consider it. What if all of their escapes so far *had* been an answer to their prayer? It would mean God *had* watched over them and cared what happened to them. Dare he hope? Dare he believe? *Dare I try again and trust in Him as Stella suggested?* When it came down to it, he had little to lose.

'All right.'

Stella became animated. 'I shall pray this time.' She closed her eyes and folded her hands together as he had seen his papa do at grace before dinner. She had become excited about her Bible these past few days, and more so each time she read. *I suppose she finds it all easier to believe than I.*

Tony closed his eyes as she prayed, but his mind did not follow her words. He couldn't help but wonder; if God had helped them, why? Why would the Almighty show interest in a worthless fool such as himself? *Well, God, here's another chance to prove You care. Help us find our way home.*

'Amen.' He heard Stella finish her prayer and opened his eyes.

'Amen.' He tried to encourage her with a smile. 'Now, hand me the gun from the satchel.'

Stella's lovely brows drew together a little. 'Why?'

'We didn't have much chance to prepare yesterday. Today, I want to be ready if we happen upon any danger.'

Her face cleared as understanding lit her eyes. She nodded and gave him the gun. He examined it and gave it a wipe over with his shirt. 'May I have the bullets and such that go with it?'

Stella fumbled in the bag and brought out the gun's ancillary equipment. She studied as he loaded the gun. When he poured gunpowder down the muzzle she leaned forward.

'What's that?'

'Gunpowder.'

She flew to her feet and slapped her thigh. 'Fiend seize it! I cannot believe I would miss such a simple thing.'

Tony stopped loading the gun and looked at her. 'What are you talking about?'

'At the stockade. I tried to — never mind.' She sat down again.

'What did you try to do?'

'I said never mind.' She folded her arms across her chest. She did not wish to discuss it for some reason.

Tony's mind raced. The stockade. She went there to 'help'. He remembered she mentioned something about a gun which she had left behind. Just now she became angry after she asked him about the gunpowder. *She missed it?*

He could not help but grin at her. 'Did your gun not work at the stockade?'

'Keep your mockery to yourself.' She scowled at him.

Tony chuckled. Amusement bubbled up from within him and he did not intend to stop it. It felt good to laugh. Except for the pain it caused his ribs. He wrapped his arms around his chest and the laugh became a gasp.

Stella glared at him, not amused his laughter was aimed at her. Her frown eventually became a smile, until he doubled over in pain. And then she leapt to his side.

'Are you all right?'

'I ... shouldn't ... laugh.' He gritted the words out between agonised breaths and waited for the pain to subside again.

'No you shouldn't laugh. The riot at Eureka was not funny in the least.' She sounded like a mother with a naughty child to scold. 'Even if the ball *did* roll out the end of my gun.' Stella caught his eye then and grinned, letting him know she hadn't been offended.

They still joked over her ignorance when he slung the satchel over his shoulder, and they headed off. He had tucked the gun into the waistband of his pants and had given Stella the knife for her own protection. Although they were both hungry, stiff and sore, their spirits were lighter and Tony even heard her hum as she walked. Somehow they both knew all would be well.

The climb up the mountain took time. The incline rose steeply before them and Tony needed to stop frequently to keep his breath as shallow as possible. The harder he had to breathe, the more painful it became. Since they had relaxed in the sun half the morning, it was close to midday by the time they reached the top.

Throats parched again, and stomachs growling in hunger, they sat on a fallen tree to rest. Tony wiped at his brow and neck where sweat ran freely. It neared the hottest part of the day. He glanced across at Stella and noticed strands of dark hair clung to her face and neck. Even in the shade of the trees, they could still feel the heat.

The gumtrees up here had white leathery trunks, a beautiful contrast to the rest of the greenery. He watched Stella approach one and run her hands across the smooth bark.

'Snow gums, I believe they're called.'

'Oh.' She nodded. 'They're quite lovely.' She turned around a full circle. 'But I cannot see much else.'

'We have to find an elevated place to see from. Perhaps boulders, or I'll climb a tree if I have to.' Not that he knew if he could manage to climb a tree.

A brief search of the area revealed a perfect rocky outcrop. They clambered onto the boulders and stood to survey the view. Tony heard Stella breathe out a long sigh. A breathtaking vision met their eyes. The clear sky meant they could see for miles around. The devastation caused by the Black Thursday fires was very evident from here. The tops of burnt-out trees stood out above the new undergrowth, resembling the stubble on an unshaven man's chin.

Tony lifted up a hand and pointed. 'You see that grey smudge on the horizon and the blue beyond it?'

Stella shaded her eyes and squinted. 'Yes.'

'I believe that is Melbourne and the port.'

'Are you sure?'

'I am.' Tony directed her attention to the right. 'You see the thin line that runs through the forest there? I think that's the road to the Bendigo goldfields.'

'So you were right? We are in the Black Forest?'

Tony nodded with a satisfied smile. 'At a guess, I would say we are on Mount Macedon.'

'Oh.'

Without thought, Tony put an arm around her waist and turned her to the south-east. He lifted his right hand next to her shoulder and pointed, his head beside hers. 'Down there is Ellenvale Station.'

'Are you certain?'

'Yes. I think if we head back down to the water, we should be able to follow it out towards home.'

Stella turned towards him then, their faces inches apart. Her eyes were wide with wonder. 'You did it, Tony. You found us a way home.'

She looked at him with such fondness. His eyes fell to her lips. For a long moment it felt as though they drifted towards each other. To kiss her would be sublime. A perfect way to celebrate this moment. But would she agree? Tony swallowed hard and stepped back, breaking the spell. 'We should ... we should go.'

Without a backward glance, he made his way off the outcrop of boulders and began the descent down the mountain. He could feel the heat in his neck and did not wish Stella to see his discomfort. Neither did he wish to see any embarrassment or dislike in her face. What would she think of him? Taking advantage of a girl alone in the bush — it simply was not done.

They hiked for hours — back down the mountain and along the small forest stream where they were able to keep from dehydration. At times they had to cross the creek to make their way easier — but always checked they headed south-east, but still they saw no end to the forest. They encountered a few snakes coiled on warm rocks that slithered away at their approach. An occasional wallaby bounded through the trees and birds took flight often at their disturbance, but they saw no sign of a road or people of any kind. The sun had begun to dip towards the horizon when they stopped for a drink and to rest.

'How big is this forest?' Stella tried to sound cheerful, but Tony could hear the worry in her voice.

He didn't quite know what to tell her in case he gave her false hope, but he believed they were headed in the right direction. 'I'm sure we'll come to the end of it soon.'

She looked at him and he could see the concern on her face. 'I hope you are right.'

'We should press on then, before it gets too late.'

'Have you rested enough?'

'No, but I can rest properly when we stop for the night.' She gave him a grim smile.

'Very well.' Tony stood to his feet.

They rounded a large boulder on the opposite side of the creek and Stella stopped short in front of him. A gasp of fright escaped her lips.

'Wha...?' But then he saw him. An aboriginal man wearing canvas pants and a headband, with scars of ritual on his chest, stood before them, a spear in his hand. Tony heard the rustle of leaves as a dozen others appeared in a circle around them. He moved closer to Stella and slid his hand to the gun at his waist. 'Stay very still,' he whispered in her ear.

He tried to draw the gun out, but the aborigine raised his spear. 'Don't you touch 'im gun!'

Chapter Twenty-One

To Angus, the Bush Inn seemed even gloomier than the Gap Inn, although it could have been his growing apprehension over the ransom. He looked at Penny who paced before the empty hearth. She appeared to be cold in spite of the heat and hugged herself as she walked. Her lips moved in silent prayer, he assumed for her brother. Then again she could be trying to encourage herself.

Mattherson sat hunched over in a chair, his elbows on his knees, and stared at the stone floor. Angus could see the muscles in his face work as he ground his teeth in tension. Gertie, on the other hand, chatted away to anyone who might give her audience — presently a young maid who cleared the tables.

He himself sat at a bench near the doorway, where he could see who approached the Inn. Mattherson had sent the soldiers out four at a time, spaced a few minutes apart, to find the ransom site and surround it. When they were ready, one ensign had been designated to return and report to Mattherson.

Angus, whilst eager to move on and a little nervous about the outcome, felt content to entrust the mission into Mattherson's hands. During their journey from The Gap, he had learned Mattherson had once been an Infantry Major, but had sold his commission a few years earlier to take up more governmental positions in the colony, and thus have the freedom to settle with his family. This knowledge convinced Angus they were in experienced hands.

He peered out the window for what seemed the hundredth time and saw a flash of red nearing the door. 'He's here.'

Mattherson jumped to his feet and strode over to the door. Penny also followed and stood beside Angus, gripping his hand.

'Mr Mattherson, sir.' The soldier gave a salute, indicating the level of respect these men had for the ex-major.

'Yes, Ensign. At ease.' Mattherson's face remained grim.

'All the men are in place, sir.'

'And the criminals?'

'There are two men, but only one appears to be armed. One of them is a burly cove who has the look of a fighter.'

'And the captives?'

'We saw three ... er ... persons tied up ...'

'What? Three?' They all seemed to say this at the same time.

'Yes, sir. They were bound and gagged. But, sir ...' The soldier shuffled his feet, looking uncomfortable.

'I wonder where the third relative is, the person who needs to make the swap.' Penny interrupted.

Angus shook his head a little then shrugged. 'Perhaps they've no' come yet. Yer note did say ye had three days, did it no'?'

Penny nodded her acceptance of this knowledge and all attention turned back to the young soldier.

'What is it, Ensign?' Mattherson encouraged him to continue.

'Sir, none of them seemed to be ... a girl.'

A deep frown creased Mattherson's face.

'Wait.' Angus put out a hand to his shoulder. 'Did ye no' say she dressed as a boy?'

Mattherson nodded. 'Yes, that's true.' He turned back to the messenger. 'Is it possible you were mistaken?'

The ensign hesitated again. 'Sir, they all wore ... beards.'

'Beards?' Mattherson looked worried all of a sudden. 'If they are all men, where is my girl?'

'Perhaps she wore a beard as part of her disguise.' Penny suggested. 'It would be a good way to hide her face.'

Mattherson stared at her in contemplation, but did not look convinced. 'Perhaps. I hope so, at any rate. Something does not feel right about this. I suppose we should hurry up and get it over with. Ensign, you can tell us in more detail as we travel.'

Angus gave him a supportive slap on the shoulder. He could

imagine the man's stomach must churn with anxiety by now. 'Never mind, mate. We'll find her.'

Gertie waved them away as they rode down the track into the Black Forest minutes later, happy to stay behind and banter with the inn staff. She wished them all success and Godspeed of course. Angus glanced sideways at Penny as they passed between towering gums, so close together they blocked out much of the light. Her eyes darted everywhere, her apprehension obvious. There were many stories about the Black Forest, most of them Angus believed to be exaggerated, but they were none-the-less scary.

He no longer carried the rifle on the strap over his shoulder, but held it, loaded and ready, across his lap while he held the reins with the other hand. It made Thunder much more difficult to control, especially with all the ruts in the road from carts which had passed through in winter, but he needed to be ready and alert. Who knew if any other thieves hid out around here?

Angus tried not to focus on the bad things he had heard, but instead looked around to admire God's creation. In truth, these trees were majestic — ancient statues which declared the Lord's faithfulness through the ages. They still showed life, in spite of the great fires of '51. It amazed him how quickly life returned to the forest after such a tragedy.

Mattherson and the ensign rode a little ahead of them, the soldier on foot beside his horse, and they discussed the layout of the swap site in more detail. Angus could only make out a word here and there and realised the futility of trying to listen. Instead, he turned his attention to his fiancée. 'How are ye managing, dear?'

Penny seemed to draw in a deep breath and release it slowly. 'I am all right — trying not to let my anxiety run away with me.' She offered him a grim smile.

'It will be over soon.' He smiled back. *Very soon.*

Moments later they noticed the outcrop of boulders and the track to the left. The knowledge a group of soldiers already lay in wait made him feel much more at ease than if they had headed in there blind. Penny, on the other hand, paled at the narrow track. Angus reined in and dismounted, urging her to follow suit.

'Er ... Mr Mattherson.' Gus waited for the ex-soldier to turn in his saddle. 'We would like to stop and pray for a moment.'

Mattherson looked from one to the other and back again. 'Right.' His face showed no emotion but he got down from his horse and joined them, directing the ensign to go and take his place surrounding the outlaws. The soldier saluted then ducked between two ferns, at once out of sight.

Mattherson stood silently by while Angus led another prayer, pleading for safety and success of the mission. Penny gripped his hand tightly and muttered an emphatic amen when he finished.

'What now?' Angus wanted to know the best plan for what lay ahead.

The man looked at them both with gravity. 'It is important neither of you act as though we are surrounded by help. We go in and do the swap as the villain directed. Once you have Tony back in your care and I have Estella, then they will carry out their orders. Unless, of course, something goes wrong ...'

'What then?' Penny's face became whiter than he had ever seen.

'They are trained men.' Mattherson tried to console. 'They will act accordingly.' He glanced at each in turn. 'Shall we go?'

Penny nodded but reached out for Angus. 'Will you hold my hand?' She appeared a little unsteady on her feet. He took her elbow and they walked down the rutted track holding their horses by the reins with their free hands, although Angus's free hand also held the rifle. Neither said a word as the narrow path crowded in on them, the long afternoon shadows making the forest gloomier and more insidious than ever. They came into a clearing where they saw three captives tied hand and foot, with flour sacks over their heads.

Angus felt Penny stagger beside him and wrapped an arm around her waist to steady her. His grip tightened on the gun in his other hand. Mattherson took Thunder's reins from him and he gave the man a grateful nod.

'I thought the ensign said they wore beards. How could he tell?' Though she whispered, she sounded a little panicked.

Angus knew it was not a good sign. 'They must have heard us arrive.' But it reinforced the fact there were probably three men beneath those sacks, which left the question: *where is Estella?*

'Ho! Who goes there?' A gruff voice called out from behind a large tree.

Angus gave Penny a little nudge. *She must play her part now. I hope she does no' faint.* He remembered how she had tended the wound in his leg months ago, without the slightest sign of wooziness. But, this was very different.

He saw her swallow and move her mouth a few times before words even came out, and then they were shaky.

'Penny ... Penelope Worthington. I have come for my b...brother, Tony.'

None of the bound men moved at all and Angus's doubts grew even graver. If Tony were one of the three, surely he would have stiffened at the very least.

'Did y' bring the money?'

Angus saw the muzzle of a rifle peep out from behind the tree, followed by a dark and greasy looking head.

'Y... yes I have.'

'Who are the other two coves with y'?'

'I am her fiancé, Angus, an' this is William Mattherson.' Angus put enough growl in his voice to let them know he was ready for a fight. Once again, none of the three captives moved an inch.

'Put down yer gun, nice an' easy like, an' don't be tryin' anythin' stupid.'

He saw the outlaw's muzzle wave menacingly and bent to comply, gritting his teeth in frustration.

'Now, girlie. Bring that package over here and put it by the rock an' I'll send yer brother over.' The greasy head protruded further from behind the tree, gaining confidence. They could now see a thin weasel-eyed man, although the rest of his face was covered with a scarf.

'I ... I want to s... see him first.' Her voice sounded weak, but it impressed Angus that she took a stand against this blackguard.

'You'll see 'im when I've got that money nice an' safe, like.'

'How do I know you speak the t... truth? You could have anyone h... hidden under those sacks.' She held her ground.

'I could just put a hole in you an' yer two mates right now. Bring it over here!' He lifted his gun to take aim.

Penny glanced back at Angus, her eyes wide with fright. He nodded to her and pulled the bag of money from the saddle bags. 'Ye'll be all ri', darlin'. Do as the man says.' How he wished she didn't have to be here. His stomach knotted up and his heart pounded at the fear in her eyes. And somehow he knew this would not be as easy as it looked.

Penny took the bag with trembling hands and with an unsteady gait, edged her way closer to the man with the gun. Angus felt like he didn't breathe until she placed the bag on the ground and ran back to his side, where he held her close.

Another outlaw appeared from behind the tree then — a very large man who looked like he'd been in a fight or two — untied one of the captives' feet and yanked him up, pressing him forward. 'Walk.' The weasel-man kept his gun trained on the blinded captive as he stumbled ahead. 'Remember, I've got me sights on 'im, so don't try anythin'!'

As the bound man came closer, Angus heard Mattherson mumble behind him. 'They're going for the money.' Sure enough, the giant crept towards the bag of cash.

'It's not Tony.' Penny whispered in panic.

'How can ye know? Ye've no' seen him since he were a lad.'

'I just know. Angus, what shall we do?' She became agitated and stepped forward to meet the shrouded man. Without hesitation, she pulled the sack from his head and studied his face. She spun around to face Angus, her eyes wild with fear. 'Tony has green eyes.'

Indeed the man before her had dark, almost black eyes. *Dear God, help us.*

Mattherson let out a string of curses and Angus went for the rifle near his feet. Before he could get it up and aimed, he heard an explosion and a bullet whistled over his head. Mattherson groaned and fell to the ground. Angus spun around to see him grip his shoulder, but he also tried to reach a pistol which had fallen from his hand.

'Penny! See to him.' He knew she was good with wounded men. 'I must go after them!'

The weasel-man and his accomplice had darted into the trees, leaving the other two captives behind. He knew the soldiers would all move out from their positions now. 'Do no' fire!' He roared at the top of his voice while he sprinted across the clearing after the outlaws. 'I repeat! Do no' fire! We need 'im alive!' They needed these men to find out where their loved ones were.

He saw the flash of red as the soldiers leaped out of their forest hideaways, with bayonets raised, and joined in the chase. Not far into the bush, he saw the two had paused at a cart and untied two Clydesdales from a tree. Neither had a saddle, but they pulled themselves up onto the bare backs. The soldiers closed in on them, but Angus raced back to his horse just in case. *Lord, do no' let them get away!*

Thunder was away almost before he swung into the saddle, as though he sensed the urgency. As he neared the place where the cart waited, he heard a shot fired. *I told them not to shoot!* He hoped the outlaw had not been killed. Thankfully he saw one of the Clydesdales off to his left. The big prize-fighter attempted to hold on to a startled horse. Obviously the animal was not used to someone of his weight, especially without a saddle.

As Angus neared, the big man fell from the rearing horse and Redcoats surrounded him. 'Take 'im back to Mattherson!' he ordered as he flew past. A few of the soldiers pointed in the direction the other criminal had taken with a shout of encouragement to catch the mongrel.

Angus urged Thunder onwards and they bolted into the heavy woods. Branches slapped at his torso and he was forced to duck beneath several of them, but the horse beneath him seemed to revel in the chase. They swerved this way and that as they rounded trees and boulders and Thunder leapt over fallen logs as though they were merely twigs. Before long they had the Clydesdale in sight, its long, heavy lope and large size made it a little slower through the thick bushland.

'Come on Thunder! We've got 'im now!' He hissed and sank his heel into the horse's flank.

Thunder seemed to understand the urgency and edged closer to the huge animal. When they were almost alongside, Angus released his feet from the stirrups and lunged at the outlaw, dragging him to the ground with him. They landed with a thud and Angus felt a small rock dig right into his ribcage, knocking the air from him. As he gasped, he rolled over to see where his enemy had fallen. The weasel-man had landed badly with a loud groan. One arm hung at a strange angle when he tried to get up and he cried out in pain.

Without concern for the broken arm, Angus threw himself at the man and knocked him back to the ground, pinning him with his weight. He peered into those beady eyes and angry blood surged through his veins, his chest still heaving. 'Where are Tony an' Estella?'

The outlaw's lips spread in an evil smile and Angus saw black rot in his mouth. 'I've no idea.' He laughed, though his laughter turned to a pain-filled coughing fit. 'An' I wouldn't tell y' if I knew. That pretty hoyden an' her chicken-livered beau can rot in hell for all I care.'

The blackguard's mockery made Angus's blood boil. He lifted up one muscle-tensed arm and pounded his fist into the man's jaw, knocking him senseless. 'That'll be the last of yer insults fer now.'

Chapter Twenty-Two

Even in the late afternoon shadows, Tony could see the dark man's sinews flex taut as he gripped the spear above his shoulder, ready to throw. From the corner of his eye, he saw the other Kooris poised for battle also. It seemed unlikely he could even get one shot off before he and Stella would be impaled by several javelins. He'd heard many-a-time they were a savage lot, and wouldn't give a second thought to ridding their land of a couple of intruders. Disappointment and regret flooded him as he realised death was imminent. His unsteady faith that God may have given them aid shattered in that moment. God had left them. *And I have failed Stella again.*

'I'm so sorry.' He whispered to her, closing his eyes against the grief which threatened to overwhelm him. He wished the aborigines would throw their spears and be done.

He felt Stella's hand flutter behind her, reaching for his comfort. It would be the last thing he could offer her. He gripped it tight and wished he had told her how much he cared for her. It was too late for that.

Too late.

He swallowed hard. It was too late to apologise to his sister. Too late to find out the truth about his father's will. Too late to make a decent and worthwhile life. Too late to put aside cowardice and live life with courage. Too late even to make anything right with God. *What a pathetic end to a pathetic life. God, I'm sorry I've been such a failure. Is there any way You can give me one more chance?*

He jumped as a voice behind him let out a stream of unintelligible language. Tony believed the man sounded angry and demanded from his friends the reason why they waited. The man directly in their path replied with a jerk of his chin, again in his own language. The man behind gave a curt answer and Tony wondered if they had discussed how they would hide their bodies.

'Why you come *Wurundjeri* land, eh? Dis *my* land.' The native before them looked fierce as he asked the question.

Tony felt Stella's grip loosen and she stepped forward, spreading her hands before in a gesture of supplication. 'To be honest, sir, we are not sure where we are. We are trying to find our way home.'

'Stella ...' Tony wanted to warn her, but the words were stuck in his throat.

'Where you belong, Miss?'

It astounded Tony the conversation continued. He had not expected the aborigine would even listen to her reply.

Stella turned back towards him with question in her eyes. 'What's the name of your home again?'

Tony swallowed and tried to calm the tremor in his whole body. 'Ell...Ellen... Ellenvale S...Station.'

Stella faced the indigenous man again and repeated his words. 'Ellenvale Station.'

One of the men behind him started on another string of foreign dialect. Tony wondered how long it would be until they decided to thrust them through. The man ahead of them grunted and jerked his chin again.

'What your name, eh?'

'My name is Estella Mattherson, and this is Tony Worthington.'

Yet again, the man behind chattered on in his language, but this time Tony recognised one word — *Penny*. He swivelled around to look at the one who spoke, his fear dropping away.

'Penny? Penny is my sister. You know her?'

For the first time, Tony saw a flash of white teeth as the man smiled at him. 'Yeah. Penny friend.'

With a short command from the man who led the group, all the natives lowered their spears. The one who had identified Penny stepped forward with his hand outstretched.

'My name Pindarri. White fella call me Pete.'

Tony could not believe his luck and almost laughed as he shook the man's hand. 'Pleased to meet you, Pete.'

'Hello Pete.' Estella shook hands with him next.

Pete peered at Tony, examining him. 'Why your face black, boss?'

As they sat around a campfire later, Stella smiled to herself. It amazed her how things had turned out for the day. Yes, her legs ached and her feet burned from many blisters which had formed, but she was alive. In the morning she had doubted what would become of them, in spite of their prayer and her fledgling faith that God would hear.

Uncertainty over Tony's strange behaviour added to her worries. He'd held her close to his chest all through the previous night, but now kept his distance, rarely even making eye contact with her. Yesterday he had held her hand all day, but today he'd only touched her if she needed help down a steep incline or over a large object, and that one moment when Mullawindju and his family had encircled them.

He *had* caught her half undressed. Stella bit her lip at the memory. That would have confirmed his worse suspicions about her. Perhaps he had resolved to brush her off as someone beneath his touch. Stella's heart dropped. *How could he misread her so?* She had hoped to convince him of her maturity and sensibility, yet she continually messed it up with her impulsive ways. *Why must I be such a dolt?*

Then there had been the moment on the top of the mountain. She had been sure he was about to kiss her. She could still recall the feel of his warm hand at her waist. She could picture in her mind the way his head lowered towards hers, his limp hair hanging over one fervent eye. Her heart had raced in anticipation and she had been about to close her eyes to receive his kiss when he had abruptly backed away. *Beneath his touch,* she reminded herself again.

There would be no way Tony would lie beside her tonight. The *Wurundjeri* people had built a large fire which they fed continually with wood. She glanced across at him where he sat with Mullawindju and talked. He pressed a poultice the natives had made to his bruises. Stella put her hurts aside. All was not bad. God had answered their prayer.

Tony had told Pete about their experience at the hands of 'bad men'. He'd shown the marks on his wrists and ankles where he'd been bound and tried to explain how they'd escaped. Shortly after, Pete had left them with the rest of the clan and gone off to find the bad men.

'How will you find them?' She had asked, incredulous.

Pete had grinned at her and his big white teeth flashed in the dim afternoon light. 'I bin trackin' you fellas long time. White fella leave big track. Pete find bad man fast, eh.'

She understood him to mean he would have no trouble following where she and Tony had been. No doubt his knowledge of the bushland and his long sinuous legs would carry him there in half the time as well.

Mullawindju and the rest had taken them back to their camp for night, since there were but a few hours of daylight left. They were accepted as though part of the family, although Stella found it difficult to look at the half-naked lubras at first. So used to women covered from neck to ankle in multiple layers of fabric was she, she found it hard to face them. *I wonder if this is how women who see me in short sleeves or raised hems feel a little.* Realisation opened her eyes to the reason some women averted their gaze from her and why her parents shook their heads in frustration. *Perhaps I should be more careful in future.*

Once she became used to their half-dressed bodies, she found the women very hospitable. They fed her and Tony various bush berries and roots, and cooked wallaby and snake. They were unusual tastes and she felt a little hesitant at first, but concluded if the food was good enough for the natives it wouldn't hurt her. And she was hungry. She hadn't eaten for well nigh two days.

Now, fed and warm, Stella could not help but be grateful that God had indeed had His hand upon them. She had no doubt with the help of the Wurundjeri people they would find their way back home. God had heard them and must indeed care for them. *I wonder if Tony realises the same.*

Like her, he must have believed they were about to die for a moment. His sorry whisper had been laced with agony. Did he believe himself responsible for whether she survived or not? Had that been his only aim — to get her to safety? Stella sighed. She didn't want to be a burden to him. She wanted to walk beside him and be together in whatever they faced. *Why can he not see it?*

A few of the young aborigines got up from where they reclined which distracted her from her reverie. Mullawindju picked up some sticks and clicked them together in a rhythm, soon accompanying it with song. The young men danced near the fire, their movements kicking up the dust as they stomped on the earth. Stella had never seen anything like it before and clapped along with the beat, laughing in delight at their display.

At one point while the young men danced, she looked across at Tony to find he stared back at her. She could not read his expression and before she even had time to guess, he shifted his gaze to the dancers. *Does he think me too effusive?* A proper lady would not behave so. Once again her impulsive nature had caused her trouble. She folded her hands in her lap and restrained from any expression of enjoyment for the rest of the performance.

'That emu dance,' Mullawindju explained when the men sat down again. 'You ever seen emu?'

'No. Never.' Stella shook her head but Tony nodded.

Stella saw the flash of white teeth again, which she had become very fond of. 'Emu big bird. Can't fly.'

Stella laughed. Now she thought about it, those men had done a very good imitation of a big bird in their dance, the way their arms had waved about. She wondered if Tony had enjoyed the dance as much as she had. It seemed she would not get a chance to ask him. The women all began to lie down for the night, leaving her a spot closer to the fire.

She looked over to where Tony sat and saw the men did the same. 'Goodnight.' She wanted to attempt some kind of communication before she lay down herself.

'Goodnight, Stella.' He offered her a smile and then lay down.

Stella rolled to her back and looked up at the stars. This would soon all be over. She would have to leave Tony and go back to her father, who would then send her away to England. A lump formed in her throat. Although many times over the past week had been scary, uncomfortable and even painful, she found she didn't want it to end. If it meant she could stay with Tony, she almost wished more trouble would beset them. *God, I know I prayed for help and You have helped us. But, now I want to stay with Tony. Is there a way You can make him love me as I love him?* She felt a tear slide from the corner of her eye. She knew she could make Tony a good wife if she were given the chance.

Penny paced back and forth before the hearth of the Bush Inn while Angus could only look on in sympathy. She was distraught. Even though they had caught the kidnappers, they still had no idea where Tony and Estella were. Gertie paced beside her for a time, squeezing and patting her hand, but she had little effect and eventually disappeared into the kitchen.

It had been a great task to get everyone back to the inn. Angus had been thankful for the cart the thieves had with them in the forest. Mattherson and Smith had been carried to the inn under the watchful eye of half Mattherson's men, while the other half escorted Burns and the three captives they'd had tied at the swap site. Angus had returned with Penny on their horses, the ransom money returned safely to his saddle bags, and Mattherson's horse in tow.

The two villains, Smith and Burns, had sworn blind their ignorance to their loved ones' whereabouts. Even with heavy persuasion from Mattherson, who refused to lie down and rest, they had not revealed any information. They would admit nothing except that the two had escaped them early yesterday. Smith often spat and cursed the man who had almost strangled him and shouted vulgar insults about Miss Mattherson.

Angus had his temper back under control and the scoundrel's rotten diatribe no longer made him feel murderous. He now pitied the man who viewed his fellow men and women with such a low opinion. *Perhaps he's had a hard life.* He remembered many of the convicts he'd served time with. They had also been filled with bitterness. Indeed, he had been very much like them before he found faith in Christ.

Mattherson had left the two men, securely guarded by his soldiers, in the washroom of the inn and sent the ensign to fetch a surgeon for Smith's broken arm and his own injury. His trouble worn features stood against his grey face as he re-entered the inn.

'We must begin a search.' Penny started at once. It mattered not that she had already gone over this with Angus.

'It is too dark.' Mattherson was abrupt and to the point. 'The light will be gone in minutes and the forest will be pitch black.'

'And they are out there in it!' Penny flung a wild arm in the direction of the Black Forest.

Mattherson's frown deepened. 'I know. Do you think me heartless? It is *my* daughter out there. But there is no way we can find them at night. We shall start a search at first light. I hope your brother knows how to survive in the bush. Estella has no idea how to handle herself out here. She's probably terrified. She's only ever lived in cities.'

Angus could see Penny's contempt rise and she wagged an annoyed finger at Mattherson. 'Do you insinuate my brother is not capable of looking after her? I can assure you Tony has plenty of survival skills and will doubtless take good care of your girl.'

Mattherson opened his mouth to protest, but Angus thought it prudent to intervene.

'Listen. Ye're both worried sick about them, and that's understandable. But it will serve no purpose to argue about it. The best we can do for Tony an' Estella is rest so we are fresh for the search tomorrow. That an' put their safety in the hands of God.'

Mattherson thumped a clenched fist onto a nearby table. 'I wish those two thieves would loosen their tongues. I am sure there is more to their tale. But yes, fighting amongst ourselves will not help.'

Penny lowered her head. 'I am sorry to fly into the boughs. I do not know what I would do if something happened to Tony. Did Smith and Burns say why they had Miss Mattherson as well?'

Mattherson grunted. 'They claim she stowed away on their cart.'

'What?' Penny looked incredulous.

Why a city-dwelling young lady would run away from home dressed in male clothes and then climb aboard a stranger's cart was beyond Gus as well.

'Then, when they found out her family name, they got greedy. But they were originally after your Tony,' Mattherson explained.

''Ere, I've brought yer supper.' Gertie entered the room with bowls of steaming broth. 'I've been helpin' the cook.'

Penny turned to Angus with a swish of her skirts and widened eyes. 'Gus, I could not possibly eat at a time like this.'

Angus stepped closer to her and stroked her arm. 'Ye need to keep up yer strength, love. Try to eat a little, eh.'

'Gertie, bring me some rum, would you. This shoulder gives me grief.' It was the first Mattherson had complained about the gunshot wound, although his pale face belied his bravado.

The three of them sat at one trestle together and sipped at the hearty soup, into which they dunked thick chunks of bread. All except Penny, of course, whom Angus knew would refuse to eat in such an uncouth manner. He grinned as she sat with her back straight and dipped her spoon very properly into the thick soup.

'Who were those three men, the kidnappers had with them? Did they give you any further information?' Penny asked between mouthfuls.

Mattherson scowled again. 'They saw our two not long after they escaped. Came to them for help, they did. But they say Burns attacked them all of a sudden, and Tony and Estella ran away again.'

'So Burns single-handedly rounded them up an' took them with him?' Angus believed it sounded farfetched.

Mattherson let out a harsh laugh. 'Burns is more than a match for three men. He's an experienced fighter, I'd say, and possibly a champion at that. It turns out those three men were wanted thieves anyway. We've got them guarded in one of the stables.'

'At least some good will come of this then.' Angus nodded with a grim smile.

Penny stared at him with an incredulous look. 'How do you remain so positive? All I can think about is my brother and that poor girl out in the darkness somewhere with no food.'

Gus gave her hand a comforting squeeze. They had to keep their trust in the Lord. Something about Smith had troubled Angus. He wondered whether he should raise this fear, but it niggled at the back of his mind. 'Smith said sordid things about your lass. Ye do no' suppose he ...?'

'If he did, there will be hell to pay!' Mattherson's face turned a deep shade of red. 'I'll strangle him myself, the worthless brute!'

Angus's gut churned with sympathy. He had not yet had a daughter, but even to imagine his sisters in the same predicament roused his wrath beyond rational levels.

Penny's glance swerved from one to the other and then she shook her head. 'No. Tony would never have let anything happen to her, if it were at all possible.' Her gaze faltered as new doubts entered her mind. 'Of course, if he were tied ...' She didn't finish her sentence, but swallowed the spoonful of soup she held and then pushed herself up from the table. 'Oh, I wish this night were over.' She moved towards the doorway. 'Excuse me, I need to go outside for some fresh air.'

When the door had shut behind her, Mattherson turned to Angus and heaved a deep sigh, rubbing his good hand over his face. 'The truth is we don't know how either of them will be when we find them. You'd best prepare her for the worst, mate.'

'Aye. But I'm goin' to hope for the best. Where are we goin' to start tomorrow? Do we know which direction they went?'

'Burns said east, but who knows if they kept in that direction. I'll get directions to their original campsite and we'll work from there.'

At that moment a high-pitched scream filled the night air.

'Penny!' Angus flew for the door, Mattherson inches behind him, pushing a pistol into Angus's hand.

Chapter Twenty-Three

By the time Angus and Mattherson made it outside, they saw Penny had a smile on her face, although her hand clasped her heart in shock. 'It's all right, Angus.' She saw the gun in his hand. 'It is only Pete. He gave me a fright because I did not see him there in the dark.'

'G'day boss.' The dark figure stepped out of the shadows with a cheeky grin.

'Who is this?' Mattherson demanded.

'Pete is a friend of mine, Mr Mattherson. He means you no harm.'

'Right.' Mattherson nodded and stepped back a little.

'What brings you here, Pete?' Penny asked him.

'Lookin' for bad men, miss. But then I seen you 'ere, eh.'

'What bad men, Pete?'

'I been trackin' bad men, miss. I track 'em all the way 'ere, too.'

Penny's eyes widened in surprise.

'Ye tracked Smith and Burns?' Angus could hardly believe it.

'That their name? I dunno. I follow 'em 'ere but. They beat up Tony. Beat 'im up real good too. 'E your brother, eh?'

Penny gasped and grabbed for Angus's hand. 'You've seen Tony? Where is he? How badly beaten is he?'

'Was there a girl with him? Is she beaten up too?' Mattherson stepped forward again and fired questions as quickly as Penny, no longer the bystander.

Pete seemed overwhelmed with all the questions.

'Hold on, hold on.' Angus tried to calm them. 'One at a time.'

He could see Penny try to rein in her excitement by taking deep breaths. 'Yes, Tony is my brother. We have been looking for him. Is he all right?'

''E proper broken up, but 'e be right again soon. 'E with my people up in them hills. Safe there, eh.'

'And Estella?' Mattherson reminded him.

'The lady bit hungry an' tired. But she all ri', boss. My Mrs feed 'er up good an' proper, eh.' Pete chuckled.

'Thank you, Pete.' Penny breathed in relief. 'You do not know how much that news means to us.'

Pete nodded then frowned and turned to Angus. 'Bad men. You catch 'im?'

'We caught 'em all ri'.' He heard the sound of a horse approach the inn. 'In fact, I think the surgeon is here to have a look at one of 'em.'

Sure enough, the rider of the horse dismounted and pulled a saddlebag of instruments behind him. 'Doctor Evans.' He nodded to the small gathering outside the inn. 'I'm here to see some wounded men.'

Mattherson greeted him. 'I am one of them. Ball to the shoulder, but it's not too serious. I would like you to see our prisoner first. He has a badly broken arm.'

'Where is he?' Doctor Evans asked.

'In the washroom out back, under guard.'

The doctor peered into a window. 'It would be better if you could move him into the tavern where I can lay him on a table. Better light too.'

'Very well.' Mattherson nodded. Without hesitation he skirted the building to fetch Smith.

'You're lucky to find me.' The doctor said to those who remained. 'Most surgeons won't come near this place at night.'

'We are grateful for yer help, doc.' Angus grinned at his serious words. It was probably true, even if a little exaggerated.

He gave a curt nod and entered the inn to prepare a table for surgery. Angus did not wish to be around to see him set a broken arm. The patient would likely yell loud enough to wake the dead, at least until he passed out. He shuddered and turned to Penny whose eyes scanned the shadows for Pete.

'He disappeared when the doctor came.' She peered into the darkness.

'I still 'ere, miss.' Pete's voice came out of the blackness of night.

'How can we find Tony?' She shaded her eyes and continued to search the shadows until the native stepped into the dim light which shone through the tavern windows.

'Don't worry, miss. I go back to my people now. Tomorrow I bring Tony an' the lady to Ellenvale, eh.'

'You will?'

'Yes miss. Not far from there, eh. They walk long time in them hills.'

'Thank you, Pete. We shall see you tomorrow then.' Penny's eyes were filled with tears as she waved him off.

Angus pulled her to him and held her close. 'Ye see. God has it all in His hands, love. Everything will be all ri'.'

She pulled away from him as two soldiers rounded the corner, half carrying, half dragging Smith between them.

Pete dashed back into the dim light and his swift legs took him straight to the door where he peered at the prisoner. He then turned to Angus and Penny with a frown. 'That man not Smith. Not Burns either. That man name Riley.'

Angus saw the villain's eyes widen in fear as he was recognised and let forth a stream of obscenities, telling Pete in vile terms to hold his tongue.

Penny gasped at the foul string of abuse, but Pete seemed unperturbed by such an outburst. 'I seen 'im with that Foxworth fella. Them two up to no good, eh.'

Tony woke to the sound of kookaburras greeting the sunlight with their raucous laughter. Gentle golden rays seeped through the tall trees and the air felt mild. It would be another warm summer's day. He stretched his tall frame, though every joint and muscle complained, particularly his broken rib. His face felt somewhat calmer since using the poultice he'd been given.

He marvelled over the change in their fortunes. He had been quite sure of imminent death when the Wurundjeri surrounded them, and yet, here they were fed and sheltered by these same people. Mullawindju had explained to him how there were very few of their tribe left since white man came, and they had to meet each person with extreme caution. Some white men, he said, would kill a black fella without compunction or hesitation. This people had a sad story of sickness and warfare which had decimated their numbers.

He sat up and gazed at the sleeping bodies around him. They had been nothing short of kind to him and Stella. He wondered what he could do in return.

The fire had dwindled to a few glowing embers, so he set about gathering more wood to stoke it up. They would need it to cook food soon. As he moved about he noticed the man, Pete, had returned during the night and now slept beside his wife. *I wonder if he found Smith and Burns.*

He smiled to himself as he marvelled over the past week. Not only had he and Stella escaped the two thugs, but had survived two days in the bush with no supplies and had now been rescued and accommodated by the native people of the area. *Perhaps God has heard me after all.* As he blew on the embers to ignite the fresh wood, he noticed Stella's satchel on the ground nearby her. When the flames caught on, he crawled over to her and pulled her Bible from the bag, careful not to wake her. He held the book in his hands and closed his eyes. *All right God, show me it is really You.* He opened the Bible and read.

'For I know the thoughts that I think toward you, saith the LORD, thoughts of peace, and not of evil, to give you an expected end. Then shall ye call upon me, and ye shall go and pray unto me, and I will hearken unto you. And ye shall seek me, and find me, when ye shall search for me with all your heart. And I will be found of you, saith the LORD: and I will turn away your captivity, and I will gather you from all the nations, and from all the places whither I have driven you, saith the LORD; and I will bring you again into the place whence I caused you to be carried away captive.'

Tony's breath caught in his throat and the book fell from his hands. How could one passage be so accurate to his life — and to his questions? His sudden movement must have disturbed Stella, for she sat up and yawned, soon focusing on him beside her.

'Why do you look so surprised, Tony?'

He could say no words. Instead he picked up the Bible and held it out to her, pointing at the words he'd read in Jeremiah. Stella read for a moment and then looked up at him with a strange light in her eyes.

'We prayed.'

'He answered.' Tony replied in a whisper, then swallowed hard.

'We've been seeking Him.'

'I think we've found Him.' Tony felt his body tremble with wonder.

'And He wants to bring us home.' Stella grinned with excitement.

Tony let out a slow breath. 'So ... what now?'

'We should thank Him.' Stella nodded as she spoke as though she had made up her mind. 'It would be the right thing to do, would it not?'

'Yes.' What else could he do but agree? Tony could hardly believe the God of the universe was interested in him enough to answer his prayer. He held out a hand for Stella to join him and together they thanked God for saving them and leading them home.

When Tony finally said 'amen' he did not relinquish Stella's hand at once, but squeezed it tight. She looked up at him with moist eyes, though her smile was broad. *She is so beautiful ... and clever ... and expressive.* He could have been knocked over with a gumleaf last night when he saw her clapping and laughing, it had made his heart pound that hard.

'Tony, I ...'

He came to himself in a rush and let go of her hand. 'I'm sorry, Stella.' His mouth went dry.

'It's all right.' The smile disappeared from her lips, but her eyes still brimmed with emotion. 'I wanted to say thank you ... for everything.' She had not pulled her hand away, but rested it on his.

Tony swallowed again. 'I ...' *Should I tell her?* 'It's ...' *Can I tell her?* 'I've ...' *What if she laughs in my face?* 'I've only done what any decent fellow would do ... haven't I?'

Her eyes were locked on his. Did she want him to know something? Did she feel the same? *It couldn't be real.*

Impulsive giggling behind them broke the spell. Stella's hand withdrew but it left a warm sensation all over the back of his hand. He turned and saw a group of ladies huddled together, pointing at them and laughing.

'What's so funny?' Stella's eyebrows drew together in a look of consternation.

A small cloud of dust rose as Pete plonked himself between them, forcing them to move away from each other a little. 'They think you two belong married.' He grinned and then chuckled himself. 'You got no Mrs yet, eh Tony? She make you good woman.'

Tony felt heat and colour rise in his face and neck and he dared not glance past Pete to see how Stella reacted. She would likely have all kinds of retorts ready to fly. She wouldn't want to be treated like property. Except ... *what was that I saw in her eyes?*

He shook his head. 'No Pete. We are just friends who happened to be kidnapped by the same people.'

Pete looked at him, his white teeth flashing. 'Whatever you say, boss.'

He clearly didn't believe him. If only he'd seen all their arguments. He needed to change the subject. 'How did you fare last night? Did you find the bad men?'

'Yep. Found them all ri'. Smith an' Burns, eh?'

'That's them.'

'But not Smith an' Burns, boss. This one called Riley. Dunno other fella.'

'I knew that wasn't their real names!' Stella waved a feisty hand in the air.

'How did you find out his real name?' Tony wanted to know.

'I seen 'im before with another bad man — Foxworth.'

'Our neighbour?' Tony was incredulous.

'That's 'im. But them soldiers got Riley proper locked up now. An' I told Miss Penny I bring you home to Ellenvale today.'

'You saw Penny?'

'Yep.' The native's dark curls bobbed as he nodded. 'An' her bloke Angus.' He turned to Stella. 'Saw your old man, too.'

Stella's eyes widened in surprise. 'My father was there?'

'They all goin' home Ellenvale today. You meet them there.'

Tony and Stella's eyes locked once again. This was it. They would soon be home, like the words in the Scriptures had promised. Exhilaration flooded through Tony. This ordeal would finally be over. Stella would be reunited with her father and ... and Stella would go back to Ballaarat. Tony felt his stomach drop. *Will this be the last day I ever have with her?*

Chapter Twenty-Four

Angus had to grin as he watched Penny ride, straight and confident in her saddle. She rode next to him but a little ahead. The worried and needful woman of yesterday had disappeared. As soon as she knew of her brother's safety, she had returned to her capable self and almost took charge of matters.

She had assisted Doctor Evans as he set Steven Riley's arm and Angus even wondered if perhaps she took pleasure in the man's agonised cries. Riley's incessant cursing could be heard well out into the darkness. She then helped the doctor clean and dress Mattherson's wound. As he had insisted, the ball had hit the fleshy part of his upper arm, and though it had bled considerably, it would heal well.

Since he had been discovered, Riley had also given them his accomplice's name, that of Morgan Brownhill. He continued to vent his spleen until pain rendered him unconscious, and named Rupert Foxworth as the instigator of the abduction.

We were right. He was behind it all.

He glanced back over his shoulder to see the platoon of Redcoats behind. While some had been left to guard Riley, Brownhill and the three bushrangers, the rest accompanied them. They planned to arrest Foxworth and take him into custody.

'Penny, how do ye feel about goin' with these fellows to watch the show at Henry's Run?' It would be interesting to see the man's reaction, since he would know little of the kidnappers' capture.

She turned back to him with a sly grin. 'I would not miss it for the world.'

'As long as you stay out of the way,' Mattherson's voice called from behind them.

'And I don't need any more patients today.' Doctor Evans rode alongside Mattherson. Penny had requested he return with them after hearing of her brother's injuries. Both of the victims would need a good check over.

Penny craned her neck even further around. 'I have no intention to do anything that would keep me from my brother, Doctor Evans.' She tilted her head back a little so her nose went up in the way Angus was so familiar with. Most of the time she behaved with much less hauteur than she had a few months back, when *everything* had been beneath her. But, it still crept out from time to time.

'Here is the turn-off gentlemen.' Penny reined in and turned Chocolate to the left. Angus noted the gleam of excitement in her eyes. She had wanted to see justice come to Rupert Foxworth for a long time.

'Are ye sure ye don't want to go home, in case yer brother gets there first?' Angus tried to lure her away, though sure she'd have none of it.

Penny looked at the position of the sun in the sky and then back at him. 'I should not think they would have arrived yet. It is far too early.'

Angus tried not to look too amused. Indeed they had left the Bush Inn at first light. Even now it had not passed mid-morning. He doubted Pete would have been in such a hurry to head to Ellenvale after his late night.

'I could ride ahead if y'd like, make sure everything's prepared.' Gertie's voice broke into their conversation.

Angus turned to look at her and shook his head. 'A girl ridin' on yer own? I do no' think so.'

They allowed Mattherson and his men to go ahead down the driveway. Foxworth would not be given the chance to run. Angus felt his heart rate rise in anticipation of this moment. The man deserved some punishment for all he had put them through in the past few months. He had deceived Penny to the point of despair, he had manipulated both of them at each turn, and he had underhandedly tried to steal the gold from Penny's land. He had deceitfully tried to win her hand in marriage in order to claim her land as his own. Back then they had not had enough evidence to have him arrested. This time he would not be so lucky.

The party dismounted at the large homestead, tethering their horses to the fence posts, where Gertie decided to stay. Angus assumed she didn't wish to face her previous employer. They climbed the steps to the verandah, Mattherson in the lead, surrounded by his soldiers with their firearms at the ready. Mattherson banged his fist on the door and the sound seemed to reverberate throughout the whole house.

Drummond, the familiar butler, answered the door with surprise. As his eyes rested on each of them in turn, they widened further. He kept his composure well, but Angus could see the concern in his face. 'How may I help you folk?'

'If you could be so kind as to fetch Mr Rupert Foxworth at once. We have business of import to speak to him about.' Mattherson spoke to the point without revealing the true nature of their visit.

Drummond gave a curt bow and disappeared within the house. Moments later they heard hurried footsteps as Rupert Foxworth came to the door, his father behind him. His steps slowed as he saw the soldiers gathered there.

'What's this about?' He sounded a little hesitant.

'Step outside please, sir,' Mattherson commanded.

Rupert gazed around at each of them, frowning as his eyes rested on Angus and then Penny. He stepped out slowly. 'Again, what is this about?'

'I should like to know the same.' Henry Foxworth's voice boomed out.

Mattherson took Rupert's arm. 'You are under arrest for conspiracy to the abduction of Mr Anthony Worthington and Miss Estella Mattherson.'

'Who?' Rupert interrupted and jerked his arm to release Mattherson's grip. 'I've never even heard of this Estella Mattherson!' Angus thought he looked genuinely surprised. He hadn't known about Miss Mattherson at all.

The soldiers raised their bayonets at the first sign Foxworth might fight and run. Mattherson regained his hold on the man, forcing his arms behind his back. 'We have two witnesses who claim your involvement. Mr Steven Riley and Mr Morgan Brownhill.'

Rupert let out a choked laugh. 'This is ridiculous! Those men are lying. I don't know what you are talking about.'

'You are the one who lies!' Penny surged forward and pointed a finger in his face. 'You thought you would get back at me by having my brother kidnapped. You shall rot in gaol for this!'

'Penny.' Angus tried to pull her back.

Rupert's eyes grew cold as he looked at her. 'The spiteful words of a spurned lover. That's all you have.'

'How dare you!' Penny raised a hand to slap him, but Angus took hold of it before she could let fly.

He pulled her to him and whispered in her ear. 'Let the authorities take care of it, love.' He looked up at Foxworth. 'Insulting a lady is no' goin' to help yer situation, mate.'

'Well, if you kept your *lady* in hand, I wouldn't even be *in* this situation.' Foxworth spat the words hatefully.

'Hold on now, gentlemen ... and lady.' Henry Foxworth intervened. He turned to Mattherson. 'Where are these *witnesses* you say you have?'

'They are held at the Bush Inn. They shall soon be transferred to the stockade at Pentridge.'

Henry rubbed his chin. 'I agree they have fabricated Rupert's involvement. I can vouch for him. He has been here with me on The Run, overseeing the shearing. How he could have been involved in a kidnapping is beyond me.'

'That's right.' Rupert nodded. 'It's impossible.'

Mattherson looked from one to the other. 'That is for you to prove in court. For now, Mr Foxworth will be taken into custody.' Mattherson nodded to his men who surrounded Foxworth, tied his wrists together and led him from the verandah.

'No! Father, help me! I am innocent!' Foxworth struggled against the men as they forced him down the steps.

'Stop fighting, son. Go with them in peace for now. I will go immediately to see a lawyer and we shall have you home again in no time.' With a cold stare at Mattherson, Penny and Angus, the elder Foxworth descended the steps and headed to his stable.

Penny watched the soldiers retreat with their prisoner in their midst. 'Where will they take him?'

'I suppose to a holding cell along the way to Melbourne,' Mattherson answered.

Angus put his arm around her waist and gave her a squeeze. 'Do ye feel better now?'

Penny sighed 'Not really. Though Rupert deserves justice, I cannot help but wish things had not come to this. Why can some men not be content with life, instead of turning to crime to fulfil their desires?'

Angus squeezed her again. 'That is a question I'm sure has been asked for hundreds of years. An' yet, men an' women go on hurtin' one another.'

'To the detriment of our society,' Mattherson agreed.

They strolled off the verandah and to their horses, where Gertie waited for them. Angus wanted to put all the nastiness behind. 'Well, this lot o' villains are dealt with fer now. Let's think about our loved ones. We've got a reunion to look forward to.'

'Right you are,' Mattherson said heartily as he mounted his horse. 'But I think I might make sure Foxworth is secure before I join you. God willing I shall reach your Ellenvale before Estella arrives.'

'As ye wish, sir.' Angus nodded and proceeded to give him directions. Minutes later Mattherson rode away from them at a canter, deftly managing his horse even with one arm in a sling.

'Let's go home.' Penny turned to Angus and Gertie with a weary sigh, then pulled herself into the saddle.

Angus grinned at her. He would soon meet his future brother-in-law.

It seemed they had hiked for but a short time when they started to descend and the trees began to thin. Stella remained very quiet but Tony could hardly look at her for the churning in his stomach. He'd never wanted to hang on to something so much in his entire life. He wished he could be sure she felt the same way. He had an inkling she had formed some kind of attachment to him, but that could be born from the desperate situation they'd been in. *She probably sees me as some kind of father figure.*

His future loomed ahead of him like a big dark hole — much as it had before this ordeal started. He would have to make decisions. He had to find out the truth about this new property he had — probably some kind of farm. Could he even run such an operation? *I know nothing about farming.* Fear and uncertainty rose in him like familiar ghosts which had haunted him for years.

While they had been imprisoned in the forest, he had needed to be concerned with nothing but their immediate needs. Now he had to think further ahead. More than anything, he wanted Stella to be part of his future. But how? Would she even concede to live on a country property, away from the fashionable city with all the things a beautiful woman cherished? Exhaustion crowded in on his thoughts, making it difficult to think up any solutions. He just had to make it back to Ellenvale first.

Tony stole a look at the precious girl as they clambered down a rocky incline and his heart leaped. She looked unhappy. No smile lit her cheerful face. He imagined she did not look forward to meeting her father. She had mentioned her frustrations with him many times. *I wonder if he is the ogre she makes out.* He remembered all the times her temper had flashed with defiance and knew her father most likely was not all at fault. He would be curious to see how they would meet again.

As they broke from the last trees of the forest a loud screeching sound interrupted his thoughts.

'Look at that!' Stella's face lit up with wonder.

Tony followed her line of sight and saw hundreds of white birds perched in trees and on the grass, some swooping between both. The noise this flock made could deafen a man. It reminded him of a bunch of cheeky children in a park. Tony stopped to watch. 'Little Corellas I think. Incredible.'

'Noisy bird, eh.' Pete grinned at them. ''E make good tucker, that one.' He smacked his lips to emphasise his point.

'You eat them?' Stella looked astounded.

'Yep.' Pete nodded and lifted his boomerang, balancing his stance, his eyes on the birds. The next moment he let the boomerang fly.

Tony was amazed at the accuracy of Pete's throw. He knocked one of the birds clean out of the air. Pete darted to where the bird and boomerang had fallen, and threw the boomerang again before the huge flock were startled too much and moved away in a great flurry of white. He managed to get five birds in a very short time.

Stella, to Tony's astonishment, did not seem perturbed by the hunt. She squealed a little at the noise the birds made as they took flight, especially when one flew inches above her head, but she looked as mesmerised as he felt. He presumed she would have objected to seeing the pretty birds killed.

'This does not bother you?'

'The aborigines need food, do they not? Who am I to tell them what they can and cannot eat?' She had not looked at him, but continued to watch Pete in action.

'I thought you might find it disturbing, that's all.'

Stella gave a little shrug. 'Should I?'

Tony looked at her warily. Was she in another testy frame of mind? *I should tread with care.* 'I don't know. Most people of the more feminine temperament often dislike the hunt.'

Her eyes narrowed. 'So, because I am not troubled by a dead bird, I am abnormal?

'That is not what I said.'

'But it's what you meant, isn't it?'

'No! I ...'

'Let's just keep going. It is too hot to stand about in the sun.' With those words, Stella continued to limp in the direction they had been travelling. He winced. *Her feet must be in agony.* He wondered if her head swam with dizziness born of fatigue as his did.

'Miss Stella likes you, eh.' Pete chuckled as he appeared at Tony's side, his quarry in hand.

Tony looked at him in astonishment as he stumbled ahead. 'She has a funny way of showing it.' He wondered how Pete had come to such a conclusion, when she had spoken with such hostility. He shook his head. *Beats me.*

Stella had one thing right though. The sun rode high in the sky and it grew hotter by the minute. Now they were away from the cover of trees, they could feel its heat on the top of their bare heads.

Ahead, across the plains, Tony could see a line of trees which snaked through the land. *Water!* He would be grateful for a drink when they got there. He could feel streams of sweat trickle down his back beneath his shirt. The relentless summer sun beating down did not help the wobbly feeling in his legs.

Pete must have seen him wipe his brow with his shirt sleeve, for he pointed to the water-way with his boomerang. 'You see creek over there?'

Tony nodded.

'White fella call that one Jacksons Creek.'

Tony stopped and gaped. 'Jacksons Creek? That runs through Ellenvale!'

'Yeah. You just gotta follow 'im. You be home soon, eh.' Pete also stopped but half-turned back towards the mountains and bush. 'I go now. You don't need Pete no more.'

Tony nodded again and put out his hand to shake the native's hand. Pete had to put his boomerang under one arm to free his hand, but then shook it with a grin.

'Thanks for everything, Pete.'

'Tell Miss Penny g'day.' He began to stride away, but then turned back again. 'An' make sure you marry that woman, eh.'

Tony could hear his laugh as he jogged off towards the forest and shook his head with a grim smile. Stella hadn't even looked back to see Pete's departure. She still hobbled along with a stoic tread, well ahead of him. He would have to manage a feeble run to catch up to her.

Stella did not even acknowledge him when he came alongside her, but kept her eyes on the creek ahead.

'Pete's gone. I know the way from here.'

At this she stopped and turned around, shading her eyes from the sun in order to try and see their friend in the distance. She waved an arm in the air, but Pete no longer looked back. 'I did not get a chance to thank him.'

Because you were too busy being cross at me. Tony wanted to scold her, but then he didn't want to finish their journey on another argument. 'Perhaps you will see him again one day.'

She looked at him for a moment and then continued to trudge ahead. They stopped at the creek to slake their thirst then followed the creek to the south. At one point they came across a place where a few stakes had been driven into the ground in a few rough squares, with red flags tied to the top.

'What is that?' Stella was curious.

Tony investigated the area and saw digging had taken place.

He looked up at Stella with a slight frown. 'I believe it might be the beginnings of a gold mine.'

'Oh. How far do you think until we reach Ellenvale?'

With a grin Tony collected a small branch from the ground. 'We are already on Ellenvale.'

'We are?' Stella watched him with her eyebrows raised.

'If I am correct, this is where my sister found her fortune.' It had not occurred to him until now she might have struck gold on Ellenvale. She must have found a lot of gold to make her so rich. He poked around in the soil and rock within the marked off area, to see if he could recognise a glimmer of gold. It appeared plenty of digging had taken place there already. He picked up a piece of quartz and examined it. *Yes!* He could see the familiar yellow vein within it.

As excitement built within, he turned to show Stella, but his heart dropped like a stone when he heard her scream. She stood in a frozen stance by the water's edge, her face drained of colour. He dropped the rock and hurried to her side. 'Stella? What is it?'

She lifted a trembling hand and pointed. 'S...snake.'

He looked to where she indicated, but could see nothing. He turned back to her and rubbed her shoulder. 'It's all right. It's gone now.'

Wide eyes rounded on him and she shook her head. 'It ... bit ... me.' As soon as the words departed her lips, her eyes rolled back in her head and she collapsed.

Chapter Twenty-Five

With a gasp of shock, Tony caught her and lowered her to the ground, trying to ignore the pain as her body fell into his ribs. His eyes darted from her leg to her face, not sure whether to check for the bite or wake her up. He patted her on the cheek. 'Stella! Stella! I need you to tell me what kind of snake it was.'

When he could get no response he moved to her feet, pulling off one boot then another. Surely the boots would have protected her ankles. Again he tapped her cheek. 'Come on, Stella. Wake up. Talk to me.' He was confident she had merely fainted. No snake's venom would have worked so fast.

He rifled through the satchel for the knife and then cut away the moleskins from her right leg, hoping he had the correct leg. Then he saw it; two small puncture wounds just below the knee. *High for a snake bite.* He swallowed his fear down. How poisonous was this snake?

'Stella!' He slapped her cheek again. 'Wake up, darling. I need you to tell me about the snake.'

Her eyes fluttered then and opened. 'D... darling?'

She heard that? It had slipped out of his mouth without thought, but he didn't want to try to explain. Even now the site of the bite began to swell. 'What kind of snake was it?'

Her eyes flickered in confusion and she shook her head a little. 'I don't know.'

'Stella, this is very important.' He needed her to think. 'What did it look like?'

Tears slid from the corners of her eyes. 'It hurts, Tony.' She tried to get up but Tony pressed her shoulder back down.

'No, it is better to lie down. I know it hurts.'

'I didn't see it.' She brought a hand up to wipe at her eyes. 'I went to get a drink from the creek. I must have disturbed it. The next thing — black, the snake was black, Tony.' Her eyes focused on him then.

'You're certain?' Tony felt his stomach twist.

'But I saw red on it, too, I think.'

'Sounds like a Red-bellied Black Snake.' *Poisonous!* He had tried to make his voice sound light, but he knew this would not be good. It explained the high bite though. Those creatures could jump. *What to do? What to do?* He recalled all the years spent on the sheep-run. There had been the odd snake bite which his father had attended to — half of them had died. Tony felt a shock through his whole being. She couldn't die ... could she? *I must do something.* What had Papa done? He tried to push the rising panic down and focus his attention on the current crisis. *Incise and suck!* That was it! He looked down at Stella. This would not be pleasant for her.

She reached out and grabbed his arm then. 'Tony, you look — am I going to die?'

I don't know. Tony swallowed down his fears. 'No.' He shook his head and tried to force a smile. 'You will be fine. But you must lie very still.'

He felt his heart hammer in his chest at an alarming rate. *Please God! Don't take her from me. Not now. Help me deliver her of this poison.* He took a deep breath and let it out, then looked at Stella with grave face. 'I have to cut you ... to get the poison out.'

He saw her swallow hard and her eyes widen in fear, but she nodded, tears still slipping across her temples into her hair.

He grabbed the leather satchel and handed her the shoulder strap. 'Here, bite down on this through the pain.' She took it, though with a little hesitation.

Tony turned so his back became a shield between her face and the bite on her leg. He did not need to see the pain in her eyes while he worked, and he supposed she didn't need to see him cut her leg. He breathed deeply again in an attempt to slow his heart down and stop the trembling in his arms. It was now or never.

The scream that echoed through the bush would surely be heard at Ellenvale homestead. Tony fought back his own tears as he continued with his gruesome task. Stella's scream subsided to agonised sobs as he leaned forward to begin to suck and spit, all the while praying under his breath she would be all right.

Leaving the wound to bleed for a moment, he moved to the water's edge, washed his mouth out, splashed his face, then drank to refresh himself. *How can I even look at her after what I've just put her through? She will despise me forever now.*

'Tony,' he heard her call in a shaky voice. 'Can you bring me some water please? My head hurts. It's too hot.'

He hesitated, but only for a moment. He knew the heat did not cause her head ache, the venom in her body had begun its attack. He closed his eyes tight to squeeze out the fear. He scooped up some water and brought it to her. She raised herself a little and sipped from his cupped hands.

When she'd had enough, he picked up the cut-away moleskins and tore them into strips.

'What will you do with those?'

'I need to bind your leg and get you home. You need a doctor.' He could not look at her for the fear he felt.

'But you sucked the poison out ... didn't you?'

How could he tell her it might not have worked? 'Just to be sure, Stella.' He tried to smile at her.

He slung the satchel over his shoulder and bent to lift her. The effort it took sent agony through his torso, but he had no choice, he had to get her to a doctor. With every step, the pressure of her body against his rib cage brought a new jolt of pain. Added to the exhaustion which already had sapped all of his energy, moments later he had to set her down again, tumbling into the dust beside her as he clasped his chest. 'I can't ... carry you,' he groaned.

'I'll walk then.' She rolled onto her side and looked at him, concerned. 'If you assist me, I'm sure we can make it.'

'No,' Tony gasped. 'You need to be as still as possible.'

'What are we to do, then?'

Tony dragged himself to his hands and knees. 'I shall have to go for help.'

Her eyes widened. 'No. Don't leave me here alone.'

Tony shook his head. 'The house should be but a few minutes away. I won't be gone long.' Panting still, he stood to his feet.

Her face paled then and beads of perspiration appeared on her brow. 'I feel sick.'

Oh dear God, no!

She vomited in the dust, then rolled back clutching her head in her hands with a groan. 'It's the venom isn't it?'

'Y... yes.' He wanted to stay with her and comfort her, but she needed help ... desperately. 'I need to go. I'll be back soon.'

She did not answer, but nodded and curled into a ball, her arms wrapped around her stomach.

Stella wanted to call out to Tony to come back. She should tell him she loved him before ... before ... *What if I die while he's gone? He'll never know.* She wasn't an imbecile. She knew the snake bite meant it was all over for her. She'd seen it in Tony's eyes. He feared for her life.

She groaned again. Her leg burned and throbbed. She glanced down at it. It had swollen to almost double its size. Her head pounded and her stomach cramped making her want to heave its contents over the ground again. Not that there was much left to cast up, but that didn't stop the urge.

When the convulsions eased off, she lay back, panting. 'God, I don't want to die.' She cried. *Why didn't I watch where I put my feet?* She had been too busy listening to Tony while she watched a kookaburra in a nearby tree.

She looked through blurry eyes into the azure sky which floated above the grey-green canopy of eucalypt. *And I have been so terse with him this morning.* She gave herself a mental thrashing. Would Tony's last impression of her be a temperamental miss behaving badly? Choking sobs shook her pain-filled body. *I wanted him to show me some affection, a sign he loves me too.* Now it would be too late. He had gone and she would die before he returned.

Death. With the mockery of kookaburras in her ears and a cheerful sun smiling down — how could that be fair? *God, I thought Your Scriptures said You wanted to lead us home. Did You answer all of our prayers so I could die by a snake bite? Why did I ever leave home?* Tears filled her eyes once again and she wiped at them with her shirt. *Abuela trusted You and I have tried to trust You, but I'm confused now. What do You want from me?*

Cramps assaulted her again and she rolled to her side and retched. Her head felt as though it would explode at any moment. It became harder to form her thoughts into a sensible stream. The vision of green and blue above her swam, mingling together into a greyish haze. *Is this it? Is this the end?* She remembered Tony calling her darling as she slipped into nothingness ... quiet, peaceful, nothingness.

Tony ran as fast as his depleted body could carry him. The urgency of Stella's situation spurred him forward, in spite of the pain and exhaustion which ravaged him. Home must be a short distance away now. *Please, God. Please don't let her die.* What else could he do but beg the Creator for help? He repeated those words with every step he took.

Papa had not cleared all the land on Ellenvale Station, but left the natural bushland on one side of the valley. He knew he would break into the clearing around the homestead at any moment. He felt nervous anxiety increase in his stomach. How would Penny react when she saw him? He hadn't seen her for almost a decade. They would hardly recognise each other. Her letters had always been pleasant. *But what if she despises me for deserting her? And I didn't come when the flood came and she needed me.* He shook his head as he ran. *I can't think about it now. Stella is all that matters.*

He stopped short in the clearing and gasped for breath. He dragged his gaze across the white-washed homestead until he saw the solitary figure on the verandah. He sucked in as much air as his angry ribs would allow and called out. 'Help! Help me!'

'Tony?' The woman answered as she stepped off the verandah. 'Is that you?'

Tony crumpled to his knees, barely able to hold on to reason. 'Yes. Penny. Stella ...' He pointed back the way he had come.

'Heavens, you look terrible.' Her face took on a horrified mask as she approached. She flung her head back towards the homestead. 'Angus! Doctor Evans! Come quick!' As she turned back to him, she frowned further. 'Where is Miss Mattherson?' Her concerned eyes searched his.

Tony gritted his teeth and braced his chest against the pain. 'Snake bite. By the creek. She needs help.'

Now he had the most pressing information out, he allowed himself to relax and fell to the ground, his mind spinning with exhaustion. Penny would take care of everything. Indeed, within moments she had sat down and lifted his head into her lap.

He heard hurried footsteps approach and a Scottish accent rang out. 'Is this yer brother, then?'

'Yes,' he heard her worried voice reply. 'But Miss Mattherson is still back there by the creek with a snake bite. Can you go and fetch her please? Doctor, will you see to my brother? I fear he is in a bad way?'

Tony roused himself a little. 'No. No. Send the doctor to Stella. I am merely tired.'

'You're more than tired, Tony, you're hardly conscious. And those bruises ...'

Tony opened his eyes and stared at her. 'Stella may be dying! See to her first. I got out some venom, but red, black.'

He saw two men frown down at him.

'Go!'

'Ri' then. We'd better go.' Angus nodded and they headed off at a run along the creek.

'I'll help you into the house then.' His sister assisted him as he sat up and held onto his arm as he dragged himself to his feet.

'Other side.' He winced as she moved to support him on his injured side.

'Sorry.' She draped his other arm around her shoulders and walked him to the house. She led him straight to a bedroom and eased him onto the bed, lifting his legs onto the mattress for him.

Penny pulled up a chair and sat beside him. She took hold of one of his hands and pressed it to her cheek. A tide of emotion welled up and threatened to engulf him. 'Penny, I am so sorry.' Broken words flowed from him. 'I have been a useless brother. I never came when you needed me. Can you ever forgive me?' He wept as all his regret surged out at once, along with relief that the recent nightmare had finally ended. Well, almost. He wished he knew that Stella would be all right.

She brushed back his limp hair so she could look into his eyes. He saw her eyes brimmed over with tears as well. 'Tony, all is forgiven. I am grateful you are here and you are alive.'

He dabbed at his eyes with his sleeve. 'It is so good to see you at last.'

'And you.' Penny offered him a warm smile and then frowned. 'But look at you. What did those villains do to you?'

'Nothing that will not heal. But you! You're all grown up.'

Penny giggled then gave him a shy smile. 'Grown up enough to get married. That was my fiancé out there. Angus McDoughan.'

Tony looked at her in surprise. 'Fiancé?'

'Yes, it is very recent,' Penny told him. 'The letter I sent probably waits for you in Ballaarat.'

Tony gave a half laugh. 'That is the best news I've heard in a while. Congratulations to you both.'

The genuine joy in her eyes struck him and he turned his face away. *If only I could have such happiness with Stella. Will she survive?* His stomach turned in a familiar knot as fear and doubt assailed him.

'I shall have Gertie prepare you a bath, and Doctor Evans will see to you when he returns. We'll soon have you on your feet again, never you mind. For now though, I think sleep is what you need.'

Tony heard the swish of her skirts as she rose and he turned and clasped her hand. 'You come and wake me the moment you know about Stella.'

'Of course I will.' She nodded and he let her go. 'Get some rest.'

Chapter Twenty-Six

Angus carried the inert form of Estella Mattherson at a quickened pace, careful not to trip upon an exposed rock or root. Her weight didn't slow him down much, but the surgeon begged him to hurry anyway, his concern evident. Doctor Evans strode ahead by two paces, often turning to urge him onward.

The young woman yet breathed, though the doctor had managed to rouse her once only to hear a confused string of words about Tony and death. Miss Mattherson had then swooned again and the surgeon had ordered he lift her at once.

As they broke into the clearing which surrounded the homestead, he saw Penny leap from the verandah and run towards them.

'Hot water, Miss Worthington, at once!' Doctor Evans commanded her.

Penny turned and flung the same words back towards the house, replacing her name with Gertie's, and continued towards them. 'Oh, the poor thing!' She gasped when she saw the condition of Miss Mattherson's clothes and the bindings on her leg. 'Is she all right?'

'I have not been able to examine her properly yet, but she is in a bad way. We must get her into the house. It seems Mr Worthington incised her already, so I dare say he's sucked much of the poison out.'

Miss Mattherson roused then, but writhed in Angus's arms so much, he had to set her down. She dropped to her knees with a groan and retched violently. She did not rise but lay on the grass with a moan then began to sob. 'Where is Papa? Tony?'

'Your father will be here soon, dear.' Penny knelt beside her and stroked her hair. 'He had to see to those evil men who kidnapped you. Tony is exhausted. He came as quickly as he could. He needs to rest.'

'She does not seem to suffer from paralysis.' The doctor's eyebrows rose. 'It's a good sign.' He crouched down. 'Miss Mattherson, can you tell me about the snake?'

She focused on the surgeon at last and Angus saw her blink a few times before she answered. 'Tony said red-bellied black snake.'

Doctor Evans straightened and breathed out a sigh of relief. 'In that case, I think she will be well in a few days. This is probably the worst of it.'

'Come, Miss Mattherson,' Angus reached a hand down to help the girl up. 'Let's get ye inside.'

Penny took her other arm and spoke soothing words. 'We'll get you cleaned up and give you a new pretty nightgown. You are about the same size as my late mother. Tony and I inherited our height from Papa. Mama's clothes shall fit you nicely. With luck we can have you snug in bed before your father arrives.'

Stella dissolved into tears again. 'I did not mean to cause a scandal. Do you think he will be very angry?'

Penny patted her hand. 'No, no. He shall be glad to see you. I meant that in those clothes it is obvious to see the ordeal you have been through. I rather think it might upset him. It shall be bad enough for him to know you have a dangerous snake-bite.'

Penny's eyes wandered to the filthy rough-sewn shirt and cut-away pants and then rose to meet his with concern. Angus knew she wondered how much the poor girl had suffered. They could see numerous scratches and bruises on every part of exposed skin.

Miss Mattherson nodded and allowed Angus to lift her again. 'My head hurts.' She closed her eyes and leaned into his shoulder. 'My stomach hurts, too. And my leg.'

The doctor glanced at them all. 'All signs of the poison.'

Angus looked up as he heard the sound of hooves pounding the ground. A horse rounded the corner of the house and William Mattherson reined in, barely waiting for the animal to stop before he jumped down. Without hesitation, his eyes searched and found his daughter. 'Oh, my poor darling girl!'

With his good arm outstretched he surged towards her. Amidst warnings to be gentle, Angus set her down again and Mattherson wrapped her in a bear-like embrace which would have squeezed the air from her lungs. Indeed, a deep groan rose from her throat and he abruptly let her go. She crumpled against him and he was forced to prevent her from falling. 'What's wrong with her?'

'Snake bite,' Angus told him. 'We were just takin' her inside.'

'No!' Wild, fear-filled eyes turned towards the doctor who put a calming hand on his shoulder.

'It is well, sir. It shan't be fatal.'

Mattherson bent his head and pressed his cheek against his daughter's head. 'You're certain?'

'Yes, sir.'

He nodded and lifted his precious cargo, despite the wound in his upper arm. He looked to Penny for direction. 'Lead on, Miss Worthington.'

Stella opened her eyes to find two unfamiliar women fussing over her. She lay on a bed in a white-washed room. *How did I get here?* Blurred images flooded into her mind. She had been carried here. She remembered voices. With a gasp, she jerked awake. 'Papa!'

One of the women came to her and stroked her hair. 'There, there Miss Mattherson. All is well.'

All is well. Could it be true? 'I'm not going to die?'

The young woman smiled. 'No. The surgeon has already examined you. You shall be sore for a few days, but you will recover. Your father waits to see you once we've freshened you up a little.'

Stella looked down along the length of her almost bare body. With warm cloths, they had removed the dust of her journey through the bush and cleaned the cuts and grazes. She felt a slight sting where they had dabbed alcohol on the worst of them. The other girl, at present, bound her blistered feet at the other end of the bed. Air hissed through her teeth as she sucked in a breath. How had she not noticed how painful they were before?

A sudden cramp gripped her abdomen and she rolled to the side to retch yet again. The lady who had spoken to her held a bowl beneath her and placed a comforting hand on her back until it was over. 'You've been through quite an ordeal, my dear. But it will get better, I promise you.'

As she leaned back against the pillow, she looked at her nurse. 'Are you Tony's sister?'

'Yes. But, you may call me Penny.' Her eyes twinkled as she smiled. 'Now, we need to sit you up so we can remove these towels from under you and put you in a nice nightgown.'

The other girl came to help her sit up. 'I'm Gertie. I'm the maid 'round 'ere. Penny an' your pa have been so worried about y'. I'm glad yer all ri'.' She gathered the towels while Penny held her steady.

'Many prayers went up, I can assure you.' Penny draped the nightgown over her head and Stella put her arms through the sleeves.

'Tony and I prayed too.'

Penny's eyebrows went up in surprise. 'Did you?'

'Yes. We are certain God guided us here. Where is Tony, may I ask?' The mention of Tony's name made her yearn to see him. The dear man had sucked the poison from her leg even after she'd been horrible to him, and she had a vague recollection the word 'darling' had passed his lips. Could it be? Did he hold her in affection after all? The only way she would know for sure was to speak to him again.

'The doctor gave him a sleeping draught. He has a few broken ribs and a broken nose, besides many other bruises. I dare say he is exhausted beyond endurance. Doctor Evans considered it best he had a long rest.' Penny lifted blankets over her and tucked her in.

He's asleep. Disappointment made her heart sink.

'And you are just as weary, else you wouldn't keep fainting on us.' She smiled again and sat on the edge of the bed. She looked up at the maid and nodded. 'Gertie, will you bring Miss Mattherson a cup of tea, please?'

'Yes'm.' The maid bounced a curtsey and bobbed out of the room.

'Now.' Penny turned her attention back to Stella. 'The doctor would have me ask you a delicate question. Do you mind?'

Stella gazed into her sombre green eyes and wondered what it could be. 'No. Ask what you must. But, please call me Stella.'

'Very well, Stella.' Penny took a deep breath and let it out. 'Did Riley ... um ... force himself on you?' Her eyes were laced with deep concern.

'Riley?'

'Oh, I mean, Smith. His real name is Riley, you know.'

'That's right. Pete told us so. And no, he did not have his way with me.' Images of that morning flashed into her mind and she felt her body tense with the memory. How close she had come to — it terrified her all over again to think about it. 'He ... he tried. But Tony ... Tony saved me ... just in time.'

Penny's eyes widened. 'He did?'

Stella swallowed hard, but her voice continued to waver anyway. 'Y... yes. You see ...'

Without warning, sobs bubbled up from within her and all the pent-up emotion which she had kept under guard for days flooded out. 'I was so scared.'

Penny wrapped her arms around her and cradled her while she cried. 'Fetch Mr Mattherson. And the doctor.' She heard the rattle of a tea cup on a saucer and knew Gertie had appeared and been dismissed again. 'There, there. It is all over now.' Penny's words gave her a little comfort, but she could not hold back the storm.

In moments her father had swung in the doorway and knelt beside the bed opposite Penny, his face etched with concern. She reached out a hand to grip his.

'I'm so sorry, Papa. I never should have run away. I will go where you want me to.'

'There, there, darling.' Her papa soothed and stroked her hair as she cried. 'Did those wicked men hurt you at all?'

She pulled her tear-stained face away from Penny's shoulder and looked at him. 'Only a very little. Tony protected me from them as much as he could, and God took care of the rest. I am more tired and sick than anything else.'

He withdrew a handkerchief from his pocket and wiped her wet face. 'I only wish to understand one thing, Estella. How did you end up with Riley and Brownhill?'

Though he had dried her cheeks, the tears kept coming. She became aware Penny had withdrawn and her father had put his strong arms around her. In a flurry of words, she blurted out everything. 'I felt angry at you for making me go to England. I ran away thinking it would be an adventure. I went to help the Redcoats at the Eureka riot, but I didn't even know how to use your gun. I saw a man killed, Papa! It was awful! Then I ran towards Melbourne to get away and I got so tired. When I saw a dray go past, I snuck under the covers to hitch a nice ride. But it turned out to be a nightmare, not an adventure. It's all my fault Tony received that beating. I have upset you and *Mamá*. I made Jemina lie for me. Papa, I have been so wrong. Please forgive me.'

A fresh bout of crying assaulted her and she buried her face on his shoulder. She still half expected him to push her away in disgust and tell her he wished to disown her. But he didn't. He held her tight. Tighter than she imagined he could. And he whispered soothing words in her ears — words of forgiveness and love. That made her cry harder. She had believed he didn't care about her at all. That he wanted to be rid of her. Had he not seen to those vile men before he came to her? But here he sat, cradling her and telling her how much he did care.

'Doctor,' she heard him say over her head. 'She is beside herself with pain and exhaustion, not to mention the trauma she has been through. Is there something you can give her?'

'I have laudanum here. It should ease her pain and help her sleep.'

Her papa held her back from him so he could look in her eyes, his own glassy. 'Take the medicine Doctor Evans prescribes, my dear. It will do you good.'

Chapter Twenty-Seven

Tony woke to a rumble in his belly. The room was dark. He climbed out of bed and went to the window. The stars were still out, but he could hear the morning birds' song already. *No more sleeping draughts for me.* He figured he'd been asleep for the good part of two days. He had vague memories of drinking water and being fed broth a few times, but the foggy haze had soon taken over again. *They must have put the draught in my water.*

He stretched each aching limb in turn. His body had become stiff with inactivity. Aside from that, he felt well rested. *Lord, I must have needed all that sleep.* It had been sublime to sleep on a mattress for a change. For almost a decade he had slept on a canvas cot, and the last week his bed had been the hard ground. The comfort of Papa's bed had enveloped him and made wakefulness impossible.

He shrugged into a shirt, careful not to inflame his still-tender ribs, and pulled clean moleskins over his legs. What had become of Stella? He had a dim recollection he'd been told she would survive. Did she still remain in the house? Or had her father taken her away? Even though the sun had barely made an appearance over the horizon, he tip-toed to the kitchen, determined not to allow anyone to send him back to bed.

The busiest room of the house remained cloaked in early-morning stillness, the smell of last night's supper and stale smoke still lingering on the air. He heard more than saw the rustle of a maid who stoked the fire for the day's cooking. She bent low and blew on the embers till a flame caught. He sat nearby, although the room was far from cold, and watched the flames dance and lick at the larger logs she placed in the hearth, the light reflecting off the young girl's face. She did not notice him there until she straightened from her work.

'Mornin', Mr Worthington. I didn't 'ere y' come in.' The maid nodded with a grin.

'I do not think I have had the pleasure, Miss ...?'

'I'm Gertie. Pardon me sayin' so, but aren't y' s'posed to be restin'?'

Tony had to smile at her impertinence. What would Penny think of a maid who spoke so to her seniors? Not that it mattered to him. He had mixed with all ranks and stations in Ballaarat. But Penny had always been a stickler when it came to propriety. 'Two days in bed is more than enough for me. If you try to send me back, you shall find me quite uncompliant.'

She grinned at him again. 'Ri' you are then. Shall I brew a cup o' tea for y'?'

'Tea would be excellent.' *Food would be good also.* But it was too early yet to ask for a full meal. 'Might there be a slice of bread around to tide me over till breakfast?'

'I'm sure I can find somethin' for y'.' Gertie bobbed a curtsey. 'I'd be hungry too, if I'd been sleepin' so long.' She moved about the kitchen preparing his food.

'Might I enquire after Miss Mattherson? Is she still here?' He knew she was not the right person to ask, but he could not wait until his sister appeared.

'Yeah. She's still 'ere. Been sleepin' as much as you. I think she's on the mend, though.'

Tony felt his heart rate quicken. She was still here, a few strides away somewhere. And she would be well after all. How he yearned to see her. It took great effort to refrain from asking which room she occupied and running off to find her. It would be unseemly to behave so. What would they all think? He had no claim on her. Perhaps they would understand the two of them had formed a bond through their hardship, but Tony knew it went deeper than that. For him anyway. He wished she felt the same. She had hinted at some kind of affection or attraction. Or had she merely tried to make him feel better at his lowest point? Or worse, had she been teasing him?

Gertie placed a cup and saucer and a small plate on the side table beside his chair. 'There y' go, Tony. That should make y' feel a little better for now.'

Tony? Did she even know her place? He feared Penny would dismiss her if she knew of the girl's impertinence. 'Thank you, Gertie. But, I should warn you, my sister will rake you over the coals if she hears you address people by their first name.'

Her face erupted into a large smile and a giggle burst from her amused countenance. 'Oh, no. She'll not do that.'

'You sound very sure of yourself. The Penny Worthington I know will not brook such impudence.' He said the words with a smile, to try and let her know he did not hold with the same attitude.

'Your sister has changed.' The maid grew serious, although her eyes still twinkled. 'We are all equals in this house.'

Tony stared at her with an open mouth, astounded by what he heard.

'What she means is,' Penny came into the room with a half-smile twisting the corners of her mouth. 'While each person knows their place — Gertie is my maid and works for me — we are all friends and refer to each other as such.'

Gertie looked at him, the twinkle still in her eyes. 'See?'

Tony gaped at his sister. 'Well, this is refreshing. What made the change?' He stood to greet her with a kiss to her cheek.

'I have learned a few things about arrogance and humility in the past few months. Did the doctor give you permission to be up?' She sat in a chair opposite him and he resumed his seat.

'I wouldn't try to send 'im back to bed if I were you, Penny. He's got a very determined look in 'is eye.'

Tony grinned at his sister's attempt at trickery. 'The last time I saw Doctor Evans, he gave me another sleeping draught and told me he planned to *leave*. I daresay it means he had the impression my recovery was almost complete.'

'Is there anythin' else y' need, before I go an' milk the cow?' Gertie interjected.

Tony nodded to her between sips of tea. 'I could use a decent bath.'

The maid bobbed a curtsey. 'Comin' ri' up.' She collected a bucket on the way out the door.

A spark shone in Penny's eye as she turned back to him. 'Doctor Evans *will* be back to check on you.'

'Or to check on Miss Mattherson perhaps? How is she, by the way?'

'Improving. She asks for you every time she wakes.'

Tony felt his stomach lurch. Could she be as eager to see him as he was to see her? He noticed Penny studied him for a response. Did she already suspect there might be an attachment? He watched as Gertie entered, tipped a bucket of water into a large iron pot and hung it over the flames, then departed again.

'I am relieved to hear she is well. Am I right to believe you struck gold here at Ellenvale? That scoundrel Bobby Smith or Riley, or whoever he is, told me you were rich.'

Penny eyed him for a moment, obviously aware he wanted to divert her attention away from Stella. 'Stephen Riley attempted to cover his identity to evade capture and to avoid the connection to our neighbour, Mr Foxworth. The discovery of gold on Ellenvale is what started this whole fiasco. The flood uncovered it on the creek bed and Foxworth happened upon it before we did. Then he proceeded to carry out a conniving plot to get it back. Tony, I am so sorry you were embroiled in this affair.'

And yet, if I hadn't, perhaps I would not have had a chance to discover the wonder of Estella Mattherson so fully. He gave a half smile. 'I am alive. I am astounded to hear you rode to my rescue.'

Penny's lips formed into a pout. 'Did you not believe I would care enough?'

Tony allowed his gaze to drop to his lap. 'I have wronged you. I should have been here. I didn't expect you to look past that.'

Penny put a hand under his chin, lifting it, and looked him in the eye. 'You are my brother. Money is not worth enough to get in the way of that.' She leaned back again. 'Besides we didn't lose it in the end and Angus rode out yesterday and returned it all to the bank.'

'I am glad to hear it. Although I expect more is to be found. I saw the claim marked out on our way here the other day. That is when St... Miss Mattherson met with the snake.'

'An unfortunate meeting, to be sure.' Penny nodded in sympathy. 'We are yet to build a mine, but we believe there will be plenty to give you a share in all we recover.'

Tony reached out and patted her hand. 'There's no need to worry about me, sister dear. I have my own property to sustain me now.' He paused to grin at her. In his waking moments, only Stella and the mysterious land had preoccupied his thoughts. 'I received a letter from Mr Harrison Blake not long before those men ... well, you know. He told me Papa left a separate property to me. Do you know much about it?'

Her eyes widened and a smile lit her face. 'Did he not give you any details?'

Tony shook his head. Gertie passed them again as she hauled a bucket of water towards his room. He turned his attention back to Penny as she spoke.

'I myself heard about it only a few weeks before your abduction and I thought it best for Mr Blake to contact you himself. Papa contracted to lease a large cattle-run near Seymour on the Goulburn River. He called it Sunworth Cattle Station.'

Tony let his eyes drop to the worn fabric on the arm of his chair and traced his finger over the faded pattern. He still found it difficult to accept his father's generosity in the face of his rebellion. 'I think Papa wanted to tell me about it when he came to Ballaarat. I did not listen to him.'

'He never spoke of it to me.'

'I was too stubborn — clinging to my grudge. I did not give him a chance. I cannot tell you how much I regret it now.'

Penny reached a hand across and placed it over his forearm. 'I know he would forgive you. If he went and purchased a whole property for you, he obviously cared about you and your future. I think you should forgive yourself now.'

'I suppose.' Tony shrugged. 'Do you know any more about Sunworth, then?'

'I believe Papa engaged a gentleman to manage it until such time as you could take over. I have copies of his reports on the progress of the business if you should like to see them. Do you think you will take it on?'

Tony straightened and pushed his stray hair back with a sigh as another bucket of water sloshed by. He looked at his sister in thought. 'There is much to consider. As I told Papa once, I have not the stomach for work with animals. And yet, I dare not refuse his bequest. I should like to honour his memory.'

'And there is the matter of a certain pretty girl who cannot think of much else but her rescuer.' Penny threw him an arch look.

Tony pressed his mouth into a grim line. 'I think she sees me as a kind of hero, or as the brother she never had. She is an only child, you know.'

The corners of Penny's eyes wrinkled as her smile grew wider. 'You may try to convince yourself of that, but *I* think there is more to it.'

Tony let his head dip forward again and pretended to examine the tea-leaves floating in his cup. Her words made him uncomfortable and his stomach churned.

'You love her, don't you?'

How could he deny it before his sister? She would see straight through his clumsy refusal. 'More than anything,' he admitted to the half-empty cup.

'Then tell her.'

Tony lifted his head to see an earnest look on her face. 'I don't know if I can. I don't know if she feels the same.'

She gripped his forearm again. 'Listen. You have regrets about Papa, don't you? You wish you'd spoken when you had a chance?' She watched him for a response, so he nodded. 'Don't make the same mistake again. Imagine the regret you would feel this time. What is the worst that could happen?'

She could laugh in my face, that's what! Penny didn't understand. Aloud, he uttered a half-laugh which sounded full of self-doubt and rose to his feet. 'I think I might go and help Gertie fill my bath.'

Retrieving the bubbling iron pot from the fire with a mitt, he avoided Penny's stare and headed to his room. He imagined she would either grin at him with one of those annoying I-know-what-you're-thinking looks, or she would shake her head in disappointment. Neither could he face. She knew him for what he was: a coward.

As he soaked his battered body in the warm, soapy water, he leaned his head against the high back of the hip bath. Penny seemed willing to forgive his years of avoidance, his neglect of her and his unwillingness to help in a time of crisis. She had been far too gracious. He did not deserve her kindness.

On the other hand, Stella either remained blind to his cowardice, or she lacked the intelligence to recognise it. No, a simpleton she would never be. She must have put him on an imaginary pedestal because he'd rescued her a time or two. She would soon learn that pedestal had false legs and would come crumbling down.

Frustrated with his jumbled thoughts, he clambered out of the tub, towelled himself off and dressed in fresh clothes. Papa's old garments. Everywhere he turned, his failures shouted in his face. That was why he had never wanted to come back here. Ellenvale was pain. *God, why did You bring me here?* God. There came that question again. Had God truly watched over them, leading them here? But why, when it proved to highlight all his failings?

He raked his fingers through his damp hair and pressed it into a form of neatness. *I should take a look at those letters Penny mentioned.* It could be a solution — move on from here to his own property, away from all that reminded him of his worthlessness. But, what about Stella?

Tony stepped into the hallway. Which room did she occupy? He looked to the right and left and noticed one bedroom door stood ajar. He crept towards it and peeked in. His heart began to somersault the moment his eyes rested on her lovely, peaceful face. They must have left the door open in case she needed something in the night. He leaned his head against the door jamb and gazed at her sleeping form. How could he leave without her? Would she agree to a life with him on a cattle run? And what would happen when she realised he was not as noble as she believed him?

'I can imagine she gave you a handful of trouble.'

The voice startled Tony and he straightened from the doorway. 'I beg your pardon. I did not hear you approach, Mr ...'

'Mattherson. William Mattherson. Estella's father.'

Of course, Tony already knew who he was, but it was hard not to feel intimidated by the broad-shouldered, grave-faced man. 'Mr Mattherson. Pleased to meet you.' Tony took the man's outstretched hand and shook it.

'She's never spent time in the wilderness. She would never have survived on her own. I commend your efforts in looking after her.'

Tony stared at him with wide eyes. This man did not know his daughter well. 'She was no handful, sir. I'm glad I managed to get her back safely. For a moment there, I ...' Tony swallowed the memory of his fear when the snake bit her. 'She really gave me no trouble at all. Indeed, she looked after *me* much of the time.'

Mattherson chuckled, winked at him, and patted him on the shoulder. 'Humble words, sir. I know my daughter.'

Tony opened his mouth to object but then decided he did not wish to argue with Stella's father — especially since they had just met. Maybe he had never recognised her strengths, or perhaps he had not wanted to acknowledge them. *Is that why Stella has been so bitter about him? Does he wish to make her into someone she is not?* Maybe he wanted her to be a pretty and demure lady of society. It almost made Tony laugh to think about it. Stella had made it clear she would not enjoy that sort of life.

'There is one thing I should like to clear up.' Mattherson shuffled his feet a little. 'You spent much time alone in the bush with my daughter. Are you an honourable man?'

Tony knew what he asked and understood a father's concern, but it still troubled him to be questioned. 'I have not compromised her, if that is what you want to know. I looked after her and kept her warm, but that is all.'

He could feel Mattherson's stare boring into his very soul. If he knew how tempted Tony had been to take Stella into his arms on several occasions, he might put his lights out with one of those huge paws. In truth, if Mattherson knew he'd held Stella through the night, he might well have him hanged from the nearest gallows. He swallowed again.

'I shall bring her to sit in the parlour later on this morning. You may visit with her then.' Mattherson gave him a pat on the shoulder, but his words were dismissive and he brushed past Tony through the door.

Chapter Twenty-Eight

Stella sipped from the china tea cup and gazed around the room. She would be thankful for a change of scenery. She had seen enough of these four walls, with one painting to break up the white which surrounded her. Papa had promised he would let her get up today — as soon as she finished her breakfast.

If she could walk unhindered, would he think she was well enough to travel? How soon would it be before he dragged her back to Ballaarat? Or sent her off to England? She shook off a shudder. Why had she promised him she would go?

She let out a deep sigh as she helped herself to a bite of perfectly poached egg. She smiled, recalling the bubbly maid who brought in her tray. *These people seem so nice.* She hoped they could stay a while longer. It would be lovely to get to know Penny Worthington better. She hadn't even seemed shocked by Stella's appearance in ragged boy's clothes — not even by the slightest blink. Neither had Angus. She had been here a few days and already she felt accepted and at home.

She wondered if Tony had reconciled to his sister. Penny couldn't hold a grudge against him, could she? She seemed too nice for that. Stella grieved that Tony carried such a burden of guilt on his shoulders. She wished he could stop thinking of himself as a worthless coward. Maybe then he would see how much she cared about him.

Would it be enough, though? Did he still see her as a trashy hoyden? Her heart fluttered when she remembered he called her 'darling'. Or had she imagined it? She had been in a swoon at the time. Had she been hallucinating? Perhaps all her hopes had materialised into a fanciful dream. She sighed again.

'Here y' go.' Gertie swept in the room with a dress draped over her arm. At least Tony would see her more feminine side. The fabric was of a muted blue, very different than the bold colours Stella preferred. Neither was it in the current style. She gave a small shrug of resignation. There was not much she could do about it. *Now if I had my sewing things ...* She shook her head. Her modifications always got her into trouble.

'Now fer some underclothes.' Gertie threw her a grin and flounced out again.

Stella hadn't worn stays for over a week. It would feel strange to put on such restrictive garments again. Men's clothes were much more comfortable in that respect. Would Tony appreciate her more in a dress? She hoped he would forget her impulsive and sometimes indecorous ways and see her as an attractive young maiden.

Some time later, leaning on Papa's arm, Stella limped to the parlour. Her leg, although it had improved, remained swollen and painful. At least no-one could see how fat her calf was — one advantage of wearing a dress.

Papa led her to a chaise lounge where she could sit with her bad leg up. 'Comfortable, my dear?' Even as he asked, he fetched cushions to prop her up.

'*Si*, Papa. Thank you.' She gave him a furtive smile. She had not been able to bring herself to ask him his plans for their homeward journey.

'Good.' He winked at her. 'There is a certain gentleman who is rather eager to see you.'

Her heart leapt in response. *Tony!* He was eager to see her? She tried to compose her features. 'I would be pleased to have fresh company — not that yours is tiresome at all, Papa. You know I didn't mean that.'

He let out a hearty chuckle. 'I know what you meant.' His face turned grave. 'Mr Worthington was very concerned for you when you arrived. He may very well have saved your life. Please give him your highest respect and show him your good breeding.'

In other words, do not behave like a hoyden. His chastisement stung, but she felt as though she deserved it. Her father remained disappointed in her unmaidenly actions. '*Si*, Papa.' She allowed her gaze to fall to her lap, feeling her cheeks burn with shame.

Her father went to the door and returned to sit in a chair nearby, where he picked up a newspaper. She had not heard the other footsteps, intent on the fabric she'd twisted around her fingers in her lap, so jumped a little at Tony's voice.

'Good morning, Miss ... Miss Mattherson.'

Her eyes shot up to his and she hoped he couldn't see the flame which still burned in her face. Did his voice sound a little unsure? 'Good morning, Mr Worthington.' She glanced across at her father and remembered his warning for her to behave with proper manners. It would be hard to go back to such formal address.

'Are you well?' He pushed his light-brown hair away from his forehead.

She smiled at that. So familiar and so dear. 'I am improving.' She didn't want to sound too positive in case her father should whisk her away to Ballaarat. 'My leg is still swollen where the snake bit me.'

He nodded and fiddled with a cane in his hand. She noted how well he looked in fresh clothes. If not for the greenish bruises on his face, he would be quite striking. She wished he could free himself of that air of defeat in the slump of his shoulders.

'This ... this is for you. Angus expects it might help when you wish to walk.' He leaned the cane at the end of the chaise, but now seemed not to know what to do with his hands.

'Won't you sit down, Mr Worthington?' Stella tried to put him at his ease. He appeared to be in discomfort. Did her father's presence make him feel awkward? Could he be intimidated?

'Yes. Thank you.' He stammered the words out and found a close chair. 'You look ... nice.'

She saw his eyes indicated her dress. *Nice?* Should she take that as a compliment? She wanted him to think her *beautiful*, not plain and simple *nice*. She glanced at her father again. She must keep her composure. 'Thank you, sir. And how do your injuries fare?'

'Aye, I should like to know, too.' Angus strode into the room. 'Good mornin' to ye.'

Stella breathed a sigh of relief. Now, perhaps they could all do away with such stiff formality. She glanced at her father who frowned briefly but put his paper aside.

'Morning, Angus.' Tony nodded to the Scotsman as he took a seat nearby. 'I feel much restored by the long sleep. My ribs and nose should heal nicely in time, so Doctor Evans says.'

'Good to hear. Good to hear.' Gus grinned.

'Did he tell you how he got the injuries?' Stella wanted everyone to know precisely what Tony had done for her.

Tony glanced her way and she saw a request to keep silent in his eyes. 'They all know Burns, er, Brownhill used me as a punching bag.'

Angus looked from one to the other. 'Something tells me we've no' heard the full tale yet. What else happened?'

Stella watched her father from beneath her lashes. He seemed intent on Tony's reply. Looking back at Tony, she saw colour seep into his neck.

'Burns, er, Brownhill, punished me for tripping him over, that's all.' Tony shrugged.

Stella gaped at him. 'But you didn't say *why* you tripped him over.' She looked at those gathered in the room, noting Penny had now appeared in the doorway. 'I was foolish enough to try and escape. Smith — I mean Riley — caught me, and Brownhill had been about to hit me to teach me a lesson. Tony deliberately threw himself at Brownhill to stop him from punching me.' She turned sympathetic eyes to her hero. 'Of course, he suffered the cruellest punishment as a result.'

The room went silent and all eyes were on Tony.

'It was nothing ... really.' Tony scuffed at the floor with his shoe, his head bowed. His discomposure was evident.

Her papa continued to stare at Tony, with an expression which Stella could not read. *What is he thinking?*

Penny went to her brother's side and clasped his arm. 'That is truly commendable, Tony. I am so proud of you.'

Angus cleared his throat. 'Ye know, that reminds me of another story.'

Attention shifted to the ex-convict whose eyes seemed to glow.

'It does?' Stella asked.

'Aye. A story from the bible. Ye see, the Scriptures say we have all sinned, an' fallen short of God's glory. It also says the payment for sin is death. We were all destined to the same end — hell an' death.

'But God stepped in by grace. He sent His son, Jesus, to die on the cross an' take our punishment for sin, so we didn't have to suffer that fate. He took the beatin' on our behalf, so to speak.' He looked at Tony. 'I'm sure *He* thinks it were nothin', too. I reckon He would do it again in a heartbeat, if He knew it would change anythin'. That's how great His love for us is.'

Silence filled the room again and Tony's eyes remained focused on the floor.

Stella felt Angus's words wash over her very soul. She knew how grateful she felt that Tony had taken the punishment for her. If God had done the same, then her gratitude to Him should be much deeper.

'Would anybody like tea?' Penny broke the silence with a welcome diversion.

Papa stood to his feet. 'Yes, thank you. But, may I commandeer your study to write a letter to my dear wife?'

'Of course you may.' Penny turned to Tony. 'How about you, dear?'

His neck still bore dark red patches. 'Not yet. I think I shall take a walk.' With a curt nod in Stella's direction, he hurried from the room.

'Gus? Stella?'

'I'll take mine in the kitchen. I must be about me chores.' Angus winked at Penny. 'Too many pretty girls in 'ere to distract me.'

'Go on with you.' Penny slapped him on the arm in mock anger, but the smile on her face belied her actions.

Penny's smile faded as she turned back to Stella. 'What is the matter?'

Stella knew she must look worried. The way Tony had walked out ... 'Perhaps I should go after him.' She made to get up.

'He will be all right. He does not like all the attention.' Penny put a staying hand on her arm. 'Besides, I dare say you wouldn't catch him in your condition.'

But she hasn't heard him say how much he hates himself. 'I really think ...'

'Trust me, dear. He will be back shortly.' Penny patted her arm as if to soothe her. 'How about some tea?'

'I should like a cup, thank you Penny.' Stella resigned herself to waiting.

'Very good. I shall return with it in a moment.'

Silence fell in the room and her mind turned back to Angus's words. Tony had saved her ... more than once. And she loved him for it. But her eyes had been opened to something new. Jesus had saved her ... for her *whole* life. She wanted to love Him for that, for her whole life. While she waited for her tea she prayed, letting her thoughts travel to heaven. *Lord, if You indeed died for me, then I want to live for You. Let me live a life which honours You and help me to honour my father as well. I am Yours Lord, to do with as You will.*

To honour her father would be a challenge. His plans for her were so different from her own desires. Or were they? She had been sure he would be angry when he first saw her. He had still been stiff and formal at times, but he had not scowled at her or accused her. Indeed, he appeared to have been shaken by the whole episode. *Could my understanding of Papa be at fault? Am I the one in the wrong?*

Penny soon returned to the parlour with a tray of tea for two.

'Penny, may I ask you something?'

'Yes, of course.' A small frown creased her brow as she set the tray down.

'Was Papa angry ... about me running away, I mean ... when he was not in the room with me?'

Penny looked thoughtful as she sat beside her. 'I think he was upset, perhaps confused. I'm sure he does not understand why you did it. He was certainly worried about you. He showed every sign of relief when Pete told us you were safe.'

'Oh.'

'Are you afraid of him?' Penny searched her eyes.

Stella shook her short waves. 'No. Not afraid. I expected him to be furious at me. I think I may have been wrong about him.' Tears found their way to the corner of her eyes.

Penny put an arm around her shoulders. 'Are you all right?'

She withdrew a handkerchief from her sleeve and blew her nose, then gave a watery nod. 'Yes, that is, I feel confused about Papa. Sometimes I think he does not like me.'

'I think you'll find he does more than that. He loves you. You are his only daughter.' Penny squeezed her shoulders for emphasis. 'Perhaps you need to sit down with him and tell him how you feel.'

Stella sniffed. 'Perhaps.' A proper conversation might be just the thing needed to sort this out. 'Thank you, Penny.'

Chapter Twenty-Nine

Although part of Tony wanted to remain at Stella's side, another part of him had to escape the homestead and be alone with his churning heart. When he saw her in a dress, once again The Vision of Ballaarat, it knocked the smallest sense of confidence right out of his head. Whatever aspirations he might have, he did not deserve someone so beautiful. Then she had to go and look at him with those wide, soft eyes, and tell the world what a hero she thought him.

He had already come undone before Angus even spoke. But that made it ten times worse. He had no idea what possessed the man to talk about Christ's death on the cross, but he knew it had stirred up dangerous emotions in him.

He sought out his mother's grave and saw his papa's newer mound next to it — and Joe's as well. Looking down at them he clenched his jaw then brought a hand up to massage it a little.

He had deliberately directed Brownhill's anger towards himself that day, with the full knowledge it would result in pain. And he had done it without consideration for himself. Most of all, he had done it because he loved Stella. She had been worth every bit of the agony. If it meant she did not have to suffer the same fate, he would take a thousand beatings for her.

Is that what motivated Christ to die on the cross? Did He love mankind so much he was willing to suffer in their place? *Do You love me that much?* Hadn't they sensed God helped them escape Riley and Brownhill? And hadn't He guided them to safety?

He dropped to his knees before his father's grave. 'But God, I'm not worthy!' He cried out. *Look at how I treated my father. I deserted my sister. I have wasted my life. How can You love me?* Deep pain swelled within his chest and for the third time in recent days, he gave in to tears.

'I'm sorry, Papa! I wish I could see you again and tell you how much. If only I could ask for your forgiveness.'

He wept bitter tears. It was hopeless. He would carry this guilt around with him forever. As he sobbed, soaking the earth with his tears, he felt a hand on his back.

'If we confess our sins, He is faithful an' just to forgive us our sins, an' to cleanse us from all unrighteousness,' a voice said.

Tony straightened, wiping at his eyes and looked at the man who had appeared behind him.

'It's in the Bible. Just thought y' should know.'

'Who are you?'

'Gordon Johns. Blacksmith.' The man offered a hesitant smile. 'Y' can't make things right with yer pa, but y' can make things right with the Lord.'

Tony swallowed the lump in his throat. How could a stranger know the right thing to say at the right time? 'Help me?'

Mr Johns knelt in the dirt beside him and with his guidance Tony poured out years of regrets and offences. Together they prayed for Christ's peace and salvation to come and Tony felt as though his very soul had been washed clean — as though the weight of guilt lifted off his shoulders.

'God really does love me, does He not?'

'That He does, Tony. More than you'll ever comprehend.'

It seemed as though hours had passed when he re-entered the homestead, though in truth it had been less than half-an-hour. However, he felt so different from when he stepped outside, he could hardly reconcile it.

He found Angus in the kitchen where he stirred a pot of food over the fire, beads of sweat glistening on his brow. 'Thank you for telling us about the crucifixion, Angus.'

The large Scotsman stopped and looked at him with interest.

'Penny had told me there was more to faith than what we have grown up with and she was right. Stella and I have seen the hand of

God in the last week or so, but what you said earlier capped it off for me. I have now made my peace with God, and I cannot tell you how good it feels.'

Angus's face lit up in a huge grin. He crossed the room in two strides and wrapped him in a great hug, letting out a spontaneous laugh. 'I knew it! I knew ye needed to hear it. That is wonderful news. Penny will be overjoyed when ye tell her.'

'Where is she?'

'Preparin' the table for dinner.' His eyes sparkled with joy. 'Since there are so many of us in the house, she needed to set up the dinin' room.'

'And Stella?'

'Still in the parlour, I believe.'

More than anything he wanted to see Stella, but his emotion-filled heart needed a bit longer to settle. He made his way to the dining room where his sister added the final touches to the table. She smiled up at him. 'Is it done?'

'Is what done?'

'What you needed to get done out there?'

How did she and Angus seem to know what took place inside of him? 'You were right about God.'

She let out a squeal of joy and threw her arms around him much as Angus had. He kissed her temple. 'Thank you, Penny.'

When she pulled away her eyes shone with merry tears. She put her hand in the pocket of her skirt to pull out a handkerchief. 'Oh, I almost forgot.' Along with the cloth, she withdrew a familiar pipe. 'You might like this back.'

Tony gazed at the pipe with a sigh. The last gift he received from Papa. It surprised him to realise the usual sense of guilt did not accompany the remembrance of his father. It felt good to have a reminder of Papa for a change. He leaned forward and pressed another kiss on Penny's forehead.

'Enough of that.' She blushed. 'Go and bring your girl in for dinner.'

'She is not my ...'

'You have but to say the word, you know. She is yours for the asking. Anybody with eyes can see it.'

Tony did not know what to say in response. He wanted to argue with her, but he figured it would serve no purpose. She couldn't understand his reservations. With trepidation he entered the parlour and almost lost his composure at the sight of her. Too lovely by far.

'Tony!' Her face lit up. 'I am sorry if I embarrassed you before. I wanted them to know ...'

'It is no matter.' He brushed her words aside and held out his hand to her, his arm rigid. 'Will you come for dinner?'

Her soft hand in his sent tingles of pleasure up his arm. And then she tucked her hand around his elbow. Oh, how good it felt to have her so close. He dared not look down at her. It would undo him for certain. He handed her the cane to use in her other hand. She looked up at him with gratitude and he felt his heart bounce around in his chest. He needed to get her to the dining room right smart before he made a goose of himself.

All the dishes had already been placed on the table and everyone stood about waiting for them. Mattherson looked pleased to see her on her feet. Tony wondered how long until her father whisked her away to Ballaarat.

'Here they are.' Penny's warm smile welcomed them to the table and they all took their seats.

There were sounds of agreement from around the table. Tony noted that the servants, Gertie and Gordon had joined them. Papa never operated the homestead this way, but he liked the way Penny included them.

Mattherson stood and raised his glass. 'To Tony Worthington, who saved my daughter. May you live a long and prosperous life.'

'Here, here!' The call went around those gathered and they all drank together.

Tony's gaze swept around the table, but the only person he wanted to look at was Stella. She joined in the toast without hesitation, a brilliant smile shining from her eyes.

When Mattherson sat, Tony stood. 'Thank you all, though I feel undeserving of such adulation. I should like to make my own toast to Miss Mattherson, who showed bravery in the midst of frightening circumstances.' He raised his glass and everyone uttered a hearty agreement before they washed down another mouthful of wine.

Stella nodded her thanks with a large smile, her eyes shining with emotion. Oh, how he could drink in that smile for the rest of his days. He wished he could kiss those sumptuous lips right then and there. He tore his gaze away and focused on his plate. She was too good for him anyway. He brushed his stray hair from his brow and served himself some food, his heart sinking in his chest.

Stella watched Tony excuse himself once again with a small frown of consternation. He had not finished his dinner and declined an invitation to gather in the parlour with the menfolk for port or coffee. He was clearly preoccupied — he'd spent a lot of time reading information about his property, so she'd heard — but she also wondered if he wanted to avoid her for some reason. He had been awkward and stiff around her and it didn't make sense. His behaviour was so far removed from what it had been in the bush.

She had noticed a difference about him, though. His shoulders were not so slumped during dinner and he had not reddened with shame when her father toasted him. None of that accounted for the way he stiffened at her touch, however. He had not even met her glance when he'd walked her into the dining room.

Perhaps he no longer found her attractive. Perhaps he never did. The unknown twisted her stomach into knots. Perhaps he had all along seen her as a child in need of protection. Now he'd seen her dressed as a lady, he kept his distance. She wished she could tell him how she felt without her father condemning her for forwardness. Would Papa take her away without her ever having a chance?

Stella tried to put her worries out of her mind. She needed to speak to Papa as Penny had suggested. The men had long gone about their business and she had resettled herself in the parlour, with naught to pass the time but to think ... and pray. *Please, Lord, help me tell Papa how I feel. And please make a way for Tony and me.*

'You wanted to see me, my dear?' Papa came in and sat before her.

Stella felt her stomach clench. Baring one's heart was a difficult thing. She swallowed. *Where to start?*

'Do you still intend to send me to England?' The words came out in a rush, and even to her own ears they sounded more defensive than she meant them.

A frown appeared between her father's eyes and he let out a tired sigh. 'Are we to go back to this again? You promised me you would heed me.'

'I thought I was about to die.' His impatience stung and she made her excuse without thought.

Papa's voice lowered, his anger barely restrained. 'So, you mean to say that only on your supposed death-bed can you be a pleasant and dutiful daughter?'

Stella gaped at him. *He thinks me unpleasant. I knew it!* 'You have *never* cared about me!' Her voice rose in hurt and anger.

'I have never ...? *You* have *always* pushed *every* boundary we set for you. Do you know how difficult it is to be at loggerheads with your only child almost every day?' He looked her in the eyes and she could see his frustration, but could there also be ... pain?

Stella's impulsive temper was already out of hand and though she saw hurt in his expression, her pounding heart lead her on. 'But you weren't even *there* every day! You left me and *Mamá* to fend for ourselves!'

Papa stood to his feet and ran his fingers through his short hair with a grunt of frustration. He paced back and forth before her several times before he stopped and stared down at her. His voice shook as he spoke. 'Why must we always come to this? You know why I ...' He paused and shook his head as if he couldn't be bothered explaining it all again. 'When will you open your eyes and see the truth and stop fighting me every inch of the way?' He turned and stalked from the room, his heavy footsteps echoing through the house.

Stella leaned back and closed her eyes with a groan. It hadn't gone as she'd planned. She curled her hands into fists and pummelled her thighs. Why did she have to go and lose her temper? She had gone about it the wrong way and now she had made things worse. On top of that, she still had no resolution to the problem.

Chapter Thirty

Tony walked for a long time out in the grassy fields where sheep once grazed, around the gardens which surrounded the homestead, along the creek, not taking much note of his surrounds. His mind tumbled with thoughts and questions. Penny had been right earlier that morning. He knew he would rue the day he let Stella depart without knowing how he felt. And Penny seemed convinced she would accept his courtship. If there was any chance she would have him, he must make his sentiments known.

Yet, the very idea terrified him. *I told you I was a coward!* Yes, he might have been able to stand up to two ruffians who threatened their lives, and steel himself to suck poison from her leg, but when it came to revealing his heart, he felt frozen with fear. One word from her could tear him apart, the one word he didn't want to hear. And even worse if she looked at him with disgust or contempt — she might as well cut his heart out and trample it on the ground. He couldn't bear it.

But if she agreed — oh, then he could take her to Sunworth and make a life with her there. He could think of numerous ways she would find her place on a cattle-run. The possibilities excited him. It would be beyond a dream come true if he could spend the rest of his life with her and start a family together. How he yearned to have her lively spirit with him. Without her, life would seem void of colour.

Well, perhaps not so bland now. His reflection turned to his new faith, which had also given him new hope. He remembered the Scriptures he'd read at the natives' camp. *Thoughts of peace, and not of evil, to give you an expected end.* The Lord had a future for him.

With or without Stella, it would be worth looking forward to. *But Lord, I pray it is with her. Please give me favour with her.*

Tony made his way back to the homestead with more confidence than he had felt for years. Whatever happened, he had the Lord watching over him now. All would be well.

He rounded the corner of the house to see Mr Mattherson leading his horse from the stable, saddled and ready to go. His heart stopped in his chest. Time had run out. He approached the man as he tethered the horse to a fence post.

'Do you plan to leave already?' He dispensed with any pleasantries. His mind felt too jumbled to be genteel.

Mattherson turned around. 'Ah, Mr Worthington. I am not leaving as such, just making a trip to The Gap for a few items. Estella is not strong enough yet to travel, but in a few days I should think she will be ready to depart, although it will be an arduous journey for her, I'm sure.'

Tony heard little of this explanation, except for his lack of faith in Stella's strength. 'I think you underestimate your daughter, sir.'

Mattherson seemed to stiffen. 'Do I, lad?'

'I have seen her climb up and down hills, through dense forest, without food and very little water, from sun-up to sun-down, without the smallest complaint. She is made of sturdy stuff.'

A slight frown creased his brow. 'People sometimes force themselves to do difficult things in the face of danger. Things they would normally not cope with. I have seen it many times in the military.'

'I am sure you have, sir,' Tony conceded, although he didn't agree in this case. 'What will you do when you return to Ballaarat? Will you send her to England as you once intended?'

Mattherson looked grim. 'Stella has made her views on that very clear, and as much as I believe it would be a grand opportunity for her, I don't suppose I'll try to send her again. Perhaps I will engage a gentlewoman, to train her in deportment and etiquette. It is necessary for her to succeed alongside me in polite circles. I'm not sure however, it is any of your business to ask.'

'With all due respect, sir, I think she would prefer a life away from politics and society.' Tony felt the heat rise in his neck and swallowed his trepidation.

'She told you this, did she?' Mattherson smirked. 'I suppose she asked you to speak for her.'

Tony shook his head. 'No, Mr Mattherson. It is just ... I have seen her in the wilderness. She did not fret in the dark of night. She did not show alarm over the strange creatures, except perhaps the koalas for a moment.' He grinned at the memory. 'She showed resourcefulness and courage. She even enjoyed the company of the natives.'

Mattherson watched him with one eyebrow raised, almost as though he were surprised. 'Go on.'

'Perhaps you expected she would be a frightened little girl out there, but there could be nothing further from the truth. She fought those scoundrels at every chance she got — by word or by deed. Her strength inspired me to hope and to find a way to escape.'

Tony realised his words had become impassioned and he saw the corner of Mattherson's mouth twitch.

'You seem to be slightly enamoured, son.'

He felt heat rise in his neck. 'Sir, if you would permit me, I could give her a wonderful future on my cattle station. I am well able to provide for her and I am sure she would be happy there.'

Mattherson watched him with keen interest. 'Do you mean to say you wish to marry her, Mr Worthington?'

'Y... yes, sir. I do.' Tony could hardly believe he admitted it — and to this intimidating ex-military man. He could feel his heart race in his chest and the heat burn in his face while he waited for an answer.

Stella grew tired of sitting alone in the parlour. She eyed the cane which rested against the arm of the chaise. *Perhaps I shall endeavour a stroll.* She stood to her feet and used the cane to support her tender leg. A shadow passed before the window and curiosity drew her to pull aside the lace curtains to see what or who passed out there.

She saw the familiar figure of Tony in conversation with her father. The vision of Tony made her heart skip a beat. Much of the tiredness had left his countenance and the defeated sag of his shoulders had disappeared. He stood tall, although there were signs of discomfort about him.

She glanced at Papa who looked stern but amused. A horse stood tethered behind him, pulling at tufts of grass. She felt her heart do a flop. Were they to leave already? It couldn't be so. *I must find out at once!* She ducked out of the parlour and through the kitchen to the verandah. She hobbled to the end of the porch and was about to round the corner when she heard her father's voice boom out.

'By all means, take her off my hands. You seem to be able to manage her better than I. And if anyone found out you spent a night alone together in the bush ... well, it is better this way.'

Stella knew by instinct they discussed her and at once became furious. *I knew Papa didn't want me!* She swept around the corner in a rage. 'How dare you try to palm me off to another to be rid of me? And merely to prevent more scandal!' She turned to Tony with a glare. 'What did he offer you?'

Tony appeared to be startled. 'N... nothing. Stella ...'

'He wants to have you on his cattle station.' Her father interrupted with a slight smirk. 'Is that not the kind of life you've always talked about?'

'So you want to put me to work out there?' Stella flung the question at Tony. Her anger carried her now, even if she knew the words had no grounds. How could they discuss her as though she were common property? How could Papa be so heartless?

'No!' Tony paled. 'You misund...'

'I am sick to the death of being told what I can and cannot do. I am a grown woman.' She felt her anger melt into tears and her words became choked. Her promise to honour her father came undone and guilt mixed with her hurt. 'How can you stand here and make plans for my future without involving me? Did you ever consider how I would feel?'

She glanced through tear-filled eyes at her father whose eyebrows were raised in surprise and perhaps a little shame, then at Tony who looked grim and shook his head. He reached out a hand to her. 'Stella ...'

She tugged her hand away. 'Let's go, Papa. Just take me home.' She turned and began the long walk up the Worthington driveway, limping with the cane.

'You are being unreasonable, Estella!' Her father called out with a gruff voice.

Unreasonable? *He has no idea how I feel!* She wiped at her eyes. How could things have gone so wrong? She had hoped Tony loved her, but instead he made deals with her father over her management. New sobs formed, making it hard to see where she planted her feet and the pain in her leg told her she would be unwise to continue. She didn't listen.

'Permission to take liberties with your daughter, sir?' She heard Tony's voice behind her. What could he mean? Did he plan to smack her like a naughty child? She quickened her step.

'*Someone* has to take her in hand.' She could hear the frustration in her father's curt response.

She heard Tony's hurried steps over the hard ground, and though she tried to hobble faster, his long legs meant he caught her with ease. She felt his hand grasp her arm from behind and she tried to fight him off. He was too strong for her though, and he soon gripped her by the shoulders and gazed into her eyes with fire like she had never seen.

'Don't you dare hit ...'

Her protest was lost as he pressed his lips roughly on hers and held them there. Confusion tumbled her thoughts until his message forced its way through her anger. *Oh! He loves me.* She surrendered to his kiss and returned it with meaning, dropping the cane to the ground beside her.

When he withdrew he looked into her eyes with adoration. 'I would never hit you, darling. I love you.'

She searched his eyes, but could find nothing insincere in them. 'But all those things you said ... I thought ...You don't think me a hoyden?'

'Never.' He stroked her cheek, wiping away the tears which had been there so recently. 'I only ever insulted you to make you angry because I couldn't bear to see you cry. I think you are a delight. I always have. And I would be more than honoured if you would be my wife.'

Stella felt her breath catch. He really wanted her. Her heart swelled with happiness. 'I can think of nothing I would rather be.'

Tony's eyes widened in pleasure. 'Are you sure?'

'Yes, Tony, I am. I love you.'

He leaned towards her and she tilted her head back to receive his kiss.

'Ahem.'

They jerked apart with a half-embarrassed laugh and turned to her father who had approached.

'May I be the first to congratulate you?'

Stella crossed her arms and frowned at him, while Tony shook his hand with enthusiasm and laughter.

'Still cross at your papa, eh?' Her father turned to her with a twinkle in his eye. He pulled one of her hands free and held it. 'Estella, you must never think I don't want you. I did not wish to be rid of you. I wish the very best for my precious daughter. In this case, I believe a life with Tony here is the very best. It is a pity you missed the first half of our conversation when he told me of all your attributes. I am certain he loves you at least as much as I and will make you a good husband. He did the right and proper thing, asking me for your hand first.'

Stella let her eyes drop to the ground. She had misunderstood her father yet again. His gruff military manner always managed to confuse her. She raised her eyes to his again. 'I am sorry, Papa. I should not have lost my temper with you.'

'All is forgiven.' He wrapped his arms around her and held her tight. 'I love you, my girl. Never forget that.'

'I won't, Papa. Thank you.' She rested her head on his chest, fresh tears spilling over her cheeks. She had been wrong all this time. He did love her. He held her for a time, stroking her hair, but eventually pulled away from her.

He squeezed her hand. 'I think I shall go and make those purchases as I mentioned I would. I should be back by nightfall.' With those words, he turned and headed for the horse.

She looked up at Tony with a sigh and he pulled her into his arms. 'My father is a good man.'

'Yes, he is,' Tony agreed. 'Not so easy to read. But his heart is soft.'

'I have been wrong about him so many times.'

'But I think you have made your peace with him now, haven't you?'

'Yes, as well as peace with God.'

'As have I.' He smiled down at her. 'It shall be wonderful to share our faith together.'

Stella sighed again. 'I cannot wait to start a life with you, Brave Tony.' She giggled.

He laughed, and his mirth brought joy to her heart. All the heaviness had lifted from him.

'Now, where were we before your father interrupted?' he murmured as he gazed into her eyes.

She reached up and pushed the stray hair from his brow. 'You were about to tell me again how much you love me.'

'Mmm.' He smiled and pulled her close.

'Oh! Oh!' Penny's excited voice rang out before she could receive Tony's kiss again. Instead, he stepped back and turned towards his sister as she hurried to them.

'What is it, Penny?'

In reply, Penny threw her arms around him in a tight embrace. 'I knew you two would find a way.' She released Tony and before Stella could prepare herself, she was engulfed in Penny's arms as well. 'I am so happy for you.'

Tony laughed. 'I see you've guessed we are to marry.'

'I am right, am I not?' Penny pulled back but kept hold of Stella's hands. 'We shall be sisters, you and I.'

It was a thought which hadn't crossed her mind as yet. She would have a sister. How wonderful. Stella realised Penny's excitement — she had no sister either. She squeezed her future-sister's hands.

'How about a Christmas wedding in Melbourne?' Penny proposed with bright eyes. 'That gives us almost two weeks to prepare our bridal clothes and such. And, of course you are welcome to stay on here as long as you wish.'

'Two weeks?' Angus strode up with a broad grin and began to shake Tony's hand. 'Too long if ye ask me.'

Tony laughed again. 'Interminable.' He threw a wink at Stella.

Her cheeks began to ache from the size of her smile. 'I think it is a splendid idea. We shall have to send a courier to *Mamá* at once to prepare for a trip to Melbourne. I'm sure Papa will be delighted to meet her there.'

'There is a very good seamstress in town who has made several of my gowns. I am sure she will do a fine job on our wedding trousseau.' Penny squeezed Stella's hand in an excited gesture.

'Stella is rather clever with a needle herself.' Tony waved in her direction.

Stella giggled. 'I think I shall leave this gown to a professional, although I may make a few modifications.' She glanced at her fiancé with an arch grin. 'But I promise not to touch the hemline.'

Tony laughed but the others returned questioning looks.

'Stella has a reputation for her somewhat ... er ... bold modifications.' Tony smiled at her. '*I* think she is quite skilled.'

'You, sir, are blinded by love,' Stella scolded, though she could not hide the smile on her face. 'No more scandalous cuts for me. I have learned my lesson.'

'I hope not, my dear.' Tony frowned a little. 'I have a grand idea to make use of your talents on our cattle station.'

'What do you mean?'

'I have been thinking. I could engage a tanner to make leather from the hides and you, my sweet, could fashion clothes from them, suitable for this Australian climate. It would mean a secondary income from the sale of cattle, along with the sale of fresh meat to the locals.'

Stella's eyes became wide and she noted Penny gaped at him also.

'What is it? What have I said wrong?'

Penny cleared her throat. 'Well, you may not have the stomach to work with animals, but you have a sound mind for business. That is a wonderful idea ... that is, if Stella thinks she can do it.'

All eyes turned to her. So much had happened in the last few minutes, it was almost too much to take in. 'I ... I would have to learn how to work with leather, but, yes, I would *love* to do that.' She let out an incredulous laugh. 'Thank you, Tony.'

'I knew you would like the idea.' He smiled at her, love in his eyes.

Angus slipped an arm around Penny's waist. 'Perhaps we might go an' make some tea, me love.' He gently turned her toward the house. 'Do we 'ave any small cakes?'

Their voices faded and she and Tony were alone again. Stella breathed out a contented sigh as he wasted no time in pulling her close. She couldn't imagine feeling any happier.

'Are you sure you will be happy on a cattle station?' He searched her eyes.

She gazed back with as much fervour as she could muster. 'Yes. I am sure. As long as I have my Brave Tony with me, I will be happy anywhere.'

A soft gurgle of laughter left his mouth as he leaned in and let his lips meet hers in a blissful message of tenderness.

Epilogue

Rupert sat on the dusty earthen floor, his back against the rough blue-stone bricks. Darkness had begun to settle into the hot, airless cell. Hopefully a cool night breeze would find its way through the tiny prison window. But, then again, fresh air was the least of his concerns.

How did I end up here?

He knew what he'd done. He never expected to be found out though.

Riley and Brownhill. He gritted his teeth. The mangy cowards had dumped him in it the moment they knew they were caught. *I should never have trusted that crooked piece of slime.* He cursed his own lack of common sense.

The chain rattled as he lifted his arm to swipe at his damp brow, the manacle biting into his wrist. He would likely suffocate in here before long. Or die of thirst. He moved his tongue around his dry mouth, searching for any sign of moisture. 'Hey!' His parched throat didn't allow for much volume. 'Anyone out there? I need a drink.'

Silence replied.

How long had he been here? It felt like days, although he had not yet spent one night in the cell. How long would it be until they moved him on? And where would they move him to? Fear gripped his stomach. Surely he would not end up in a penal settlement, or worse, at the end of a rope. What was the punishment for abduction, anyway?

Father — his sorry excuse for a father — was his only hope. Would he even bother? He dared not think what Father's reaction would be next time he saw him. A cold shiver worked its way up his spine, in spite of the oppressive heat.

His thoughts were broken by the sound of cart wheels rolling and creaking to a stop outside. Several voices met his ears along with footsteps and other noises he could not exactly recognise. Another prisoner perhaps? He stood to his feet and pulled at the chains, although they were fixed to the wall.

The bolt in the iron door rattled as it was unlocked and opened, revealing dim twilight outside. 'Hey there, Foxworth. Got some company for y'.' The guard offered a mocking grin.

Behind him, two Redcoats entered the tiny cell, bearing a heavy chest between them. They gave him a scathing glare as they deposited the box at the other end of the room. It didn't take a genius to realise what his new 'company' was — the gold being escorted from Bendigo to Melbourne.

Rupert sank to the floor once again and the guard deposited a mug of water and some stale bread by his side. Moments later the bolt slid back into place with a clang and all became silent.

It seemed fate intended to mock him. Gold. The very thing he had striven for over the past few months. It now sat only feet away from him and he could not touch it. A laughable failure, that's what he was.

Rupert chewed the bread, washing it down with water, although the fear in his gut made him sure it would not stay there. What would become of him now? Would anyone be able to save him? His guilt was evident. Riley and Brownhill made sure of that.

Through the long night ahead, with only the intermittent hooting of an owl and the sing-song noise of cicadas to listen to, regret slowly found its way into Rupert's soul. It grew into deep remorse as fear of his punishment took hold. By morning, with barely any sleep, dread had weakened him so much he lacked the strength to stand when he heard horses draw up outside.

Muffled voices exchanged words for a few moments. Then the lock rattled as the guard turned the key. The grinding of the bolt being slid back met his ears seconds before rays of early-morning light blinded his eyes. Rupert raised his arm to shade them. 'Where are you taking me?' His voice sounded as weak and unstable as his legs felt.

The guard thrust a key into the lock on the wrist irons and turned it. 'Yer free to go,' he grunted.

'Free?' How could that be?

'C'mon. Get up.' The guard pulled him to his feet, although Rupert had difficulty making them co-operate, feeling as they were made of jelly. The guard walked him to the door, supporting most of his weight.

At the door, the vision which met his eyes made all strength leave him and he collapsed to the ground. Father. On a horse with a spare mount in tow. And the look on his face ...

'Seems a bit weak.' The guard spoke. 'Dunno if he's sick or what.'

Sick would be a good excuse. But would it save him from what was to come? Rupert struggled to find his voice. 'What happened?' He slowly raised his eyes to his father's.

'The two witnesses have managed to escape, and the aborigine who corroborated their story is nowhere to be found either. Therefore, none can charge you with wrongdoing and you are free to come home with me.'

Although his father wore a cheerful expression, his eyes told a completely different story. Rupert knew he might be free from the hands of the law, but he was yet to receive his punishment in full. The guard helped him to his feet again and Rupert managed to pull himself onto the horse. As he nudged the horse to follow his father away down the road, he wondered if this fate were preferable to a life in prison. Only time would tell.

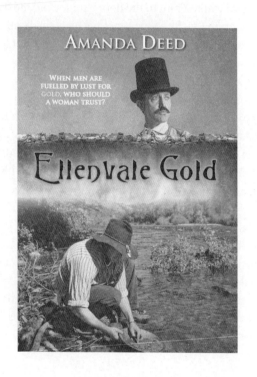

Ellenvale Gold

ISBN: 978-1-921633-53-9

It is the time of Australia's harsh rogue-filled goldrush of the 1850's when Miss Penelope Worthington suddenly finds herself orphaned, isolated and alone. With a large sheep station to run single-handedly, she has little option but to enlist the aid of a mysterious stranger.

Henry's Run
ISBN: 978-1-922074-28-7
With murder hanging over Rupert
Foxworth's head, can he make some drastic
changes to his life before it's too late? Will
he be able to find the love he has yearned for
in his pretty cousin who has come to visit?

Coming 2013, to continue the story
from *Ellenvale Gold* and *Black Forest
Redemption*

The Greenfield Legacy

Meredith Resce, Paula Vince,
Amanda Deed, Rose Dee
ISBN: 978-1-922074-43-0
RRP: $19.95

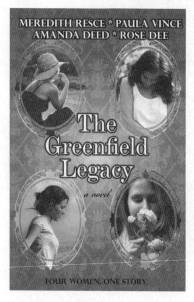

How can one decision cause so much pain? Can it also bring hope?

Mattie was in love with Billy, but she was too young to wed.

Navy is a young woman who has never known her family.

Brooke wonders if it is too late to connect with the man she loves.

Connie cannot forgive her mother as too much has happened.

Is it time for it all to be set right?

This absorbing family drama, set in South Australia's beautiful McLaren Vale wine region, is written by four of Australia's outstanding Christian fiction authors who have brought you best-selling and award-winning novels.

About Amanda

Amanda Deed resides in the South Eastern suburbs of Melbourne, and keeps busy dividing her time between being a mum, a finance administrator and a writer of historical romance. Her debut novel, *The Game*, won the 2010 CALEB Prize for fiction. For more information, go to www.amandadeed.com.au.